# CROSSING THE ICE

### BY

## JENNIFER COMEAUX

Crossing the Ice
by Jennifer Comeaux

Copyright 2014 Jennifer Comeaux
ISBN 978-0-9904342-1-4
Cover Art Designed by Sarah Schneider
Cover Models: Alexandria Shaughnessy and James Morgan
Photography by Ann Bowes-Shaughnessy

*To all the skaters who have inspired me with their beautiful performances.*

# Chapter One

*March, 2009*

There was nothing quite like the sound of ten thousand people gasping at once.

Especially when it was because my butt had just slammed into the cold, hard ice.

I scrambled to my feet and caught up to my partner Mark as fast as my skates could take me. I'd dreamt of this day all season — skating in front of our home American crowd at the World Championships in Los Angeles. But the dream had quickly become a nightmare. Two falls already in our free skate and we still had one more throw jump remaining.

*Courtney Elizabeth Carlton, you are going to land this throw if it's the last thing you do!*

Mark set his hands on my hips, and we glided on a backward curve until he sprang me into the air. The bright lights and the large Staples Center crowd blurred around me as I pulled my arms in tight and spun three times. My right blade hit the ice for the landing, but my body tilted dangerously forward.

A surge of panic took hold of me, shaking me into action.

I touched the ice to steady myself, and I sighed with relief as I avoided splatting again.

*Small moral victory.*

The final furious notes of Tchaikovsky's first piano concerto guided us to the end of the program, and the crowd gave us a warm and sympathetic ovation. Mark lowered his eyes to the ice, his sandy brown curls flopping over his forehead. He was already blaming himself for our mistakes. I'd skated with him for nine years, since I was twelve and he was fourteen, and I could read him better than anyone.

I reached up on my tippy-toes and put my arms around his shoulders. At five foot four I was tall for a pairs skater, but Mark still towered over me. He gave me a tight hug in return, and we took quick bows to all four sides of the arena. I was thankful my dad hadn't been able to get away from the Boston accounting firm where he worked, so only my mom was in the audience. Hopefully Dad hadn't found a live internet feed of the event. He had enough stress to deal with at his job without watching us give our worst performance of the season.

Our coaches Emily and Sergei greeted us with quiet hugs as we exited the ice. I held onto Em and let her familiar lavender perfume surround me. She'd always been as much like an older sister as a coach to me, and I needed her comforting embrace now more than ever.

"I don't know what happened on the flip," I mumbled against her blazer, thinking back to my fall on the first throw jump.

She patted the back of my beaded gray dress. "We'll look at it on the replay."

While we made our way to the kiss and cry, the designated area where we'd wait for the scores, I noticed a grim look pass between Em and Sergei. The young married couple had coached us our entire career, so I could read them just as well as I did my partner, and I knew exactly what that look was all about.

Our placement here, along with that of the other American team, would determine how many pairs the U.S. could send to the Olympics the following season. In order for the U.S. to field the maximum three teams, Mark and I needed to finish no lower than seventh or eighth here. The current U.S. champions had already skated well and had done their job in helping to secure three spots. Now everyone was looking to us to do our part, but with our two falls, the chances of us finishing top eight were… well, I'd go out on a thick limb and say less than zero.

The four of us squeezed onto the bench in the kiss and cry, and the camera in front of us lit up. Mark lifted his hand in a feeble wave. "Hey, everyone back home. Love you, Zoe." He blew a kiss to his long-time girlfriend.

I peered up into the stands, searching for Kyle, my own significant other, who was a competitor in the men's event. I'd had to miss his short program earlier, but we'd met up at the hotel, and I'd been ecstatic to hear he was in second place. At least one of us had given the home crowd a reason to cheer.

The image of Mark and me in the kiss and cry appeared on the super-sized video board hanging over the rink, and our weak smiles showed clearly on the HD screen. I looked down and smoothed my blond hair and the two braids woven through my up-do. Next to me Mark fiddled with his water bottle and muttered questions to Em about our failed jumps. The judges were taking an extremely long time with the scores.

When the numbers finally came up on the screen, my stomach dropped. They were worse than I'd expected. I bent forward and held my head in my hands while Sergei rubbed my back. Peeking through my fingers, I got a glimpse of our placement and cringed at how far we'd fallen in the standings. I could already hear the fans on the internet message boards discussing our ineptitude and bashing us for not coming through for American pairs.

We moved backstage, and after Mark and I put on our media-friendly faces and met the press, Sergei and Em circled us into a small huddle. Sergei's blue eyes deepened with conviction as he looked back and forth between Mark and me. Many of my fellow skaters swooned over him and declared him the hottest coach in the sport, but to me he was just the guy who'd coached me since I was a kid. Sure, he was good-looking, but he was like my second dad.

"This wasn't the ideal way to end the season, but you can learn from this," he said. "As soon as we get home next week, we'll go over everything that happened here and find out where we need to make adjustments. Then we'll put this behind us, turn the page, and get started on planning for next season."

Mark and I both nodded. One of the things I loved most about our coaches was their positive attitude. They never belittled us, and they didn't let us dwell on bad performances.

Em put her arms around our waists. "Enjoy the rest of the week here. Watch as much of the skating as you can. Let it inspire you."

I nodded again more fervently, my spirits lifting as my thoughts went to Kyle. Watching him reel off powerful quadruple jumps and triple-triple combinations always inspired me... in very different ways. It made me both want to work on my jumping technique and to have my way with him. And once he was finished competing the next night, I planned to finally do the latter.

**** 

The following night Mark and I were back at Staples Center but only as spectators. Mom had already flown home, so I'd enlisted my partner to help me cheer on Kyle. First we had to contend with the throng of people milling on the concourse. With Mark close behind, I snaked through the

4

masses, zig-zagging around the lines for concessions and souvenirs.

After passing the McDonald's stand, we entered a small clearing in the crowd where we could finally regain our personal space. I was about to let out a breath but then stopped.

Coming straight toward us were Stephanie and Josh Tucker, the brother and sister pair team who'd finished two spots behind us in fourth at nationals. For a moment I was confused as to why they'd be at the event, and then I remembered they lived in L.A. How could I forget? We'd competed against them for years, and Stephanie flaunted their wealth and Hollywood connections every chance she had. Josh, the older of the two, had always been much quieter. I could count on one hand the number of times we'd spoken since we'd shared an awkward experience as teenagers.

I didn't feel like making small talk, especially after our disastrous skate the previous night, so I put my head down and veered to the right. I didn't make it two steps before Stephanie called my name.

Groaning inwardly, I pivoted to face them. Anyone who saw them together would know they were siblings. Two years apart in age at twenty and twenty-two, they both had the same rich shade of brown hair, clear blue eyes, and creamy skin. Even the long slope of their noses was identical. But there was something different in their eyes. Stephanie's examined me with critical scrutiny, while Josh's watched me with guarded interest. I stood taller and straightened the denim jacket I wore over my green sundress.

"Josh and I were just talking about you two," Stephanie said in the fake-nice voice that seemed so natural to her.

Josh slanted a dark glance in her direction, but she paid him no attention as she continued, "We're so excited about moving to Cape Cod and working with Emily and Sergei."

Moving to Cape Cod? Our training site? Working with

*our* coaches?

"Come again?" I sputtered.

"They told you we're going to be training together, didn't they? We finalized all the details earlier this week."

I stared open-mouthed at her, my voice stuck in my throat. Mark and I were Emily and Sergei's only senior team. *We* were supposed to be their priority for the Olympic season. This had to be a mistake. I looked at Josh, and he avoided my gaze as he bent his head, shaking it ever so slightly.

"They haven't said anything to us about it," Mark piped up beside me.

"Oh." Stephanie touched her French-manicured hand to her mouth. "Sorry, I guess we weren't supposed to share the news yet." She couldn't sound any less sincere in her apology.

"So you're moving across the country?" I asked.

"After Josh graduates from UCLA in May," Stephanie replied. "We think Emily and Sergei are the best coaches to help us get on the Olympic team."

Josh continued to stay silent, alternating between shooting subtle daggers at Stephanie and looking anywhere but at Mark and me. He shoved his hands in the front pockets of his dark jeans and turned halfway toward the approaching crowd like he was ready to escape the conversation.

"They are the best," I said, realizing how dazed I still sounded.

Stephanie folded her arms and gave me a pointed glare. "It's a shame there will only be two spots for pairs on the team."

My face filled with heat, and I hated that my pale cheeks likely revealed my emotions.

"We gave it everything we had," Mark said, mimicking Stephanie's pose. "It was a tough competition."

She hummed softly in response, and her eyes narrowed, her critical gaze sharpening. "It wasn't—"

"We should get going." Josh finally broke his silence.

Well, I didn't know much about him, but being willing to shush his sister earned him some points in my book.

"Right. We have to head upstairs." Stephanie showed us her glossy ticket. "We have seats in one of the corporate suites."

Of course they did. I refrained from rolling my eyes at her obvious display of showing off.

"Enjoy," I said tersely.

I watched as they walked away, Stephanie's ridiculously high heels clicking loudly. Josh pushed his hand through his hair and appeared frustrated as he spoke to his sister. She waved her ticket at him as if she was dismissing whatever he said.

"What the hell?" Mark said. "How could Em and Sergei take them on without talking to us about it?"

I had no answer for him. I couldn't wrap my head around this. Em and Sergei had talked all along about doing everything they could to help us get to the Olympics. For them to bring in one of our main competitors and not even discuss it with us didn't make sense. Even though Mark and I hadn't been as successful the past few years as had been expected of us, I didn't think our coaches had stopped believing in our potential.

"There has to be more to the story," I said as I headed for the nearest section of seats, sidestepping a boisterous group of teenagers.

Mark followed and joined me on the steps down the aisle. "Like what?"

Again I didn't answer him as I concentrated on searching for two empty seats. We didn't have tickets, but our credential badges let us squat anywhere we could find an open spot. I scooted past a few spectators chomping on pizza and nachos and headed for two seats in the middle of the row. Mark sat beside me and continued his line of questioning.

"What possible justification could they have for doing

this?"

I stared blankly at the Zamboni circling the ice. "Maybe the federation pressured them into it. The Tuckers could've thrown some money at the fed and set it all in motion."

I didn't want to believe that Em and Sergei would voluntarily split their loyalties between us and another team. They weren't just my coaches; they were family. When Dad had lost his job on the Cape and he and Mom had to relocate to Boston for his new one, Em and Sergei had given me a place to live. I'd been staying with them and their two-year-old twins for almost a year.

"We should text them to see if they're here." Mark pulled his phone from the back pocket of his khakis.

I covered his hand with mine. "We can find them tomorrow. I need to put all my focus on sending good vibes to Kyle."

His forehead creased, but he put the phone away. "I don't know how you guys can even say you're dating when you never see each other."

"We video chat and text and email..."

"That's not the same as hanging out with someone in person."

"Well, I can't help that he lives in California. I don't exactly have the money or the time to fly out here whenever I want."

"I'm just saying... you got together at Worlds last year and you've only seen each other what, twice since then?"

"Three times." I corrected. "But you don't have to physically be with someone all the time to have a connection with them."

The wrinkle in Mark's brow deepened, but he didn't say any more about my relationship with Kyle. I gratefully accepted his silence and turned my attention to the stream of people filing into the seats below us.

The first group of men took the ice, and competitor after

competitor performed his four-and-a-half minute program. As the time inched closer to Kyle's free skate, my nerves began to twitch, and I chewed on my thumbnail. Kyle had never won a World medal, so standing on the podium would be a huge deal for him.

He stepped onto the ice as the last skater of the event, and the building shook with cheers, my screams among them. Mark plugged his ears and I swatted his arm, to which he laughed and yelled with his deep voice, "Let's go, Kyle!"

I resumed gnawing on my thumbnail as Kyle circled the rink, taking his time in getting to his starting spot. His burgundy shirt clung to his slim torso, and his tight black pants did the same on his even slimmer hips. He was the definition of a California boy with shaggy blond hair, blue eyes, and the perfect tan that I wished I could attain. His looks had definitely attracted me first, but it was his gentle nature that had made me fall for him. I loved the sweet texts he'd send me like *Wishing I could give you a hug, Beautiful* and *I miss your gorgeous green eyes.*

Kyle settled into his opening pose with one arm stretched toward the audience, and the music of Bach filled the arena. His deft strokes took him across the ice in a blaze, and I held my breath as he approached each jump and exhaled deeper every time he landed cleanly.

The minutes raced by, and I edged forward in my seat, anticipating the final few energetic moments of the program. Kyle finished with a dizzying scratch spin, and I jumped up, hands slapping together. The crowd joined me with a thunderous standing ovation, so loud I could barely hear the announcer booming Kyle's name.

The atmosphere turned tense as we waited for the scores to be announced. The current leader had skated lights-out and was the reigning World champion, so I didn't expect Kyle to surpass him, but there was always a small chance. I folded my hands and stared at the spot on the video board where the numbers would appear.

A victory wasn't meant to be as Kyle's marks came up just short of first. I hoped he'd still feel good about his awesome skate. I had to wait over an hour to see him since he had numerous obligations at the arena, but as soon as we were reunited in the hotel lobby, I threw my arms around him and didn't let go.

"You were amazing!" I cried.

He hugged me back and then slowly worked himself out of my embrace. "I think that was the best I've ever skated."

Two tipsy fan-girls raced over and asked Kyle for a photo, which I took while they cozied up to him. As they walked away giggling, I grabbed one of Kyle's two huge bags full of stuffies and other gifts thrown by the fans.

"I'll help you bring all this to your room," I said.

"You don't have to do that."

*Does he not want me to go up to his room with him?* We hadn't spent much time alone together that week because of our busy schedules, but I'd hoped this would finally be our chance. Maybe he just didn't want me to carry his stuff.

"I've got it." I smiled and slung the bag over my shoulder.

Kyle hesitated before following me up the escalator to the elevators. His silence on the way upstairs unnerved me even more, but I rationalized that he was probably still decompressing from the frenzy at the arena.

Once we reached his room, I set down the bag and took a peek at the bed. Kyle and I hadn't gotten that far in our relationship (I hadn't gotten that far with *anyone*), but I felt like I was ready. I'd thought about this for a while, and I wanted him to be my first.

*Surely, he wants it too, right?*

I walked over to where he stood in front of the desk, and I slipped my arms around his narrow waist. Softly touching my lips to his, I waited for him to respond and pull me close.

Instead he stiffened and unwound my grip.

"Court, don't..." He raked his hand through his hair.

I took a rocky step backward and shook my head. "I don't understand."

"I wanted to wait until after we competed to tell you."

"Tell me what?" I asked shakily.

He stared at the carpet for what seemed like an hour before he finally answered, "I met someone."

My stomach flipped upside down, and anger quickly chased the hurt.

"Have you been dating her behind my back?" I demanded. "Who is she?"

"She works at my gym. We started talking one day, and then we kept talking longer—"

"Is that all you've been doing? Talking? Or did you hook up with her?"

He took a tight swallow as he avoided the furious burn I felt in my gaze. "We've been seeing each other."

I balled my hands into fists at my sides and inhaled and exhaled a deep breath. "So that's a yes, then."

"I didn't want to break things off with you over the phone. I thought the right thing to do would be to wait until after the competition and tell you—"

"The right thing!" I shrieked. "The right thing would've been to not sleep with some other girl while still acting like my boyfriend."

"I'm sorry. I really didn't want to hurt you."

I choked out a bitter laugh. "Well, it's too late for that. I can't believe I was stupid enough to think you were worth..."

I glanced again at the bed, and a sickening sensation swirled in my gut. I stormed away from Kyle and then spun around, stopping just before the door.

"You're not worth a second more of my time."

# Chapter Two

"He cheated on you?" Mark paused with his sandwich aimed at his mouth. "That little prick."

I poked and prodded my chicken Caesar salad but didn't know if I could stomach actually eating it. My insides had been twisted since the previous night when Kyle had dropped his bomb on me and exploded all my hopes for us to smithereens. I'd thought soaking up some L.A. sunshine at an outdoor café might make me feel better, but there was apparently no quick cure for heartbreak.

"I hope you told him off," Mark said.

"I don't even remember what I said. I was just so blindsided."

I put down my fork and pressed my fingers to my temples. To think I'd been ready to lose my virginity to Kyle. My eyes misted from both the hurt and stupidity I felt, and I pushed my sunglasses higher on my nose. The sidewalk next to our table had heavy traffic of skaters and fans walking from the hotel to Staples Center. This wasn't the ideal place to start crying.

"Coco!" a little girl's voice squeaked behind me.

I turned to see Em, Sergei, Em's Aunt Debbie, and the twins approaching us. Neither Quinn nor her brother Alex could say my name when they'd first started talking, so I'd been Coco to them ever since. I took a deep breath to push down the ache in my chest before I reached over the low railing and ruffled Quinn's curly blond hair.

"Hey, Cutie."

She and Alex were the two most adorable toddlers I'd ever seen with their matching golden locks and big blue eyes. But I'd expected no less with the gorgeous parents they had.

"Court, why aren't you at the men's small medal ceremony?" Em asked as she shifted Alex on her hip. "Isn't it going on outside Staples?"

The ache flared again, and I lowered my head. "Oh... um... Kyle and I broke up," I mumbled.

"Oh no. What happened?" she asked.

"I don't really wanna talk about it right now."

"He screwed around on her," Mark announced.

Em covered Alex's ears, albeit too late. I gaped at Mark and kicked his shin under the table.

"Ow! I was just trying to save you from telling the story again."

"Screwed around." Quinn giggled.

I cringed while Sergei just shook his head.

"I'm so sorry, Court," Em said. "If you want to talk later, call me. We can go do something, just you and me."

I gave her a little smile. "Thanks."

"Scre-e-e-wed!" Quinn continued to laugh as she arched her neck to look up at Sergei. "What screwed, Daddy?"

Sergei crouched to her level. "When we get to the arena, would you rather have ice cream or a chocolate chip cookie?"

Her eyes grew even bigger, and her smile did the same. "Cookie!"

*Oh, to be a kid again and be so easily distracted. Life was so much simpler then.*

"There's actually something else we need to talk to you guys about," Mark said. "We ran into the Tuckers last night."

The weight on my chest grew even heavier. I'd pushed the issue of our new training mates to the back of my mind after the other earth-shattering news I'd received.

Em and Sergei exchanged concerned glances, and Sergei turned to Em's aunt. "Can you take the kids ahead? We'll be there in a few minutes."

"Sure. We'll go look for those cookies." She took Quinn's hand and did the same with Alex once Em set his little sneaker-clad feet on the sidewalk. She traveled with them to almost every competition to help out with the twins, so she was used to babysitting in a pinch.

"Thanks, Aunt Deb." Em bent and kissed the tops of the twins' heads. "Be good."

She and Sergei came around the railing and borrowed two empty chairs from a nearby table. They both looked nervous about starting the conversation.

"So, Stephanie said she and Josh are moving to the Cape," Mark said.

Em sighed and pushed a few strands of dark blond hair from her face. "We asked them not to tell anyone before we had a chance to talk to you next week."

"I don't think Stephanie really cares about our feelings," I said.

Sergei's mouth pressed into a line. "I'm sorry you had to find out that way."

"How'd they talk you into coaching them? Are they paying double your rates?" Mark asked.

"No, it's nothing like that," Em said. "When they asked us, our first instinct was of course to say no. We value our relationship with you so much, and we don't want you to ever question your trust in us. You guys are so special to me — you were the first team I ever coached."

I flashed back to our first lesson with Em, when Sergei

told us he'd asked his then-student to help him coach us. Working together was one of the things that had brought them closer off the ice and had led to their romantic relationship. I'd wanted them to be a couple from the very beginning, so I always loved that I was a small part of the reason they'd gotten together.

"We weren't going to say yes to coaching the Tuckers, but then we talked about it, and we think this will be good for you," Sergei said.

"How's that?" I asked.

Em leaned forward and folded her hands on the table. "Having one of your biggest competitors training alongside you can only make you better. And honestly, I think you need a little kick in the butt. You need to see what your competition is doing, how hard they're working. We think it'll inspire you to work that much harder so you can make a strong push for the Olympic team."

"You don't think we're working hard enough?" Mark asked.

"To get to the Olympics, you have to step it up another gear," Sergei said. "I know you both have the competitiveness and the talent to get there. You just need to train every day with that fire in your belly, and having the Tuckers there will fuel that fire."

I understood what they were saying, but I still couldn't grasp how we could all be one big happy family. The issue of loyalty hadn't been addressed.

"There are only two spots on the team, and since Rebekah and Evan have won nationals two years in a row, they have one of them almost locked up," I said. "So we'll be going against Stephanie and Josh for the one remaining spot. How can you fully support both of us?"

"Because we want you both on the team and we believe it can happen." Em's voice took on its "coach pep talk" tone. "Nothing is guaranteed for Rebekah and Evan. If you all put in the work, you can be in those top two spots."

"You have to believe it, too," Sergei added. "You can't go into next season narrowing your odds."

It was easy for Em and Sergei to have confidence. They'd been on top of the world at the last Olympics with Sergei coaching Em and her partner Chris to the gold medal. But as much as Mark and I had tried to emulate them, we didn't have their superstar talent. We'd had to set more modest goals.

Mark took off his shades and wiped them on his T-shirt. "Why are Stephanie and Josh moving this late in their career anyway? They've been with the same coach since they were kids."

"They want us to help them with their jump technique. They've had a lot of problems with consistency and under-rotations," Sergei said.

I looked down and spun the chunky bracelet around my wrist. "I hope they're not going to mess up the good atmosphere we have at the rink. Stephanie is... well, it doesn't seem like her attitude will fit in with our group." *In other words, we don't want to deal with her bitchiness every day.*

"We wouldn't have agreed to coach them if we thought there'd be major problems. You don't have to be best buddies with them, but I think you can all get along," Em said.

Mark bumped the toe of my sandal and shot me a look across the table that said he wasn't convinced. I wasn't either, but the deal was done, and putting up resistance wasn't going to get us anywhere.

"If you think this will help us, then we'll do our best to make them feel welcome," I said, knowing exactly what Em and Sergei wanted to hear.

"Thanks, Court." Em touched my arm. "And I promise this won't change the amount of time and attention we give you. We're committed to you just as much as we always have been."

Mark and I both slowly nodded. Em's and Sergei's eyes

were hidden behind their sunglasses, but I could feel the intensity with which they watched us. They could probably tell we were still skeptical.

"Do you have any more questions?" Sergei asked.

We turned our nods into equally slow head shaking.

"Okay. Well…" Sergei pushed back his chair. "We'd better catch up to Aunt Deb before the kids talk her into buying more than cookies."

Em stood and squeezed my shoulder. "My offer still stands if you need to talk later. About anything."

They headed in the direction of the arena, and I took a sip of my lemonade. Tilting my head back, I let the warmth of the bright sunshine spread over my face. This was supposed to be my week in paradise, a trip I'd highly anticipated since the moment we'd qualified for Worlds back in January.

"I thought this week would be so amazing. Visiting fabulous L.A., competing with the best in the world, hanging out with my boyfriend… and what happens? We bomb in the free skate, Kyle tells me he's been cheating on me, and we find out we have to train with the most disliked pair skater in the country. It's like the nightmare that won't end."

Mark picked up a potato chip and stared at it a moment before popping it into his mouth. "What do you think about Em saying we need to work harder?"

I took a longer drink from my glass. "Maybe she's right. Maybe we need to push ourselves more. We could add another hour a day on the ice or in the gym."

"I guess I always thought we were doing enough."

"It was probably enough to get where we are, but is it enough to make the Olympic team? To beat Stephanie and Josh, who are likely going to get better with Em and Sergei coaching them?"

"No way am I losing out on the Olympics to them," Mark said.

"My sentiments exactly. We have to do whatever it takes

to be in Vancouver next February. We're not missing out by one place again."

Finishing fourth at nationals in 2006 when the U.S. had sent three teams had been the most painful experience of my life. We'd been in the perfect position to be in the top three, but then we'd had a meltdown in the free skate. I still got a lump in my throat every time I thought about that night.

We only had one more chance to get on the Olympic team. I was going to start my college career the next year, and Mark wanted to get engaged and work with his dad at his auto shop.

I wasn't going to let the Tuckers move in, use our coaches for one season, and steal our dream. *Hell to the no.*

# Chapter Three

I pushed open the rink door and took a moment to breathe in the cold air. With things about to change at our training base, I wanted to hang onto the familiarity of the place. I'd had two months to get used to the idea of the Tuckers skating with us, but it hadn't made me any less anxious about their arrival, which would be happening in a few minutes.

Mark was just starting his morning jog around the rink, so I quickly stashed my rolling bag in the locker room and followed his path. Someone had already turned on the stereo, and "Poker Face" echoed off the sky-high ceiling. Normally, Lady Gaga got me going in the morning, but today it was just making me jumpier.

As I completed my first full lap, the blue double doors from the lobby opened, and Stephanie and Josh entered. Stephanie dragged a Louis Vuitton bag, carried a matching purse, and wore a pair of sunglasses that were five times too big for her bobble head. Josh looked much less "L.A." in his plain black fleece jacket and black pants.

I slowed to a stop near them, and Stephanie propped her

glasses atop her head. "Where's the locker room?" she asked.

*Hello to you, too.*

I swallowed my irritation and pointed behind them. "It's the second door."

Without so much as a nod of thanks, she turned and marched away. Josh lingered and looked all around the large building.

"This is really nice. A lot newer than our rink in Burbank."

The complete one-eighty from Stephanie's frigidness to Josh's friendliness threw me, and I needed a second before I could answer, "Yeah, everything had to be redone after the snowstorm caved in the roof a few years ago."

"I remember hearing about that."

We stood for a few awkward silent moments, and I had a déjà vu flash from when we'd met as young teens. I could see us so clearly in the small room, fidgeting anxiously, all alone with nothing to say to each other.

Josh motioned with his thumb to the locker room. "I should warm up."

I nodded and was about to resume jogging, but Josh's quiet voice calling my name halted me. "I know it has to be weird having us here, but we're not here to get in your way. We just want to get better."

The way his eyes didn't waver from mine made me believe he was sincere. I was pretty sure his sister didn't share his amicable feelings, though.

"That's what Mark and I want, too... to get better. There's no reason why we shouldn't all be able to do that without getting in each other's way."

His lips twitched into the faintest hint of a smile as his eyes continued to steadily hold my gaze. Another round of uncomfortable silence followed, so I quickly pivoted and took off at a faster pace than usual. Glancing backward, I saw Josh disappear into the locker room. He and Stephanie might share a number of physical features, but they couldn't be more different personality-wise. I was curious to see their training relationship. Stephanie had drama queen written all over her, but Josh didn't seem like the type to put up with that kind of nonsense.

After a few more laps and my standard stretching routine, I headed to the locker room to put on my skates. Mark sat on the bench along the far wall, lacing up his boots and chatting with one of Em and Sergei's junior teams. I sat beside him and slipped my feet out of my sneakers and into my skates.

"Did you talk to them?" Mark asked.

I knew who "them" was without asking. "Just for a second."

"I walked past Stephanie and she wouldn't even look at me." Mark pulled the knot tight on his laces and stood in front of me. "We need to bring our 'A' game today and show them we're not affected by them being here."

"We need to bring our 'A' game every day."

"True, but today we have to really be on. We should do full run-throughs of the short and long — let them see we already have our new programs in good shape."

I stopped tying and held up my hands. "Slow your roll. We just finished putting together the long last week, and Em said she still wants to change up the middle section. Let's not rush things just to make a point."

I could just see us trying to do a full run-through of a program we barely knew and doing more harm than good. That would be a great way to show how much we were on top of our game.

We went out to the ice and were joined shortly after by two junior teams and Stephanie and Josh. As we all warmed up around each other, I kept an eye on the newest addition to our morning session. They had a balletic style I envied — classic lines like the great Russian teams of the past. Mark and

I had taken ballet classes over the years, but we just weren't naturally elegant. We were known as an athletic team with speed and power who had to work hard at looking graceful.

After we all sufficiently loosened our limbs, Sergei and Em hopped onto the ice, and Sergei skated over to Mark and me while Em headed for Stephanie and Josh. We stood in opposite corners of the rink like boxers huddled before a fight.

I faced away from them and put all my attention on Sergei. I had to lose that mentality and realize the biggest competition we had was ourselves. We had to do just what I'd told Josh — focus on getting better. That was the only way we'd have a shot at the Olympics.

Over the next couple of hours, Mark and I worked on a new jump combination with Sergei then choreography with Em then sections of our new programs on our own. I noticed Stephanie listening attentively to our coaches and following all their instructions, so maybe she had a decent work ethic after all. We'd see how she'd handle triple run-throughs later in the summer.

During our mid-morning break, I grabbed my phone and an energy bar from my locker and went up to the lounge overlooking the ice. Stephanie and Josh sat in front of the big window with a couple of skating moms. Stephanie was eating some kind of cracker while Josh hungrily spooned his yogurt. I took a seat at a nearby table and started my morning ritual of checking all my social media sites. Mark plus a group of my training mates descended on the table and were noisily discussing the latest comic book movie when Em strode to the center of the room and clapped her hands together.

"Since I have a lot of you here, Sergei and I want to invite you all to a barbecue Sunday at our house. We're celebrating Memorial Day early since we'll be here Monday."

"Free food?" Mark said. "I'm there."

"Sergei's the grill master," Kenny, one of the junior skaters, said.

Everyone else chimed in with positive responses until Stephanie spoke loudly above the din, "Will there be options besides meat? I follow a strict vegan diet."

The room went silent, and Em hesitated a moment. "Sure. We'll have lots of vegetables and salad and fruit. And if you tell me what kinds of dishes you like, I can make something for you."

"Vegan meals aren't easy to make," Stephanie said in a condescending tone.

My eyebrows shot up, and a couple of throats cleared around me. No one questioned Em's culinary skills. She was as proud of her cooking as she was her skating accomplishments.

"I think I can whip something up," Em said, not missing a beat. "I'll email everyone the directions in case you don't remember how to get there. Or if it's your first time." She smiled at Stephanie and Josh.

She breezed toward the narrow stairwell, and the rest of us lingered a bit longer, finishing up our snacks before we had to get ready to put in another two hours on the ice. Once we donned our skates, Mark kept bugging me again to do run-throughs of our programs, and I continued to refuse. We couldn't spend the next seven months trying to one-up Stephanie and Josh on a daily basis. That would take way more energy than simply concentrating on doing our best.

By the end of the second hour, my face was caked with sweat, and pieces of my hair that had escaped my ponytail stuck to my forehead. Mark and I had done repetitions of our new triple toe-double toe-double toe combination until I'd lost count of the number. We were still out of synch on the takeoff of each jump, but we were landing them, which was the most important thing. Josh and Stephanie weren't having the same success. Sergei was reworking their jump technique, and I winced on every hard fall they took. I knew what it felt like to slam into the ice that many times in one session, and it was a level of pain I didn't wish on anyone.

The big clock on the back wall ticked closer to one o'clock, and Em shouted, "Free-For-All Friday!" to which a chorus of cheers rang out from the group of us on the ice. All of us except Stephanie and Josh, who looked completely lost and confused over our excitement. Em skated over to the stereo next to the ice, and Josh glided over to me.

"What's Free-For-All Friday?" he asked as he wiped his glistening face with a towel.

I leaned against the boards and recaptured the stray hairs in my ponytail holder. "At the end of every Friday session, Em puts on a random mix of music, and we all skate for fun and make up choreography. We go two at a time with everyone getting a turn."

"That sounds kinda awesome."

"It is. We look forward to it every week. Em and Sergei skate together sometimes, too, which is a lot of fun to watch."

"Mark and Kenny, you're up first," Sergei said.

"Give us something good, Em," Mark said as he pushed off from the boards.

The rink came alive with "Viva La Vida," and Mark and Kenny took off in opposite directions. I recognized most of Mark's steps from the footwork sequence in our long program, and I shook my head. The whole point of the weekly exercise was to let loose and be original. My partner was awesome at following directions, but creativity didn't exactly flow freely from him.

Halfway through the song, Em cut the music and called out, "Stephanie and Courtney."

We gave each other cursory glances, and I straightened the straps of my tank top. I hoped we wouldn't get a slow song where Stephanie could show me up with her perfect balletic positions. We established our starting spots far across the rink from each other, and the upbeat R&B sound of Ne-Yo's "Miss Independent" burst through the speakers. I smiled and shook out my arms.

Stephanie was smiling even more confidently, and my excitement dimmed. Free-For-All Friday wasn't meant to be competitive, but the direct stare Stephanie aimed at me felt like she was saying, "Game on."

She began moving expertly to the beat, and I got started a few seconds later, watching her as I pushed hard into the ice. She'd probably taken hip-hop dance lessons from world-famous choreographers in L.A.

Speeding across the center line, I broke into quick steps to match the chorus. My gangly arms flailed back and forth as I did my best to interpret the rhythm. When I looked up, I noticed Josh's eyes following me, and my muscles tensed. I turned away from where he stood behind the boards and subdued my movements. I was used to only a familiar audience witnessing my spastic dancing.

When Em halted the song, I let out a long breath and beat Stephanie to the ice door. Sergei directed Josh and junior skater Denise to get ready, and I grabbed my water bottle and took a long swig.

"Mi Mancheri" was Em's next song choice, and my eyes stayed on Josh just as his had on me. He moved like liquid across the ice, becoming one with the passionate violin. The expression on his face was so serene, and he looked totally in his element. Seeing him alone without Stephanie made his ability even more apparent. He was a true dancer on the ice. The lean of his body over his deep edges, how effortlessly he expressed the music through his long limbs, down to his fingertips and pointed toes...

I backed away from the boards and took another long drink to wet my dry mouth. The younger girls were also staring at Josh, completely captivated. He didn't seem to notice as he flew around the rink, lost in his own world.

I studied his movements and the way he carried himself. Most of the guys I knew with that much artistic style and sensitivity to the music were gay. And Josh seemed to be a sensitive person off the ice, too. He was either gay or way more evolved than the straight guys I knew. Either way, it didn't matter because I had more important things on which to focus.

But it was an intriguing question.

****

A light breeze blew across Em and Sergei's back patio as I set bottles of mustard, mayo, and ketchup on the large round table. With the breeze came the mouth-watering charcoal smell from Sergei's grill, and my stomach rumbled. A few of my training mates had arrived and were milling about the back yard, and I hoped the rest would hurry up so we could chow down.

Sergei's fifteen-year-old daughter Liza opened the sliding patio door, and I spotted a familiar item in her raven-colored hair.

"Is that my headband? You've only been here a day and you're already stealing my stuff?" I tugged playfully on her long braid.

Her mother, Sergei's former skating partner, had driven her from New York for her annual summer-long stay on the Cape. Liza visited many weekends throughout the year and skated at our rink when she was in town, so we'd had a close relationship since she'd become a part of Sergei's life six years ago.

"I love your mom's creations." Liza adjusted the bright blue headband over her hair. "All her stuff is so pretty."

"She's making more jewelry and fewer accessories now," I said of my mom's home crafting business, an extra source of income that helped fund the astronomical cost of my skating.

"Did she make this?" Liza touched the maroon and gold woven bracelet I wore.

"Yep, Boston College colors, which I'll hopefully be draped in next year." I crossed my fingers.

"You'll get in. You were super smart in high school. And your dad went there."

"Let's hope the admissions office agrees," I said and took a closer look at Liza. "You should keep the headband. It matches your eyes."

"Really?" she squeaked. "Thanks!"

"Coming through… hot plate," Em warned as she emerged from the kitchen carrying a ceramic casserole dish.

She placed it on the table, and Liza lifted the glass cover. "What is that?"

"Spaghetti squash pesto lasagna."

Liza leaned over the dish. "Sounds kinda fancy for a barbecue."

"It's for Stephanie. She never gave me any vegan suggestions, so I found this recipe online."

"Ten bucks she doesn't eat it," I said.

"Be nice." Em pointed her potholder at me as she went inside.

The high-pitched giggles of Quinn and Alex filled the air, and I turned toward the yard. Mark and Kenny were racing across the grass with the twins on their backs. They had a lot of space to play in the expansive yard. A wrought-iron fence surrounded the rear of the property, and just beyond it was a sparkling blue pond.

When I turned back to the patio, Liza had disappeared and Stephanie and Josh had taken her place. Once again their outfits greatly contrasted — Stephanie in a crisp white shirt and pants, looking like she was going to a garden party, and Josh in a green T-shirt and khaki cargo shorts.

"Did you find the house okay?" I asked.

"We would have if *someone* had GPS in their car." Stephanie's oversized sunglasses glared at Josh.

"Getting lost is one of the fun parts of being in a new

place. It lets you see things you might not otherwise." His normally soft voice had a stern edge to it.

"I didn't need to see three dead end roads," she said and clomped in her wedge heels over to the ice chest on the edge of the patio. After plucking a bottle of water from the pile, she descended the steps to the yard and zeroed in on Denise, who happened to be from a wealthy Boston family. Did Stephanie have information on all our bank accounts?

Josh moved toward the ice chest. "Do you want something to drink?"

"Um... sure. I'll take a diet lemonade."

Water dripped from the plastic bottle, and Josh wiped it with his shirt before handing it to me. While he uncapped his sports drink, I said, "It's easy to get lost around here. I've lived on the Cape all my life, and I still discover little hidden areas."

"I'm looking forward to exploring it all while we're here. What I've seen so far is really nice."

"Coco!" Quinn ran onto the patio and stopped at my side. "You see my horsee?"

"He might be in my room. Remember you were playing with him there last night?"

She looked up at Josh and cocked her head to one side. "Who you?"

He grinned, and it was the first time I'd seen him completely relaxed off the ice. His blue eyes brightened and crinkled in the corners, and he crouched on one knee on the wooden planks.

"I'm Josh. I'm one of your mom and dad's new students. Who are you?"

"I'm Quinn." She stuck out her hand. "Nice to meet you."

He laughed, and so did I.

"Nice to meet you, too, Quinn." His hand swallowed hers.

She looked back up at me. "I go find my horsee."

Before I could blink she'd raced inside. Josh glanced over

his shoulder at the door and chuckled. "That's one cute kid."

"She's a riot. She's not afraid to talk to anyone. Em and Sergei are going to have their hands full when she's a teenager."

"You said you have a room here?" Josh asked.

I nodded as I swallowed my lemonade. "My parents moved to Boston last year, and making that commute would be a pain in the butt, so Em and Sergei offered to let me stay here."

"That's pretty cool of them."

"Yeah, I couldn't afford my own place, so they really saved me."

Sergei bounded up the steps and slapped Josh on the shoulder on his way inside. "Hope you brought your appetite."

"It smells great," Josh called after him.

"So you're not a vegan, too?" I asked.

"No, I couldn't live without burgers. I've been having In-N-Out withdrawals since I left L.A."

I laughed. "I can give you the names of some places around here with good burgers."

"That would be great." His eyes brightened even more. "I need a lot of restaurant recommendations because I don't cook and Steph only makes vegan stuff, so I'll be eating out most of the time."

"The place where I work has really good food. I usually eat dinner there before my shift."

"You wait tables?"

I took a quick sip of my drink. "I used to, but now I'm behind the bar."

"That must be an interesting job."

"It's not as fascinating as it sounds. Most of the people who sit at the bar are loners avoiding a table for one."

He smiled and glanced downward. "Well, I'm one of those loners, so you might be seeing me soon."

I was about to reply, but Sergei returned with a large empty platter, and Em followed close behind with a matching one. They announced lunch was ready and started transferring the chicken and burgers from the grill, while everyone else swarmed the patio table to get plates. I cut into the lasagna and helped myself to a serving then watched as Stephanie took a long look before bypassing it for the salad bowl. Josh stood next to her, shaking his head as he spooned a big helping of the lasagna onto his plate.

We all found places at the picnic tables set up on the grass, and Quinn squeezed between Liza and me. Em had cut up her chicken into bite-sized pieces, and Quinn popped one into her mouth and looked across the table.

"Hi, Josh," she said as she chewed.

"Sweetie, close your mouth when you're eating," Em said.

Josh smiled and put down his burger. "Hello again, Quinn. I haven't seen you in so long."

She giggled. "You silly."

"This lasagna is *soo* good, Em," Liza said loud enough for the whole table, including Stephanie, to hear.

I suppressed a laugh with a bite of hamburger, while Em raised an eyebrow at Liza. But Liza added even louder, "Yum-O!"

"Mommy best cook in da whole world," Quinn said.

Em reached over to wipe barbecue sauce from Alex's chin. "I promise I didn't bribe her to say that."

"Everything really is delicious," Josh said.

Quinn kept us entertained with her ramblings as we ate, and afterward everyone scattered around the yard again. I plopped down on the patio swing, and Liza joined me with two of Em's homemade fruit popsicles.

"Grapefruit or pomegranate?" she asked.

I chose pomegranate and took a bite of the cold sweetness. The slushiness stung my tongue.

"Josh has definitely raised the cuteness level at the rink," Liza said, her gaze trained on him.

He stood beside Sergei on the grass, his hands in his pockets. His eyes were doing that crinkling thing again as he laughed. He was indeed very cute... always had been. And he was very fit. I didn't like when guys were too beefy, and he had just the right amount of muscle filling out his T-shirt. But gay or straight, he was the competition, and eye candy was all he could be.

"I wish he was my age," Liza said.

"Like your mom would let you go on a date. She freaks out when you talk to a boy."

She sighed. "A girl can dream."

"I'm not sure he's into girls anyway."

"What makes you think that?"

"Just the way he skates, and he has that whole sensitive thing going on."

"Not every guy who points his toes when he skates is gay. I don't get that feeling from him at all." She licked pink slush from her thumb. "He just seems like a sweet guy."

She took one last slurp of her popsicle and hopped off the swing. I continued to watch Josh until Stephanie stepped into my line of sight and made herself comfortable next to me. As comfortable as she could be in her fancy outfit.

"I thought I should come over and give you some advice," she said.

*Oh, this should be good.*

"I saw you checking out my brother, and I wanted to let you know you're wasting your time because it's never going to happen."

I didn't know whether to be curious or insulted. Curiosity got the better of me. "Why? Because he's gay?"

She let out a tinkly laugh. "You think he's gay?"

"I wasn't sure..."

"I heard Kyle was cheating on you, so I guess your

judgment of men does need a little work. But, no, Josh is most definitely not gay."

Heat rose to my scalp, and I looked down at my Converse. *Damn small skating world and its gossip mill.*

"Well, thanks for clearing that up, but I'm not interested in Josh," I said.

"Good because he's way out of your league. He's going to law school at UCLA next year, and he has a place waiting for him at our dad's entertainment law practice in Beverly Hills. It's a whole different world from the one you're living in."

"Oh, I bet it is," I said with bite.

"Then you clearly see you should forget about pursuing him."

A scalding response burned my once-frozen tongue, and I couldn't hold it in. "As I stated before, I'm not interested in your brother, and the only thing I *clearly* see is you are a total bitch."

Her mouth fell open, and I stood and walked off the porch, not giving her a second look.

# Chapter Four

I looked at my watch and sighed. Only a half hour had passed since the last time I'd checked the time. Weeknights at the restaurant were so slow, especially since tourist season hadn't kicked into high gear yet. Only two customers sat at the long bar, and one of them was a famously low tipper. I wouldn't be adding much to my skating fund tonight.

One of the waitresses, Meredith, walked up to the bar and leaned her elbows on the polished wood. She was my age and taking classes at Cape Cod Community College, and we were two of the few employees who worked at the restaurant year-round. I'd grown apart from my high school friends who'd gone away to college, so I was happy to have met her. Neither of us had a lot of free time with skating, school, and work, but we tried to do fun things together when we got the chance.

"My section is officially a ghost town," she said.

"It's been dead over here all night, too."

She looked down and brushed some lint off her black tie, part of the white button-down, black tie, and black pants uniform we wore. We also each had our hair pinned up in a neat bun — mine blond, hers brunette. We couldn't have any stray hairs falling into the food. The only splash of color I had on me was on my teal dangly earrings. I always wore a pair of Mom's colorful handmade earrings to add some life to my uniform.

"What are you doing this weekend?" Meredith asked. "We should go to the beach."

"I'm working the day shift on Saturday because I'm babysitting that night for Em and Sergei."

"You always babysit when they go out. They can't find someone else?"

"Liza's going to a sleepover, but I always offer anyway. It's the least I can do since they let me live with them rent-free."

My peripheral vision showed someone taking a seat at the other end of the bar. I turned and found Josh giving me a little smile and wave.

"Who's that?" Meredith straightened up with interest.

"That's Josh. He's part of the new team that trains with us. The brother and sister I told you about."

"You didn't mention he's a total hottie."

Maybe because I was trying not to notice how much of a hottie he was. "Well, he's a customer now, so I need to take his order."

I grabbed a menu and silverware from under the bar and placed them in front of Josh. "Hey, what can I get you to drink?"

"Scotch neat and just leave the bottle."

He wasn't smiling anymore, and I froze in place. "Um... okay..."

His straight face cracked, and he broke into quiet laughter. "I was just joking."

My shoulders relaxed. "I thought maybe skating with Stephanie might have driven you to drink." I bit my lip and stammered, "I mean... I... sorry, I know she's your sister and all."

"No, you're right. Steph's not the easiest person to get along with."

Since I'd called her a bitch at the barbecue, she'd pretended I was invisible at the rink even more than before. It was nice I didn't have to talk to her but also extremely awkward when we found ourselves alone in the locker room.

"I don't know how you skate with her *and* live with her," I said.

"It's why I don't mind going out to eat every night. I had more of my own space at our parents' house, so being in tighter quarters here with her is taking some getting used to."

"Can I get my check?" grumpy Mr. Mayer, the low tipper, called out to me.

"Sure." I turned to him and then back to Josh. "What can I really get you to drink?"

"I'll just have water. Thanks."

I printed Mr. Mayer's bill from the cash register behind the bar and then delivered Josh's glass of water. Since he was still examining the large menu, I went back to Mr. Mayer's now-vacated spot and opened the black check folder. On the tip line, the old man had written one dollar.

"Seriously?" I said.

Meredith was walking past the bar and stopped when she heard me. "Uh-oh. How low did he go this time?"

"He had a thirty dollar steak, and he tipped me one buck." I slapped the folder shut. "That'll pay for less than a minute of my lessons."

"Cheap ass," Meredith said before resuming her path to the kitchen.

I put on a smile and took Josh's order before I cashed out my other customer, leaving Josh as the sole patron at the bar. He looked beside him at the line of empty seats.

"Should I be worried about the lack of people here?" he asked. "I'm trusting your claim that this place has good food."

"It gets really busy on weekends. There's a guy that plays the piano on Friday and Saturday nights, and all the old geezers come out. It's a totally happening scene."

"Sounds entertaining. Anything's more happening than what I'd be doing at home."

"And what would that be?"

He took a sip of water and thought a moment. "Probably listening to my iPod on full blast so I don't have to hear Steph watching reality TV at volume level fifty."

"You should come check it out this weekend then. The piano guy's actually pretty good if you can put up with some of the cheesy songs he plays."

He leaned slightly forward. "After a lifetime in skating, I've become immune to cheesy music."

One of the waiters interrupted us, asking me to fill a drink order for his table, so I slid down the bar to get the wine. As I poured two glasses of red, I glanced at Josh and caught him watching me. He quickly looked away to the TV behind the bar. Was I being too friendly, encouraging him to come back to the restaurant so soon? I didn't want to send the wrong signals. He just seemed like he could use the company. I'd gladly help anyone get away from Stephanie.

I scooted into the kitchen to see if Josh's dinner was ready and came out carrying a tray with his grilled salmon and asparagus. His eyes grew big as I set down the plate, and I parked myself in front of him, waiting for him to take a bite.

"You're going to stand there and watch me eat?" he asked.

"Until you tell me how you like it."

He smiled and tasted a piece of the fish. His eyes stayed on his plate as I sensed he wasn't comfortable being watched. His strong jaw moved slowly, and I found myself studying his mouth for the first time. He had nice, full lips. The kind that were made for kissing…

*Jeez, what are you, thirteen again?* I backed off and picked up a dishrag to wipe a nonexistent spot from the bar.

Josh finished chewing and waited a long moment, not giving me any hint of his opinion as he continued staring downward. Finally, he placed his fork on the plate and looked up at me.

"It's excellent," he said.

I pumped my fist. "Success!"

"You'll have to tell the owner you've recruited a new regular."

"I will. Maybe he'll give me a ten cent raise."

He cut into his asparagus. "How long have you been working here?"

"About two years. My dad was laid off from his job, and things got pretty tight, so I looked for something that could fit into my training schedule."

"Is he still out of work?"

"No, he found a job in Boston — that's why my parents moved. It's just not as good a position as he had before so I needed to keep working." I folded the dishtowel and hung it under the bar. "They've been really good to me here, letting me take off for competitions and always giving me the dinner shift on weekdays."

"It still has to be tough working all night after skating all morning."

"There are some mornings I really hate the alarm clock." I laughed. "But I try to keep a consistent schedule — leave here by ten, in bed by eleven, so I can get eight hours of sleep."

"Your life sounds as exciting as mine." He smiled.

"At least you've been to college already. You must've had some exciting times there, right? Frat parties, football games…"

He stared at his glass and traced the rim of it with his thumb. "With skating always coming first, I didn't really have the typical college experience. It was pretty much train, go to class, eat, study, sleep."

I eyed him with one brow skeptically raised. "Not even one night of drunken debauchery?"

He slowly shook his head. "I've never had a drop of alcohol."

"Really? You knew how to order a scotch."

"It's my dad's favorite drink."

I studied him harder, and he looked down and reached for his napkin. I'd thought I had limited social experience, but Josh might be even more inexperienced than I was. Even I had gone through the ritual of sneaking into a club and getting sloppy drunk (okay, it had only been once, but still).

"Wanna try some vodka?" I joked and pointed to the line of bottles behind me.

His smile returned. "I'm good, thanks."

"Okay, you just let me know because I make a mean Moscow Mule. At least that's what my customers tell me."

I gave him space to finish his meal while I organized glasses at the other end of the bar. When I went to refill his water, he was on his last piece of fish.

"I'll be tempted to have this again this weekend, but I'm curious if everything else is just as good," he said.

"So you're definitely gonna come for the big entertainment?" I realized after I spoke how excited I sounded.

Josh apparently picked up on it because his grin grew a little wider. "I'm psyched for the blue-hair crowd and the cheesy music. Sounds like this will be the hottest spot on Cape Cod."

I laughed and moved over to the cash register. "Can I get you anything else? We have some yummy desserts. Not that I eat them on a regular basis," I added hastily.

"I'll wait and splurge this weekend. Gives me something else to look forward to." He paused and grimaced. "How sad is it that one of the highlights of my week is dessert?"

"Hey, I've been known to take an hour to eat a piece of cake just to make it last. There's no shame in anticipating and appreciating dessert."

I gave him his check and carried his plate to the kitchen. When I returned, he was standing and putting his wallet into the back pocket of his jeans. I brushed aside the twinge of sadness I felt because he was leaving and marched confidently toward him.

"Thanks again for the recommendation," he said. "I'll see you tomorrow."

"Bright and early!" I chirped a little too enthusiastically.

He walked away, and I bopped myself on the head with the bill folder before opening it. As I counted the cash, I realized Josh had left double the expected tip. *What the hell?* Was he pitying me?

I squeezed the money in my fist and hurried for the door. Josh was a few steps into the parking lot. I called his name, and he spun around.

"What is this?" I held up the cash. "I didn't tell you about my dad losing his job because I was looking for a handout. I don't need your charity."

He looked stunned. "I... I didn't... that's not why I did it. I heard you say that old guy only gave you a dollar, so I wanted to give you what he should have. What you deserved."

The tension in my body melted, and I softened my voice. "You didn't have to do that. You can't cover every cheapskate that comes in here. You'll be broke by the end of summer."

His lips twitched upward. "It just didn't seem right."

"Well, thank you. Mr. Mayer owes you a drink. A non-alcoholic one." I smiled. "And I owe you an apology for getting all defensive."

"Don't worry about it. It's forgotten."

I let out a breath. "Good."

We stood quietly, making the crickets chirping around us sound even louder. Josh fiddled with his keys and took two small steps backward.

"So… goodnight again." He slowly walked in reverse toward the row of parked cars.

"Goodnight."

When he eventually turned to his car, I went inside and thumped myself on the head again, that time with the heel of my hand. What was it about Josh that threw me off balance and made me act like an idiot? If anyone else had left me a humungous tip, I'd be dancing around and bragging to Meredith.

Me and hot rich guys apparently weren't a good combination.

****

When Friday night at the restaurant came and went and Josh didn't show, I hid my disappointment behind the smiles I gave my customers. And there was a steady stream of them all night long. I was dragging the next day during the lunch shift and needed to sneak in a nap before Em and Sergei left for their dinner reservation.

With Liza gone for her sleepover, the twins and I had the run of the house. We played hide-and-seek and then built Lego animals until their bedtime. While we played I sometimes sat back and just watched Quinn and Alex because their interactions fascinated me. Children's behavior in general fascinated me, but the twins' behavior with each other was even more interesting. As they figured out the building blocks, they seemed to be able to communicate with each other without even saying anything. I'd heard about twin intuition, but I'd never realized at how young an age they felt it.

Quinn and Alex had their own bedrooms, but Quinn had been sleeping in one of Alex's twin beds since they'd graduated from their cribs. I tucked them in under their blue comforters and went to turn off the lamp, but Alex tugged on my sweatpants.

"Read to us?" he asked.

I brushed the tuft of blond hair over his forehead. "Sure, my sweet boy."

I picked up the book on the nightstand. It had kittens and puppies on the cover.

"Daddy read dat last night," Quinn said.

"I'll get something new then," I said.

I chose another book from the hundreds on Alex's tall bookshelf and settled on the plush carpet between the two beds. As I read the story about farm animals and sounded out all the required "moos" and "cock-a-doodle-doos," the twins' eyes drifted shut, and I trailed off reading before I reached "The End." After switching off the lamp, I headed for my own room, which had formerly been the guest room, and collapsed on the bed. Not yet nine o'clock on a Saturday night and I was ready to crash. Even the senior citizens who hung out at the restaurant had a later bedtime.

My phone sat on the nightstand, and the red light was blinking. I grabbed it without moving my head from the pillow and clicked to read the text message.

Meredith: *Your hottie friend is here. He looked bummed when I told him you weren't working.*

An immediate smile came to my lips. I read the message again and started typing.

Me: *He so wants me.*

Me: *I'm totally kidding (in case you didn't get that).*

I laid the phone on the bed and pressed my cheek to the cool pillowcase. There'd been a time many moons ago when I'd thought Josh *did* want me. Well, in the innocent way a fourteen-year-old boy wants a thirteen-year-old girl. Mark and I had competed against Josh and Stephanie at the Indy Pair Challenge, and a group of us were hanging out afterward in Mark's hotel room when boredom had turned into a cliché teen movie.

"Let's play *Seven Minutes in Heaven*," my friend Sarah said.

*"What the heck is that?" Mark asked.*

*"You know, when each girl picks a boy's name out of a hat, and they have to go into the closet together for seven minutes."*

*I chewed on my thumbnail and peeked up at the three boys in the room. No way did I want to go in the closet with Mark. That would be so awfully awkward. And his buddy Tim wouldn't be a much better option. He was annoyingly loud and always making stupid jokes.*

*And then there was Josh.*

*He was s-o-o-o cute but so quiet. He hadn't said a word to me, but I'd caught him staring at me a lot. What would I do if I had to go in the closet with him? I'd never kissed a boy. Do I open my mouth? I'd seen people on TV do that. Would my braces get in the way?*

*Sarah's friend Christy had already written the boys' names on scraps of paper and tossed them into Tim's baseball cap. Tim slid the closet door open and waved his hand in front of his nose.*

*"It smells like Mark's stinky shoes in here," he said.*

*"Then we can go in the bathroom instead," Sarah said.*

*She shoved the hat in front of me, and I hesitated before sticking my hand inside. My fingers touched all three pieces of paper, and as I picked one I prayed silently, Please be Josh. Please be Josh.*

*I opened the paper, and my heart started beating in triple time.*

*"Josh," I said quietly.*

*He was leaning against the desk with his hands in his pockets, and his eyes locked on mine for just a second before he lowered them. It didn't look like he was going to move. I crumpled the paper in my sweaty palm and shifted my weight from one sneaker to the other.*

*"Go get it, man." Tim punched Josh's arm.*

*Josh pushed away from the desk and waited for me to walk ahead of him to the bathroom. My legs were shaking worse than they had at nationals. Josh turned on the light and closed the door behind us, and I stood beside the sink, trying to breathe normally. Did I need to breathe when he kissed me? Or was I supposed to hold my breath? Oh my God, there were too many things to think about!*

*Josh stuffed his hands back in his pockets and glanced at the* floor before looking up at me. *"We don't have to do anything."*

His voice was so soft and quiet I could barely hear him. But what he meant was obvious.

My heart dropped into my stomach. He didn't want to kiss me. Whatever the reason he'd been staring at me earlier, it wasn't because he thought I was pretty or interesting.

I bent my head so he couldn't see the redness I felt on my face. *"O… okay."*

The seconds of silence that followed seemed like hours. I could see Josh shuffling his feet as I kept my head down.

*"You skated great today,"* he said.

I looked up. *"You watched us?"*

He nodded. *"I really liked your program."*

*"Thanks."* I smiled a little.

Silence set in again, and I wondered how many minutes we had left. I glanced at the mirror so I could look at Josh without him noticing. He seemed nice and not stuck-up like his sister who I'd met in the locker room. I sighed and frowned at my reflection. Maybe if I was wearing make-up he would've liked me better. But Mom would only let me wear lip gloss off the ice.

I tried desperately to think of something to say, but I couldn't come up with anything that wouldn't sound totally lame. So we continued to stand there, not speaking and not making eye contact. My face and neck were so hot, and I feared I'd start visibly sweating. Hadn't seven minutes passed yet?

When Sarah knocked on the door and called for us to come out, I practically bulldozed over Josh to leave. Everyone in the room watched us closely, and Sarah waggled her eyebrows at us.

*"Did you guys have fun?"* she asked.

I sat on the bed and nodded with a forced smile while Josh just went back to leaning against the desk. Yeah, that was fun. If by fun you mean the worst seven minutes of my life.

I turned over on my back and stared up at the slowly-spinning ceiling fan. God, I wouldn't want to be thirteen again for all the money in the world. At least Josh and I could converse like normal people now. But after all the years I still wondered why he hadn't kissed me. I mean, I'd been a little awkward, but I'd thought I was reasonably cute. Couldn't he have just given me a peck? According to Stephanie, he wasn't gay, one of the possibilities I'd previously entertained. So that wasn't it.

Who knew what went through the mind of a fourteen-year-old boy. From my recent dating experience, I obviously had no clue what even twenty-one-year-old boys were thinking.

# Chapter Five

"You need more tension in your arms, Court," Em said as she bent my elbow to adjust my hold on Mark's shoulder. "Remember the videos we watched online?"

I did indeed remember the countless tango videos we'd watched after we decided to use Tanghetto's version of "Enjoy the Silence" for our short program. But watching the experts do the dance and actually capturing the flavor of it ourselves were two very different things.

I tightened the muscles in my arms and gripped Mark's hand harder. Em left us at the end of the rink to restart the music, and we began our straight-line footwork sequence again, for what seemed like the hundredth time in the past hour.

We'd only gone a quarter of the way down the ice when Em stopped the music. Again. Stephanie and Josh glanced our way as they glided past us with Sergei on their heels.

Em reeled off another long list of corrections to our posture, and I silently cursed myself for finding this music even though I loved it. Em seemed to be forgetting that we were competing for a spot on the Olympic team, not the mirror ball trophy on *Dancing with the Stars.*

When the afternoon session mercifully ended, I couldn't untie my skate laces quickly enough. Being on the ice felt more natural and comfortable to me than anything else in my life, but there were some endless training days when I wanted to take off my skates and never look back.

I ran up to the lounge to get my cup of yogurt from the fridge and then headed outside for a few minutes of sunshine. Settling on the front steps of the rink, I tilted my head back and soaked in the Vitamin D. The rays kissed my bare shoulders, feeling like a soothing warm bath.

"Looks like we had the same idea," a soft voice said behind me.

I curved my neck and saw Josh tearing open his own yogurt. He sat on the other end of the steps, leaving a clear path between us.

"Summer days on the Cape are the best," I said. "But this is what it's like all the time in L.A., isn't it?"

"Mostly. Except for a few cold snaps. You know, like sixty degrees." He smiled.

"It sounds amazing, but I think I'd miss having seasons. The leaves changing, the snow melting…"

"I'm looking forward to seeing the snow," he said before taking in a spoonful of yogurt.

"We'll see how excited you are after shoveling your driveway a few times."

He laughed along with me and then turned quiet. With the rink set far back from the highway behind rows of trees, there was no noise except for a few tweeting birds.

"You guys have been working on your tango a lot this week," Josh said.

I swiveled my spoon around in my cup. "The finer details of the program are taking a little longer to come together."

"Have you worked with any dancers off the ice?"

"Sergei mentioned finding someone, but I don't really

have room for it in my budget."

He nodded with a sympathetic smile, and we went back to eating our snacks. The silence was broken when Josh cleared his throat and looked up at me.

"I um… I studied the tango in school, so maybe I could help out. I'm not a pro or anything, but I know the basics pretty well."

I paused with my spoon in the air. "You studied it in school?"

"I minored in dance."

"Oh." I bobbed my head up and down. "That explains a lot about your skating."

He wrinkled his forehead, and I rushed to continue, "You're really in touch with the music when you skate."

His eyes brightened before he lowered them to the stairs. "Thanks."

"I appreciate your offer, but I know what Mark would say if I suggested it to him. He'd think you have some ulterior motive for helping us."

"Like what? Teaching you the wrong way to tango to sabotage you?"

"As ridiculous as it sounds, his mind would go there. He's that paranoid sometimes."

Josh appeared to fall deep into thought. "I could just show *you* some things if you want. It might still be helpful."

For a moment, Mark's paranoia seeped into my brain and I wondered why Josh was being so generous to a competitor. His clear blue eyes stared back at me, and the question remained no more. I saw nothing but genuineness.

"Sure," I said. "I need all the help I can get."

"Do you have time later before you go to work?"

I hesitated before answering. I didn't want him showing up at Em and Sergei's house because then I'd have to explain why Mark wasn't present, and Em would want him to be involved. And then I'd have to talk to Mark and he would get all suspicious. No, that was more drama than I cared to create.

"Why don't you meet me at the restaurant? I usually get there at four to eat before my shift. We can use the back deck. It closes after lunch until dinner so no one will be out there."

"Cool. I'll meet you—"

"Josh, Dad wants to talk to you." Stephanie stood in the half-open doorway to the rink, holding up her phone.

Josh's face tightened, and he rose from the steps. "See you later."

Stephanie glared at me before following Josh inside, and I rolled my eyes. Not more than a minute later, Mark came through the glass doors and stood over me.

"What were you so chatty with Josh about?"

*What did I say about paranoia?* "I didn't know I had to report all my conversations to you."

"I just think it's best to keep our distance from him and Stephanie."

I stood and brushed the seat of my black stretchy pants. "I have no problem keeping my distance from Stephanie. In fact, the distance can't be great enough. But unlike her, Josh is a decent human being, and there's no reason to be rude to him."

"I didn't say to be rude, but I've seen you guys talking every day and getting too friendly isn't a good idea. I don't want you going soft and losing your competitive edge."

"I'm not going soft," I said, raising my voice. "I'm working my butt off every day harder than I ever have, and I can have a conversation with someone without it affecting my *competitive edge.*"

I stormed into the rink and spent the next hour releasing my frustration over Mark's moodiness with an intense workout in the gym. My abdominal muscles burned as I did crunch after crunch to increase my core strength. As a pair girl I had to have wicked strong abs to hold myself up in the overhead lifts, and I could outlast most guys in a sit-up challenge.

Josh was lifting weights on the opposite side of the long room, so we didn't talk again before I left the rink. A few hours later he knocked on the locked door of the restaurant, and I put my sandwich down to let him inside. He was wearing a gray T-shirt and black gym shorts, looking like he was ready for another workout.

"I'm almost finished eating," I said as I led him over to the bar.

He left one stool between us and peered at my plate. "What you got there?"

"It's a special veggie sandwich Chef makes for me. It's not on the menu."

"Looks good. Not as good as the steak sandwich I had last weekend, though."

I speared a cherry tomato from my side salad. "Was the meal worth sitting through our piano guy's old-school playlist?"

"Definitely. Like I said, I can tune out bad music." He rotated his stool to face me. "What was a little disturbing were some of the older ladies hovering around me. I swear one of them tried to hit on me."

I laughed. "Oh yeah, you have to watch out for the divorcées and the widows on the prowl. They have no shame and will pounce on the first hot guy they see."

Josh's lips curled upward, and he looked down at the bar. Heat flamed my face as I realized what I'd said. *Real smooth. Why don't you tell him he has a smokin' body and get it all out in the open?*

I gulped down some water and coughed into my linen napkin. "Did they um... did they scare you away from coming back this weekend?"

"Nah, I think I can fend them off." He picked up the drink specials menu from the bar and kept his focus downward, appearing to read the list. "Are you working

Saturday night this week?"

So he wanted to make sure I was going to be there. Interesting. Or not. Maybe he simply liked seeing a familiar face. It couldn't be much fun eating alone every night.

"I'll be here," I said.

"Cool." He smiled and tapped the menu on the bar.

I took a bite of my sandwich and chewed rapidly. Now I knew how self-conscious Josh had felt when I'd watched him eat. He turned to look at the TV behind the bar, and I shoveled down more of my dinner. *Slow down. You don't want indigestion interrupting your tango.*

After I finished my last bite, I waved my finger at Josh's outfit. "Are you going to work out again after this?"

"Sort of. Steph and I do hot yoga a couple times a week."

"Em's into that, too. Do you go to the same studio?"

"I've never seen her. We go to a place Steph found in Centerville."

"Em's asked me to go with her a few times, but working out in oppressive heat sounds like torture to me."

"You should try it. It feels better than you think."

"I'll stick to my air-conditioned exercise routine." I took my plate and glass behind the bar. "Let me drop this in the kitchen and we can get started."

I pushed open the swinging door, and Meredith left her conversation with Ronnie, the restaurant owner, to meet me at the counter.

"Is your dance teacher here yet?" She shimmied her hips.

"Yes, he is. And you will not spy on us and make fun of us."

She put on an exaggerated insulted face. "I wouldn't make fun of you. Okay, maybe a little. There are just too many *Dirty Dancing* jokes waiting to be told."

"No spying." I pointed a finger at her.

"Yes, Baby." She smiled. "Have the time of your life."

"Ha. Ha. You're hilarious."

I turned and went out to the bar, pushing aside thoughts of bodies pressed together, gyrating to the beat. No such dancing would be happening here. This was going to be a simple lesson on technique... during which Josh would be touching me and standing very close to me.

The suddenly quick pitter-patter of my heart stopped me in my tracks, and Josh looked at me curiously as I did a one-eighty and hurried back into the kitchen. I aimed straight for my purse and gazed into my compact mirror. No spinach in my teeth. No breadcrumbs on my chin. I stashed the compact and popped a mint into my mouth. I couldn't have sandwich breath while sharing dance space with Josh.

I smoothed my tie and my ponytail and returned to the bar with a smile. "Sorry, I had to check on something."

Josh followed me through the wood-paneled dining room to the French doors leading outside. The marsh grass surrounding the deck swished in the breeze, and the late afternoon sun reflected off Nantucket Sound. It would've been beautifully serene if not for the ridiculous anxiety that had begun to churn in my stomach.

"So... the tango," Josh said. "It's a bit different from the usual ballroom hold. Have you done any ballroom dancing?"

I shook my head. Slow dancing at my prom was the extent of my partner dancing, and that had been more swaying while standing still than anything.

"Good. Then you won't know the difference." He smiled. "If you've watched videos, you've seen the tango has a close hold."

He took a tentative step toward me but kept his arms at his sides. "But I'm not sure how close Emily and Sergei want you and Mark to be."

I got a stronger whiff of his cologne, which smelled expensive. And sweet. Like him. *Oh, dear God.*

"Um... we need to be pretty close in some parts of the program," I said.

He shifted nearer, sliding his hand around to my lower back, and the heat from his touch radiated through my cotton shirt, my skin, and into the deepest cells of my body. I didn't dare look up because there would be only a narrow space between our faces. Between our mouths…

*Tango! Focus on the tango.*

Thinking I should demonstrate what I did know about the dance, I clutched Josh's right shoulder and extended my other arm out to the side like I'd seen the pros do.

"Let's move this a little lower," he said.

He gently pried my hand from his shoulder and placed it around the top of his bicep. The muscle was solid under my fingers, and I resisted the strong urge to squeeze it.

"How tight should I hold onto you?" I asked.

He took a noticeable swallow and glanced at my grip. "That's… that's good."

"Em was telling me to have more tension in my arms, so I wasn't sure if I was supposed to hold on tighter or just hold my arms straighter or…" *Nice rambling.*

"You'll want to keep your right arm tense because it helps you follow your partner's lead." He grasped my right hand, pressing our palms together, and my pulse sped even faster. "I know you're not actually doing the full dance on the ice, but I'll show you how it would look and feel."

*It feels terrifying yet totally amazing.*

He was a head taller than me, so I was still staring at his shoulder, and I remembered seeing some of the women in the videos tilting their heads toward their partners. "Should I look straight ahead or…"

"You can turn your head slightly to the right. Just make sure your posture stays straight."

I looked inward at his chest, not moving anything anywhere else. I had no problem keeping the required tension in my body. I was one humungous ball of tension.

Josh pulled me a little closer to him, and his chest

expanded and contracted at a swifter pace. Was he feeling nervous, too? I wished I could put my hand against his heart to see if it was beating as fast as mine.

"The first step I'll go forward with my left foot and you'll go back with your right," he said. "Then I'll go forward with my right and you back with your left."

His hand lightly squeezed mine as he led me through the steps and showed me the next ones, counting out, "Slow, slow, quick, quick, slow." I followed his lead, keeping my posture mega stiff, but every slight movement of his hand on my back, even just the faintest brush of his fingertips, made me tingle. It threatened to turn my stiffness into total mush.

We completed a full circle and repeated the pattern, moving faster with each repetition. Josh was a commanding lead, but there was also a softness to the way he pressed my hand and glided me around the deck. His little bits of instruction as we danced were also delivered softly and patiently.

I got lost in the flow of the steps and felt more at ease until Josh stopped and we were just standing there, holding onto each other. Then the rush of nervousness returned. Josh inched nearer, and his fingertips grazed my spine, sending a thrilling wave of heat through me. Too thrilling.

"Was that okay?" I asked as I let go of him.

"Yeah, you did… you did great." He shoved his hands in his pockets. "Did you get a good feel for it?"

I nodded. "I think I was definitely too rigid before. I mean, there has to be some rigidness, but I was like a robot. It helped to do the dance with someone who's comfortable with it."

"I'm glad I could help." He smiled. "I love teaching this kind of stuff."

"Maybe you can moonlight as a dance teacher when you're in law school."

His smile faded into a thin line. "Or maybe I could just

ditch law school," he muttered.

I wasn't quite sure how to respond to his sudden mood change and the revealing comment he'd made, but I wanted to know more.

"Is working with your dad not something you want to do?"

"It's what I've always been expected to do, so…"

"But if there are other things you'd rather pursue—"

"I should get going. I have to meet Steph." He stepped back and moved toward the door. "Let me know if you want to practice again. Anytime."

He gave me a smile and was gone before I could even reply. I stood looking at the door with what must've been a befuddled expression because the first thing Meredith said when she came outside was, "What's that face all about? Did it not go well?"

"No, it was fine. He…" My body recalled the sensation of being held in Josh's strong arms, and a tiny shiver shook me. "He gives good tango."

"Oh, really?" She flashed a knowing grin. "So, he's hot and a great dancer. That's a pretty sweet combination."

"And one that I will not be getting all mixed up with." I held up both my hands.

"Why not? Because you compete against him? I watched you for a minute when you were dancing, and I saw a little somethin' somethin' between you."

I'd felt a little *somethin' somethin'*, but it was a moot point. "There's a long list of reasons why nothing will be happening between Josh and me, and yes, him being a competitor is one of them. Not that there's interest from either of us in going there."

"You know if he was a regular guy you met here in town you'd be all over it. From what you've told me, he is so your type."

Meredith was right. Whenever she and I went to the

movies, I always fawned over the quiet, not-so-suave heroes while she went for the cocky, smooth-talking ones. I had to think of Josh like a character in a movie — completely unattainable.

"It doesn't matter if he's my type because we're just acquaintances."

"Hmm…" Meredith put her arm around me and steered me toward the door. "That's a shame because you'd be awfully cute together."

I shook my head at her, but I couldn't help conjure up the image of Josh and me hand-in-hand as a couple. My head leaning against his shoulder and his crinkly-eyed smile beaming at me. Damn, we *would* be cute together.

Now I mentally shook my head at myself. Why did I always have to crush on the wrong guys?

# Chapter Six

With my leg stretched across the bleachers, I shifted the ice pack on my knee and winced at the bite of cold on my skin. I'd somehow managed to land on my knee during a nasty fall on a triple toe loop, and Sergei had made me call it quits for the day. Mark continued to practice our jumps without me, but he wasn't my focus as I watched the action on the ice.

Em was working with Josh and Stephanie on their long program, and Josh was helping create much of the choreography. Usually Em took charge of designing our programs, but I noticed her taking many of Josh's suggestions. The ballet music of *Daphnis and Chloe* was perfect for Josh and Stephanie's gorgeous lines, and they were planning to show them off with lots of spirals and other beautiful positions I wished I looked half as good doing.

"Hey, Kid."

I hadn't even seen Em's former partner Chris enter the rink, and there he was standing at the bottom of the bleachers.

"Long time no see." I started to get up to hug him, but he stopped me.

"I'll come to you." He climbed up and wrapped me in a

bear hug. "Looks like you had a fun morning."

"Slipped off my toe and had an awkward splat. It should be okay Monday, I think."

"Want me to take a look at it?" he asked.

Chris was studying to be a sports trainer, and he liked to diagnose all our aches and pains when he visited, but I didn't think this was anything worse than a bad bruise.

"That's okay. It's already feeling better with the ice." I patted the pack of cubes. "Are you and Aubrey down for the weekend?"

"Yeah, we're both taking a full class load in summer school, so we can only make it here on weekends. I think everyone else in Boston had the same plan with the traffic we were in this morning."

"How are the wedding plans going? I think a New Year's Eve wedding is uber romantic, by the way."

"Well, it was the night we had our first kiss, so as Mr. Romance I had to insist we get married then." He smiled, showing off his matching dimples.

"I'm glad you did. I'm going to need a party around that time to take my mind off the biggest competition of my life."

"You and Mark are gonna kill it at nationals. Em's told me how hard you're working."

I was glad to hear Em recognized the added intensity in our training. "Our programs are really coming together. It took a while for us to get comfortable with the tango for our short, but I feel so much better about it now."

I hadn't mentioned to anyone *why* I felt more comfortable with it. In the three weeks that had passed since my lesson with Josh, I'd continued to watch videos online, but the experience of doing the dance with him had made it much easier to grasp. It had also given me the memory of being close to him, feeling his strong hands guiding me. A memory that had been hard to shake.

"Just keep pounding it," Chris said, bringing my

attention back to the rink. "Day after day until it feels like you were born to do the programs. Then when it's time for nationals, it'll happen just like you practice every day."

"I thought we were in position to do that four years ago, and we fell apart. I wanted it so bad that I completely locked up. I just couldn't stop thinking about how I was so close to reaching the dream I'd had all my life."

"I had that same feeling the first time Em and I were trying to make the Olympic team. It was like I was so tight I couldn't breathe. But I just kept reminding myself that I could do the program in my sleep, and all I had to do was stop fighting myself. And we nailed it." He grinned.

I looked up at the huge blue banner with Em and Chris's names that hung above the rink. It was only one of a few banners bearing their names and accomplishments, but it was the biggest. The one with the Olympic rings emblazoned on it.

"Was being at the Olympics as amazing as you thought it would be?" I asked. "I mean, I know winning the gold medal had to be super amazing, but what about just the experience of being there? Em doesn't talk to us about it much because she wants us to focus more on the process of getting there."

He glanced at Em working on the ice and scooted closer to me. "You can't tell her I told you this."

I made a cross over my heart and mimed zipping my lips.

"Top three experiences of my life," he said quietly. "Number one — falling in love with Aubrey."

"Aww."

"Number two — winning gold in Torino. And number three — walking in the Opening Ceremony at our first Olympics. It felt like... like I had the power to do anything in that moment. I know it sounds cliché, but I really was on top of the world." His voice relayed the awe he'd experienced. "Trust me when I say it's everything you've ever dreamed of and more."

My throat tightened, and my eyes went back to the

banner. "That's what I was afraid of."

****

My bruised knee had me hobbling that night at the restaurant, and I was still walking gingerly on Saturday. I was relieved when the usual dinner crowd trickled in slowly. Josh showed up as one of the early arrivals and perched on what had become his barstool. He'd been arriving earlier and earlier when he came to the restaurant, which was a couple times a week, and he'd also been staying later and later. I enjoyed talking to him, but it wasn't helping my crush situation. Especially when he came in looking all sexy-but-not-knowing-it like tonight. He had on a black blazer, sleeves pushed up, over a white Beatles T-shirt. Dark jeans and Converse rounded out his outfit. Any guy who wore Converse scored extra points in my book.

I wiped my hands on my apron and carried the water pitcher over to Josh to refill his glass. He thanked me and peered over the bar.

"How's your knee?" he asked.

"It's still a little sore, but I'll be back on the ice Monday. It sucked sitting out yesterday when we were having a really good practice before I fell."

"You've been looking great on the tango."

I smiled. "Thanks to my awesome teacher."

His cheeks reddened, and he returned my smile. "I just got you started. You've done all the rest."

Meredith breezed by with an order for a vodka sour, so I grabbed the cocktail shaker and scooped some ice. After filling it with vodka, sugar syrup, and lemon juice, I went back to Josh as I shook the mixture.

"I saw you yesterday working with Em on your choreography," I said over the clacking of the shaker. "Have you always helped design your programs?"

"Just the last few years. Our old coach was pretty territorial and didn't want to give up control, but she finally gave in when I wouldn't stop bugging her with ideas."

"From what I saw, you have some great ones."

"Thanks. Emily's awesome to work with. She makes us think about each movement in a way I hadn't before. It's giving me all kinds of new creative inspiration."

"You sound really passionate about it." I hesitated bringing up his career path after the way he'd reacted the last time I'd mentioned it, but I was hoping he'd open up more. "I know you said you've always been expected to be a lawyer, but if you have other talents…"

He took a long drink of water and slowly set down the glass. "My dad would probably disown me if I said I wasn't going to law school. It's a done deal anyway."

"What do you mean?"

"I've already been accepted at UCLA. They deferred my enrollment until next fall so I could come here."

I didn't like to think about Josh moving back to L.A. even though I knew it was going to happen. It was just one of the many reasons I should be trying harder to kill my attraction to him. How did a girl go about doing that, anyway?

I poured the cocktail into a glass and placed it on the edge of the bar for Meredith. A couple of customers required my attention, so it was a few minutes before I returned to Josh with another question.

"Have you ever told your dad how you feel about—"

"You know anyone who can play the piano?" my boss Ronnie boomed at me as he came out of the kitchen. "Barry's sick."

"Uhh…"

Josh slowly raised his hand. "I know how to play."

Ronnie stared hard at him. "You any good?"

"I've… I've been playing since I was a kid."

Ronnie gave him another long look. "Well, you're the

only option I got. We'll take care of your dinner, and you can keep all your tips."

"I can pay for dinner."

"Nonsense. You give me a couple hours work, I give you a free meal."

"Sounds fair to me," I piped in.

Josh nodded. "I can start in a few minutes."

"Barry's sheet music is in the piano bench," Ronnie said. "If you know any other popular songs, feel free to get creative. Just keep in mind who your audience is."

Josh and I smiled at each other, knowing very well the crowd's demographic. Ronnie moved from behind the bar to greet two regulars, and I turned to Josh with my arms folded and my head cocked to the side.

"So, you're an athlete, a dancer *and* a musician? If you tell me you're a skilled artist, I'm gonna have to hate you."

He laughed. "I can barely draw a stick figure."

"Whew." I swiped my hand across my forehead.

"Even if I was the next Picasso, though, I wouldn't have told you." He paused and held my gaze. "I don't like the idea of you hating me."

My stomach fluttered. Josh didn't often make extended eye contact, but whenever he locked those sinfully blue eyes on mine, I became a mesmerized puddle of swoon.

"I um... I could never really hate you." I broke away from his gaze as my heart beat in double time, and I scrambled to laugh off the whole thing. "You're too good a tipper."

I zoomed away and kept myself busy with the other bar patrons, not returning to Josh's spot until he'd departed for the piano. I picked up his empty plate and found underneath it my tip and a beverage napkin containing a doodle. Looking closer, I saw it was a stick figure person playing a very lopsided piano. Written below it was — *Any requests?*

I grinned and slipped the napkin into the pocket of my apron. After clearing the dishes, I plucked a dollar bill from my purse and went over to the piano.

"There shall be no judgment passed on my request." I dropped the money into the empty glass on the piano. "I'd like to hear 'Over the Rainbow.'"

His eyebrows rose with amusement. *"Wizard of Oz* fan?"

"I was obsessed with it as a child. I drew a yellow brick chalk road down the sidewalk by my house. There was also a very unhealthy attachment to a stuffed dog named Toto, but I digress..."

Josh chuckled, and I continued, "I know the sheet music for the song should be here because I've heard Barry play it."

He cracked his knuckles. "I don't think I'll need it."

He set his fingers lightly on the keys and rattled off the first few bars before looking up at me with a smile. I rested my elbows on the shiny black lid of the piano and leaned forward.

"You really know that song by heart?"

"If I tell you something, you promise not to hate me?"

*Dude, if you only knew how far I was from hating you.*

"You're some kind of musical savant, aren't you?" I asked.

"I have this thing where I can learn music by ear and never forget it."

"And I ask you again — why are you going to be a lawyer?"

"Courtney!" one of the waiters called to me from the bar.

"Oops, I gotta go. I'll be waiting for my song!"

I scrambled back to my post and hurriedly filled the drink order waiting for me. Josh looked very serious as he flipped through the song book. Soon the sounds of dinner chatter and clinking utensils were joined by the melodic tinkling of the piano, and I immediately recognized the song as "I Could've Danced All Night."

Mrs. Cassar, one of our weekend regulars, slid onto a barstool and spun it so she faced the piano. "I've seen that boy here before."

She was a brassy lady who always cracked me up, a widow who wanted to spend all her husband's money in as many creative ways as possible.

"His name is Josh. He actually skates at my rink."

"He's simply adorable." She ogled him shamelessly. "I could put him on a cracker."

I giggled and poured Mrs. Cassar's customary glass of merlot. She took the glass in hand, but her eyes never left Josh.

"If he skates as well as he plays piano, he must be marvelous," she said between sips.

"He does. He and his sister are a really beautiful pair."

"He skates with his sister? Isn't pairs skating supposed to be *romantic*?" She breathed out the last word, which made it sound rather comical.

I snorted. "Mark and I have never been romantic. We've tried and failed to pull that off on the ice."

"You should team up with *him*." She pointed at Josh. "If I was fifty years younger, I'd strap on a pair of skates and grab him myself."

"It's a little too late for us to change partners," I said, still laughing. "The Olympics are in seven months."

As I went down the line, checking on my customers, I thought about Mrs. Cassar's idea of Josh and me skating together. I knew what dancing with him felt like. Skating with him might send me into sensory shock.

When I heard the opening notes of "Over the Rainbow," I turned to the piano and Josh sent me a bright-eyed smile across the room. I felt my own face lighting up, and I couldn't stop grinning as I filled the sudden barrage of drink orders.

Mrs. Cassar went over to talk to Josh between songs, and I noticed he had the attention of many of the other women in the room. His tip glass was already overstuffed. Barry didn't get that much love in an entire night.

As Josh resumed playing, Mrs. Cassar returned to her barstool and smoothed her wrinkled hand over her fiery red hair.

"He's a very polite young man," she said. "Turns out we're almost neighbors in Hyannisport. I told him to call me if he ever needs anything."

"Like a cup of sugar?" I joked.

"Or some other kind of sugar." Her penciled eyebrows danced.

I burst into laughter and could only shake my head. I roared even harder when she stopped by the piano later on her way out and patted Josh's cheek. The redness on his face was visible from across the room. I was itching to tease him about it when he met me at the bar at closing time.

"I heard you got a phone number tonight." I giggled. "Mrs. Cassar is quite a fan."

He turned pink again as he laughed. "She's an interesting character."

Ronnie walked up and slapped Josh on the shoulder. "Great job tonight. Plenty people asked if you'd be back."

"Sure. If you ever need me to fill in, I'd be glad to."

"How about playing on Thursday nights? Same deal — I'll pay for your dinner."

Josh thought about it for only a few seconds. "Yeah, I can do that. There'll be some weeks where I have skating stuff, but I can give you my schedule."

Even more time I'd be spending with him. Common sense fought the giddy feeling bubbling inside me, but it was losing badly.

Ronnie bid us goodnight, and I slung my purse over my shoulder. "Look at you, scoring a regular gig."

"Maybe I can slowly work in some cooler music... make Thursdays the most happening night of the week here."

"Is Stephanie going to wonder why your dinners last hours?"

He shrugged. "She knows I like to get out of the house."

I was pretty sure he hadn't told her he'd been hanging

out at my place of employment multiple times a week. If he had, she would've been giving me even dirtier looks than her usual glares, and she probably would've treated me to another lecture about how I wasn't good enough for her brother.

We walked together out to the parking lot, and the cool mist from the thick fog dampened my face. I pulled my keys from my purse as we neared the few cars remaining in the lot.

"You'll have to let me know if you have any more song requests," Josh said.

"You said you can learn music by ear, right? So if I give you any song, you can learn how to play it just like that?" I snapped my fingers.

"You name it, I'll play it," he said with a determined look in his eyes.

I smiled. "I'll start working on my list."

I turned toward my car, and Josh headed in the opposite direction for his. As I hit the unlock button, I heard Josh say, "Court."

I wheeled around. He'd never called me Court before. I liked it. A lot.

He shoved his hands in his pockets and shuffled his feet. "Have a good Sunday."

"Thanks. You too."

I slowly walked backward to my car and climbed inside, wincing as I bent my knee. Turning the ignition, the only response I received was a sickly, sputtering whirr. I repeated the motion three times, but there was no sign of engine life in sight.

"Come on, stupid car." I slapped the steering wheel.

Who knew how much repairs would cost, not to mention the hassle of being without a vehicle. I tried once more to start it and groaned when it failed on me yet again.

A tapping sound on my window startled me, and I jumped. Josh stood next to my door.

"Trouble starting?" he asked as I opened the door and

stepped out.

"I don't think it's the battery because it's making a noise." I pressed the lock button on my key fob. "I guess I'll get it towed to the shop tomorrow."

"You know a mechanic who's open on Sunday?"

"Mark's dad owns a shop. He won't be open, but he'll let me leave the car there so he can work on it Monday. I can't be carless for too long."

"I can give you a ride home," he said.

"Oh, I don't want to make you go out of your way. I'll go ask Meredith if she can take me."

"I don't mind at all." He waved for me to follow him as he started toward his car.

I hung back for a moment but then followed him. He opened the passenger door of the black sedan before walking around the front of the car to the driver's side. I slid into the dark leather seat, and when we were both buckled in, I got that nervous feeling that I'd had when we'd danced. We weren't nearly as close as we'd been then, but sitting in the small car in the dark with the fog all around us, it felt just as intimate.

Josh turned the key, and music blared through the speakers at an ear-splitting level, just the way I liked it in my car, too.

He quickly powered off the stereo. "Sorry."

"No, I listen the same way. Was that Muse? I didn't recognize the song."

He didn't directly answer as he drove us toward the exit. "Um... yeah."

I was confused by the hesitation in his reply, so I reached for the jewel case atop the stack of CDs under the stereo.

"Wait." His hand shot forward and grabbed mine.

An electrifying sensation sped from my hand to every nerve ending in my body. The car had stopped moving. Everything had stopped moving. Except Josh's thumb, which brushed lightly over my knuckles, creating a whole new and even more stirring sensation inside me. I couldn't breathe.

Josh pulled his hand away and gripped the wheel like he was on a roller coaster, holding on for dear life. "Sorry, I um... I'm just not supposed to show anyone the CD."

"Oh." I took slow breaths, still trying to shake off the buzz of Josh's touch.

He resumed driving, deftly maneuvering the stick shift as we accelerated onto the main road. I saw him glance in my direction a couple of times.

"If you promise not to tell anyone I have it..." he said.

I shifted in my seat so I was angled toward him. "You can trust me."

We stopped at a red light, and he looked into my eyes. My attempt to breathe at a normal pace suffered a massive setback. When his gaze flickered momentarily down to my mouth, I became sure I was going to need CPR.

A horn honked behind us, and Josh turned back to the road.

*Damn green light.*

"The CD is an advance copy of Muse's new record," he said. "It's not being released until September, but my dad got it for me. I didn't mean to get all weird. It's just that if any of it gets leaked, he could get in a lot of trouble."

"I totally understand. I definitely won't say anything."

He braked and made a careful left turn. "Are you pretty familiar with the band?"

"Yeah, I know most of their songs, even the early stuff."

"You have to hear this song." He flipped on the CD player and pressed the track button a few times. "It's like nothing I've ever heard."

He set the volume loud but not where we wouldn't be able to talk over it. The beat of the song did indeed sound very unique. While my ears were fully engaged with the music, my eyes were fully engaged with watching Josh drive. There was a graceful power in the way he handled the wheel and the stick shift, much like how he handled himself on skates.

He pointed to the stereo. "This is the part I thought you'd really like."

The beat slowed, and the lead singer began crooning a familiar tune, one that brought up memories of being on the ice.

"That's from *Samson and Delilah!*" I said.

Mark and I had skated our long program to the opera score three seasons ago, so I'd heard this melody every day for months at the rink. But I'd never heard it like this, woven into the middle of a rock song.

"I love this so much," I said.

Josh smiled. "As soon as I heard it, I thought of you."

I turned my head fully toward him, but he wouldn't look at me. His smile had faded, and he quietly cleared his throat.

"You know, since you um… since you skated to it," he stammered.

Yeah, *three years* ago. And tons of other skaters had used the music over the years, including a lot more memorable names than Mark and me. But I was the first person who came to mind when he heard the song.

There went my fluttery stomach again.

The fog rolled in thicker as we rode beside one of the many ponds in the area. Josh leaned slightly forward and slowed the car while going through the sharp curves.

"It's the next left?" he asked.

"Uhh… yeah."

I wouldn't mind if he slowed down even more so I could be in the car longer, and not just because I wanted to listen to more of the CD. Em and Sergei's house soon came into view, though, and Josh parked in front of the driveway.

"You should hear the rest of this." He ejected the disc and popped it into its case. "Keep it as long as you want."

He handed the CD to me, and I asked, "Are you sure it's

okay?"

His mouth curled upward. "I trust you."

He treated me to another long look, my third of the night. Not that I was counting. That kind of look was just usually so rare from him that I felt something had changed between us. Or I could be totally overanalyzing everything.

I opened the door and set one foot on the pavement. "Thanks so much for the ride. I really appreciate it."

"No problem." He patted the stick shift. "Hey, let me give you my number in case you need a lift while your car's in the shop."

He took his phone from the cup holder and pressed a few keys. "What's your number? I'll text you and then you'll have mine."

I bit my lip to keep from smiling. If he was trying to be smooth, he'd pulled it off excellently. I recited my digits and heard my phone ding in my bag a few seconds later.

I waved goodbye as I stepped out, and I put the CD in my purse before unlocking the front door of the house. Josh didn't pull away until I was inside. I went through the foyer to the living room, and Em and Sergei were cuddled together on the couch, watching TV.

"Why didn't you come through the garage?" Em asked.

"My car wouldn't start, so I got a ride home. I'll get it towed tomorrow." I loosened the knot on my uniform tie as I headed for the stairs. "Have a good night."

"'Night," they said in unison.

Upstairs Liza's bedroom door was closed, so I moved quietly past it to my room. I couldn't wait to get showered and comfy in my pajamas so I could listen to the CD. As I lathered my strawberry-scented shampoo in my hair, I hummed the aria from *Samson and Delilah*, hitting all the high notes.

Once I was dry and cozy under my comforter, I slid the CD into my laptop and plugged in my headphones. I flopped back against the pillows, blasted the music so loud Mom

JENNIFER COMEAUX

would tell me my eardrums would burst, and closed my eyes.

The epic sound of the lead singer's voice mixed with the unique and vibrant beat took me out of my bedroom and into a rocking concert hall. Every song was fabulous and surprising. Just when I didn't think the record could give me any more surprises, the next song began with only a slow piano. The beautiful, emotional melody immediately made me think of skating.

With Josh.

I saw us so clearly. I could even feel his hand around mine as it had been in the car for that brief moment. We were alone on a fresh sheet of ice, doing crossovers perfectly in sync. He pressed me up into a soaring star lift, carrying me swiftly across the rink, and then brought me down securely into his strong arms. We were so close his warm breath fanned over my lips. The music kept building around us, but we were both completely still as our momentum took us over the ice. When we finally glided to a halt, Josh leaned into me and his lips—

*Stop!*

My eyes flew open.

*This isn't going to happen, so you need to stop daydreaming about it. You CANNOT fall for him.*

I drew in a deep breath and covered my face with my hands. Who was I kidding? I was already falling for him. So freaking hard.

70

# Chapter Seven

I listened to the piano song over and over on Sunday and itched to text Josh my thoughts on the album. But all I did was stare at his number on my phone. Texting him would add another dimension to our friendship, and I was already thinking about him enough without constantly waiting for my phone to buzz.

When Monday morning came I reluctantly packed the CD in my skate bag to return it to Josh. Even though he'd said to keep it as long as I wanted, I didn't want to take advantage of his generosity. Too many people were around during our morning warm-up for me to give it to him, so when I went into the locker room later and saw his bag open on the floor, I quickly slipped the disc inside.

"What are you doing?"

I jumped back and spun to see Stephanie just inside the doorway. She stalked over to me and narrowed her steely blue eyes.

"Were you taking something from Josh's bag?" she asked.

My first instinct was to laugh because Stephanie acted too

ridiculous sometimes to be real. She was like a character in *Mean Girls*. I pressed my lips together to hold in the laughter, and I backed away from her.

"Because I'm not rich you automatically assume I'm a thief?" I said. "Sorry to disappoint you, but I was returning something."

"What were you returning that you had to put in his bag instead of handing it to him?"

"It's just a CD he let me borrow."

Stephanie crossed her arms. "Josh doesn't let anyone borrow his music. He's a total freak about keeping it in perfect condition."

My heart ballooned with a big *Aww* that Josh had made an exception for me. Stephanie's suspicious glare quickly snapped me out of happy-sappy land, though.

"Well, he loaned one to me, so I guess that makes me special," I said, knowing how much it would irritate her that Josh and I had become friends.

"Didn't I explain that you have no chance with him? You're just going to embarrass yourself if you keep sniffing after him."

*Sniffing after him?* If anyone was doing any sniffing it was Josh, who kept showing up at my workplace. The words were on the edge of my tongue, but I clamped my mouth shut. Telling Stephanie about our time together at the restaurant would taint it somehow. Plus, I had the feeling Josh didn't like his sister knowing all his business.

"I really don't give a crap what you think, but you're way off base anyway," I said.

Josh walked into the room, carrying his skates, and he stopped when he saw Stephanie and me facing each other with scowls. "What's going on?"

Stephanie relaxed her posture and picked up her bag. "We were just chatting."

Josh glanced at me as if to corroborate Stephanie's

statement. I kept mum and sat on the bench.

"I'm going to the spa," Stephanie said as she passed Josh. "Don't forget yoga is an hour later today."

I thought back to Josh telling me I should try it, and I smiled wickedly to myself at how much I'd piss off Stephanie if I did.

"You know, I've been thinking about giving hot yoga a try since Em swears by it," I said. "I might see you there tonight."

The tightness returned to Stephanie's face. "It's not really for everyone. You'd probably hate it."

"I think you'll like it," Josh said with a subtle smile.

"Don't you work nights?" Stephanie tapped her foot.

"The restaurant is closed on Mondays."

She stared me down and let out a little huff. "I have to go."

She blew out of the room, and Josh looked back and forth from me to the door. "So, what did I miss before I came in?"

"She saw me putting the CD in your bag, and she was questioning me about it."

"You could've kept it longer."

"I didn't want to hog it," I said as I toyed with my maroon and gold bracelet. "I listened to it all day yesterday. I think I played 'Exogenesis Symphony Part 3' at least ten times."

Josh's eyes lit up. "That's one of my favorites, too."

We smiled at each other, and I quickly focused on examining my bracelet as if some of the threads were loose. They were all perfectly intact.

Josh bent to pack his skates in his duffel. "Do you need a ride to the yoga studio?"

"Um... I can probably borrow Em's car. It's on Route Twenty-Eight in Centerville?" I'd grown up in that area, so I was familiar with the strip mall where the studio was located.

"Yep, that's it." He walked backward to the door. "Call

me if you end up needing a lift."

He told Liza hello as they almost bumped into each other in the doorway. Liza bounced over to join me on the long bench, her long black ponytail swaying behind her.

"I landed the double Axel-triple toe," she said while doing a jig.

"That's awesome!"

"My goal is to have it consistent by the time we leave for camp."

The U.S. Skating Federation held a camp in Colorado Springs every summer for its top athletes, and we had to perform our programs for feedback from the powers-that-be. It was a nerve-wracking experience because if they hated our programs, we'd have to scrap them and start all over.

"That's only a few weeks away," I said.

"I can do it," she said with no hesitation.

I smiled at her confidence. Liza might be only fifteen and in her first year as a senior-level skater, but she was a definite contender for the Olympic team. The girl could reel off triple-triples better than many longtime senior ladies.

"You know how you should celebrate your accomplishment?" I said. "By going to hot yoga with me tonight."

"Huh?"

"It'll be a great energy release." I did my best to cheerfully sell it.

The confusion on Liza's face said I hadn't done a good enough job. "How many times has Em asked us to go with her and how many times have we said no way?"

"I know, but we've done regular yoga before and liked it. Stephanie and Josh were telling me about it, and I want to check it out." I looped my arm across her shoulders. "And I need a buddy."

"Since when do you talk to Stephanie?" She lifted one eyebrow.

*Busted.*

"Okay, so maybe I want to go just to annoy her because she doesn't want me there. But I still need a buddy."

I gave her a big hopeful grin, and she studied me as she slowly tapped her chin with her finger. "I do like the idea of annoying Stephanie."

I squeezed her into a hug. "That's my girl."

\*\*\*\*

"I think Em was offended that we've always turned her down and now we're doing this on our own," Liza said as we stored our bags in the yoga studio's locker room.

I picked up my mat and towels. "We can go with her another time."

The strap of my loose tank slipped down my shoulder, and I hiked it back into place before pulling open the practice room door. Sticky air hit my face and seeped into my lungs. The first thing I saw was a shirtless guy stretching and another one beside him. *Interesting.* There had never been any shirtless men in the few standard yoga classes I'd attended.

I looked to the back of the room where Stephanie and Josh stood talking. I took two steps in their direction, and then Josh tugged his T-shirt over his head, halting all my motor skills.

*Holy Batman.*

The view was even better than I'd imagined, and I'd imagined it an embarrassing number of times lately. Josh's chest and stomach were smooth and cut lean and hard, and his long shorts sat just low enough on his hips to give a peek of the V leading down...

"This might not be so bad after all." Liza giggled and looked around.

I touched my face. I was already hot, and I hadn't done any exercising yet. *Yeah, hot and bothered.*

Josh noticed me and broke into a smile, and I unstuck my feet from the floor to go forward. Liza followed close at my side.

"I'm glad you guys could make it," Josh said.

Stephanie rolled her eyes and walked away. *Good riddance.*

"We're super excited to try something new," Liza said, still preoccupied with checking out our surroundings.

Meanwhile, I struggled to keep from checking out Josh's body now that I had an up-close view. Looking at his gorgeous smile made it easier to distract myself. I set down my stuff and fanned my tank top, sending a warm breeze over my sports bra.

"You might want to take that off," Josh said.

I stopped fanning. "What?"

"A sweaty shirt will weigh you down. I learned the hard way when I wore a T-shirt once."

"Oh. Yeah, I didn't think about that."

I paused and then grabbed the hem of my shirt. Josh's eyes stayed on me as I pulled the top over my head. He glanced downward at my bare stomach, so quickly it was barely perceptible, but I'd caught him. And there was definite appreciation shining in his eyes. The heat in my face spread lower.

"Should we set up?" I asked.

Liza and I lined up our mats next to Josh, and Stephanie situated herself on his other side. I took a long drink from my water bottle and tucked a loose strand of hair into my ponytail holder. The humidity in the room felt like a muggy cloud sinking over me.

The instructor took her spot at the front of the room and demonstrated the first pose, a simple standing position to warm up. I tried to go to a peaceful place mentally, but all I could think about was the blistering heat. And I only grew warmer as we moved through the various poses. When we transitioned to the ninth position, I found myself facing Josh's back, and my thoughts finally drifted away from the temperature.

Josh extended his arms out on both sides, and the muscles in his back flexed in turn. I imagined exploring the contours of each one of those muscles, trailing my fingers across his hot, slick skin. My body flushed even more, and I looked away from him, breaking my pose. Liza glanced at me, and I quickly went back into form and closed my eyes. Staring at Josh wasn't going to help me feel calm. Quite the opposite was happening as my heart rate had kicked up another notch.

The temperature seemed to be rising, and I became more jittery with each pose. Sipping water wasn't providing enough sustenance. I had only eaten a light snack earlier as Em had recommended, and I worried the heat with the lack of food were taking its toll. Why had I thought this was a good idea? I'd almost passed out at a Red Sox game once on a sweltering July day. My body was used to spending its days in an ice rink, and it was currently screaming at me, *What the hell is all this heat?* We were close to the end of the class, though, so I didn't want to make a scene by leaving (and having Stephanie gloat that I couldn't hack it). I could power through a few more minutes, right?

I shakily performed the final two positions and toweled off my sweat-caked face as soon as class ended. My head felt very light and fuzzy, and I looked toward the door. *Air. I need air.*

Josh turned to me as he wiped his own face. "What did you think?"

His voice seemed a great distance from me, and black spots began to blur my vision. My legs didn't feel as if they were part of my body anymore.

"Court?" he said, sounding miles away. "She's really pale."

I tried to move for the door but stumbled and Josh

grabbed me. He wrapped his arm around my waist and steered me to the exit.

"We're gonna go outside, okay?" He held my water bottle up to my lips. "Try to drink some water."

I took in a little bit of the liquid and continued to drink as Josh helped me sit on the bench in the hallway. The cooler air made me feel like I could breathe again... like I wasn't smothering in a rainforest.

"Put your head between your knees," Liza said as she sat beside me.

Bending forward, I rested my forehead on my knees, and the blood in my body rushed upward, giving me further relief.

"I'll go get a wet towel," Josh said.

Liza rubbed my back, and I breathed deeply, slowly regaining the clarity of my senses. I lifted my head slightly and saw Stephanie standing in front of me.

"You are so pathetic," she said. "I bet you pulled this little stunt just to get Josh's sympathy."

I blinked a few times and gingerly straightened my back. Stephanie looked down at me with a snarl of disdain.

"You think she's faking it?" Liza squeaked. "What is wrong with you?"

"I know the only reason she came was to get closer to Josh."

I shook my head in disbelief. "No, the reason I came was to irritate the hell out of you. Almost passing out wasn't part of the plan, but I'm glad I succeeded with my goal."

Josh returned and sat next to me, and he pressed the cold towel to my forehead. "You feeling better?"

I put my hand on the towel to hold it myself, and our fingers touched, shooting a tingle down my spine. I knew for sure I was better because I hadn't been able to feel anything when Josh's arm had been around me a few minutes ago.

"Much," I said.

"Do you want something to eat?" Liza asked. "I think I

have some trail mix in my gym bag. I'll go get it."

She scurried toward the locker room while Josh watched me with concern. I leaned back against the wall and gave him a little smile.

"Sorry for all the drama."

"You don't have to apologize. I'm just glad you're okay."

Stephanie made some kind of noise in her throat. "I told you this wasn't for everyone. I hope you won't make the mistake of coming back here again."

"Steph." Josh glared at her. "Jeez, back off."

"What? You want her fainting in the middle of class next time? Having to call 911?"

"I won't be coming back." I set the towel on my thigh. "I listen to my body when it gives me a warning."

Stephanie smirked. "Well, it's good you have a little bit of sense."

She left just as Liza came back with a plastic baggie of trail mix. I devoured a handful of nuts and chased them with a gulp of water.

"I can take you guys home and bring Em back to get her car," Josh said.

I waved off his suggestion. "I'm fine to drive. The cool air and food was all I needed."

"You sure?"

I nodded. Josh and Liza went into the practice room to retrieve our stuff we'd left behind, and I sat quietly and ate a few more almonds. A few people leaving the class stopped to ask if I was okay, and I gave them all solid assurances. When Josh and Liza returned, we went to the separate locker rooms to change into dry, non-disgusting clothes. Em wouldn't want our sweaty grossness all over her leather seats.

We all emerged within a minute of each other and walked out to the parking lot together. The sun had dipped low over the trees, filling the sky with deep orange, and the evening breeze felt vitally refreshing.

"I should've been the one apologizing earlier," Josh said. "I feel bad that I talked you into coming."

"Don't be silly. I wanted to come."

"I'm still kinda hot," Liza said. "I might take an ice bath when we get home."

I laughed and said goodnight to Josh, and he touched my shoulder.

"Take it easy tonight," he said.

I smiled as a much more pleasant warmth filled me. "I will."

My face couldn't turn off the smile, and Liza stared at me as we got into the car.

"Hmm..." she said loudly.

I quickly made my expression blank. "What?"

"Oh, nothing," she said with a little giggle.

She pulled out her phone, saving me from further scrutiny, but she'd definitely picked up on something. Or *somethin' somethin'* as Meredith would say. I was dealing with enough questions from myself about my feelings for Josh. The last thing I needed was questioning from other people.

# Chapter Eight

I took the last bite of my grilled chicken and looked at my watch. Thirty minutes remained before the start of my shift, so I sat back and gazed through the restaurant's large windows. A couple of sailboats floated on the calm water, making me wish I was lying on the beach instead of cooped up inside.

The kitchen door swung open, and Josh entered the dining room with one of the waiters. Suddenly I didn't care about being cooped up. If I was on the beach, I wouldn't get to see Josh looking beyond hot in a black button-down shirt and bright red tie. He was still rocking the jeans and Converse, but he'd obviously dressed up for his first night as the house entertainment.

"You're here early," I said.

"I wanted to practice a few of the songs in Barry's book."

I folded my napkin and gave him a teasing smile. "Nice tie."

He grinned and adjusted the knot around his collar. "I figured I'd class it up a bit."

He sat on the piano bench and began to page through the sheet music. I carried my plate and glass into the kitchen, and when I returned I set about making sure the bar was stocked and ready for opening. As I formed short stacks of beverage napkins, a familiar quiet melody froze me in place.

Muse's piano song.

I looked over at Josh, and he was concentrating hard on the keys, bringing the beautiful tune to life. I circled around the bar and slowly approached the piano. As Josh played, I watched his brow furrow as the notes became more intense, his lips press together as the music drew to a climax.

He kept his focus downward until he hit the final note, and then he looked up with a shy smile that turned all my insides to mush.

"That was amazing. How long did it take you to learn it?" I asked.

"Um… a couple of days. I started working on it Monday night."

*The day I'd told him it was my favorite song on the album. No biggie.*

"It sounded incredible," I said.

"Thanks. It's all I've been doing the past few nights. The perks of having no life." He laughed.

"You really should do something with that skill… other than playing in an old restaurant on Thursday nights."

He lowered his head and shrugged. "It's good to have as a hobby."

He flipped through the song book, and I excused myself to go back to work. I placed the napkin stacks along the bar, keeping one eye on the piano. How could Josh's parents ignore his talent and not encourage him to explore his options? If I had an artistic wunderkind, I wouldn't push him to be a lawyer.

The restaurant was busy right from the opening, so I didn't have much time to talk to Josh while he ate his free dinner. As soon as he finished eating, he reclaimed his spot at the piano and gave the room a more elegant feel with his smooth tinkling of the ivories.

I was filling a mug with beer from the tap when I saw someone waving from the corner of my eye. I turned and discovered Liza along with Em, Sergei, and the twins. Em and Sergei were staring at Josh and murmuring, but he was too wrapped up in playing a new arrangement of "Over the Rainbow" to notice them. Of all nights, they had to come when Josh was on the piano? They hadn't been to the restaurant in months.

The hostess showed them to a table, but Em and Liza didn't sit. They came straight to the bar.

"Since when does Josh play the piano here?" Em asked.

I toweled off a wet spot on the polished wood. "He just started."

"How come you didn't mention it?"

Liza watched me closely with a hint of a smile, and I hoped she wasn't about to burst into giggles.

"He uhh… I don't think he wants Stephanie to know, so if you could not say anything at the rink…"

She gave me a questioning look but kept quiet and left for her table. Liza stayed with me and broke into a full-blown smile. I waited for the commentary to come.

"You like Josh," she said.

*And there it is.*

I reached behind me for a bottle of vodka. "Of course I like him. He's a nice person."

"No, you *like* like him."

I let out a solo peal of laughter. "You did not just say that. I haven't heard that since seventh grade."

"I don't hear you denying it."

"Don't you need to go order your dinner? Your table is waiting for you."

"Still not denying," she sang as she walked away.

*Great.* Now she was going to hound me until I caved, which would probably be sooner rather than later. I'd never been good at hiding my emotions.

The activity at the bar died down over the next hour, and after the twins finished eating, Sergei brought them over and sat them on adjacent stools. His arms surrounded them as he stood behind them. Quinn and Alex were the only underage patrons Ronnie allowed.

I smiled and rested my elbows on the bar. "You two are my cutest customers by far."

They laughed, and Alex said quietly, "You prettiest bartender."

"Aww." I touched my hand to my heart. "You're gonna be a hit with the ladies one day."

"He already has an admirer at pre-school," Sergei said. "This little girl follows him everywhere."

"Fast forward thirteen years and imagine your life with two sixteen-year-old heartbreakers in your house." I laughed. "Good luck with that."

"My hair turns gray just thinking about it."

"I want dat drink!" Quinn pointed to the martini in front of her neighbor. "It's pink!"

"That's a drink for grown-ups, Sweetie," Sergei said.

"How about I make you both some chocolate milk?" I suggested.

"No, I want dat one!" Quinn shouted and bounced in her seat.

"Aquinnah Rose," Sergei said firmly as he bent between the twins. "We do not yell in public like that. And Court was very nice to offer to make you something special."

She dipped her head. "Sorry."

I noticed Alex looked remorseful, too, even though he hadn't done anything wrong. Yet another fascinating facet of their twin behavior.

"Why don't we go say hello to Josh and let Court get back to work?" Sergei helped the kids climb down from the stools.

"Bye!" I waved.

The three of them stood beside the piano until Josh finished playing the theme from *Ice Castles,* and he motioned for Quinn and Alex to sit with him on the bench. They both looked up at him open-mouthed like he was a rock star. I had to get a picture of the adorableness, so I ran into the kitchen for my phone and quickly snapped a shot from behind the bar.

*Should I text it to Josh?*

I had a witty comment all ready to go with the photo, but again I wasn't sure if I should open up that extra line of communication. I tapped the phone screen with my fingernail.

*Oh, what the hell.*

I typed in his name and scrolled to the message area.

Me: *So you're a hit with the toddler crowd, too. You're a demographics phenomenon.*

I hit Send before I could chicken out and slid the phone into my apron pocket. It wasn't a moment too soon because Liza was headed in my direction. She would surely have something to say about me taking a picture of Josh.

"I was thinking." She leaned against the bar and lowered her voice. "If you and Josh hook up, it would be so *Romeo and Juliet*. You know, since you're on rival teams you're like the warring Capulets and Montagues."

I gaped at her, trying to find the right response to her ridiculous metaphor.

"We read it last year in English class," she added. "*So* good."

"Josh and I are not Romeo and Juliet."

"Two teams, both alike in dignity, in Cape Cod where we lay our scene," she said dramatically.

I recognized the prologue to the play because I'd had to memorize it and recite it in front of my own freshman English class. I'd never thought my life would inspire a parody of it.

"You better not say stuff like that around Em and Sergei," I said. "I don't want them thinking something's going on with me and Josh because nothing's going on. We're just friends."

She must've heard the I'm-not-messing-around tone in my voice because her face turned serious. "I won't. They were talking during dinner about Josh working here, and I didn't say anything."

"What were they saying?"

"Just that it was weird you didn't mention it. But they do think it's good Josh has found something fun to do away from the rink."

Mr. Mayer lifted his hand to catch my attention, and I nodded to let him know I was coming. "I have to get back to my customers."

I stayed busy until closing time, and a few co-workers walked out to the parking lot with Josh and me, so we didn't have a chance to do much chatting. He didn't say anything about the photo, and I wondered if he hadn't checked his phone or hadn't found my message amusing. God, that was why I knew texting him was a bad idea. The obsessing had already begun.

I tried to put the text out of my mind, but when I was in my bedroom later undressing and my phone dinged, I dove across the bed, shirt half-unbuttoned, to read the message.

Josh: *LOL just saw your text. Now I need to win over the 18-49 demographic. Will you be my first fan? ;)*

I smiled and sat on the bed. As I reread the message, I chewed on my thumbnail. *How do I respond?*

The first thing I had to do was wait a few minutes. I couldn't look too eager.

*What?* I smacked my hand against my forehead. *You're not dating. Those rules don't apply.*

But his message sure felt like an invitation to flirt, especially with the winky face. As much as I knew I shouldn't join the game, I'd never wanted to play anything so badly.

Me: *You keep playing "Over the Rainbow" every week, and I'll be the president of your fan club :)*

I put the phone on the comforter and stood to resume

stripping off my uniform. While I pulled the bobby pins from my hair, I heard the magical ding.

Josh: *I'll do whatever I have to do to make you happy.*

My knees went weak, and I dropped onto the bed. *Dammit, stop being so irresistible!* I groaned and sank face-down onto the comforter. Why did he have to be my competitor? And even if he wasn't, he was moving all the way across the country in less than a year. I'd done a long-distance relationship, and it had been a total disaster.

Josh was so sweet, though, and I found it physically impossible to be anything other than receptive to him. That was the biggest problem. I lifted my head and stared at the phone, contemplating my response. In the end, my gut told me the safest bet would be to keep it simple.

Me: *:)*

**\*\*\*\***

I wasn't making any smiley faces the next afternoon at the rink. My triple Salchow had abandoned me for the day, and ice caked my butt after every run-through Mark and I did. Making my struggles harder to swallow was watching Stephanie and Josh nail the first full run-through of their long program. Their programs were finally complete, and every day I could see their jumps getting stronger. Sergei and Em's strategy of going back to basics with the technique was slowly paying off.

When I watched Stephanie and Josh, conflicting emotions battled within me. My eyes were automatically drawn to Josh, inspiring fluttery feelings, but when I looked at Stephanie, competitive rage burned in my chest. I'd never wanted to beat anyone more in my entire skating life.

"Free-For-All Friday!" Em threw her hands in the air.

I let out a long breath and felt some of the tension drain from my shoulders. Skating for fun would be the perfect way to forget my rough day. Everyone cleared the ice, and Em stationed herself next to the stereo.

"Court and Josh," she called.

I perked up even more. In the six weeks since Stephanie and Josh had been training with us, Josh and I hadn't yet shared the ice for Free-For-All Friday. He let me go ahead of him through the ice door, and we took our places at opposite ends of the rink.

Em pressed a button, and "Love Is Blindness" by U2 began playing. *Really?* There were thousands of songs Em could've chosen, and she had to pick a sexy one? How was I supposed to concentrate on doing my own thing with Josh skating to this around me?

I took a few long strokes to match the music, gliding toward center ice, and Josh did the same, watching me the whole way. After we crossed paths and spun around, his eyes remained on me, and I couldn't look away. I skated faster and carved deeper edges as the electric energy from him made me feel more in touch with myself and the ice.

The guitar riff in the song neared, and I built up additional speed. Josh and I flew toward each other, and I leapt into the air, extending both my legs on the split falling leaf. My breath caught in my throat as Josh did the exact same move at the same moment. I looked over at him, and he wore the expression I felt on my face — one that said, *Did that really just happen?*

Em cut the music a few seconds later, and Josh and I simultaneously arrived at the ice door, both of us breathing hard.

"Great minds," he said with a smile.

I laughed and stepped carefully onto the mat. "That was really freaky."

"Yeah, freaky," Mark said from beside the boards. He didn't sound as amused as Josh and I were.

I passed Stephanie on my way to the bleachers, and she

looked at me like I was gum stuck under her designer shoe. When Josh sat beside me, she started to come join us, but Em called her to the ice with Mark.

"I wish Free-For-All Friday was also Monday through Thursday," Josh said.

"I know, it's so cathartic." I took a sip of water. "There's something so freeing about just floating with the music and not having to follow any rules."

"Em and Sergei must be skating today." He gestured to them stretching by the boards.

"Ooh, get ready for a show. They are *awesome*."

"It has to be a pretty amazing feeling for them, skating together."

Mrs. Cassar's comment about pairs being romantic popped into my head. Em and Sergei were the definition of romance on the ice, and that's why I loved watching them so much. When I'd seen the movie *The Cutting Edge* as a ten-year-old, I'd become enamored with pairs and had dreamt of skating with my one true love. I learned later that happened much more often in movies than in real life.

"I've always wondered what it would be like to skate with someone you're dating," I said. "If there would be just this crazy amount of energy."

Josh turned to me and held my gaze. "I bet it would feel incredible."

I tingled down to my bones, and I thought about the sparks I'd felt when we'd just shared the ice as two separate skaters. I couldn't imagine how mind-blowing actually skating *with* him would be. The feels would be off the charts.

Stephanie and Mark sat below us to put on their skate guards, and I quickly turned back to the ice. I needed a water refill, so I went to the fountain near the entrance and stayed there to watch the next couple of pairs. The less I had to listen to Stephanie's mouth, the better.

When Em and Sergei shed their guards I returned to my

seat so I'd have a prime view of their performance. They only participated in Free-For-All Friday every few months because they didn't have a lot of time to create programs and to practice, but what they put together was always special.

They stood at center ice with their arms around each other like they were getting ready to slow dance, and Kenny whistled loudly. A few more of us contributed some catcalls. Liza started the music, and I recognized it as "Remember When It Rained" by Josh Groban.

Sergei dipped Em backward to begin, and I sat totally mesmerized at each fluid movement they made. They were so connected, looking at each other every step of the way. And the way they looked at each other... the love between them gave me chills.

"This is a bit much," Stephanie said, taking me away from my happy place.

"What's wrong with it?" Mark asked.

"I don't need to see them groping each other."

I rolled my eyes. "They're not groping each other. It's a classy, romantic program."

She pulled the ponytail holder from her hair and flipped her long brown locks over one shoulder. "I just don't see why they need to skate at all."

"Because they love doing it, and we can all learn something from watching them."

"I'm not sure what I could learn because I'm certainly not going to skate like that with Josh." She wrinkled her nose.

"You mean you don't wanna get your sexy on with your brother?" Mark asked.

Josh appeared on the verge of gagging, and Stephanie gave Mark the same disgusted look she'd aimed at me earlier. She mercifully left us so I could enjoy the final moments of Em and Sergei's skate in peace.

We all treated them to a standing ovation, and Sergei kissed Em's forehead before they bowed to us with beaming smiles. We kept applauding until after they'd exited the ice.

"That was really beautiful," Josh said.

"Right?" I said.

"You don't think it's a waste of time like your sister?" Mark asked.

Josh sat and leaned over to untie his boots. "Emily's an Olympic gold medalist, and Sergei probably would've been one, too, if he'd had the chance. Just watching them skate in circles would be educational."

Mark folded his arms. "It must've been your idea to come train here."

"No, it was actually Steph's."

That didn't surprise me. She knew the best chance to top us would be to work with Em and Sergei, even with her snarking about them.

"Do you go along with everything she wants?" Mark asked.

Josh stopped and stared at him. His clear blue eyes didn't blink. "We made a mutual decision after a long discussion."

Mark continued the stare-down for a few more moments and then walked away. I climbed down the bleachers and caught up to him as quickly as I could while clomping in my skates.

"What's with the attitude?" I asked.

"What's with you jumping to his defense?"

"I'm not. It's just... Stephanie already hates us enough. You don't need to piss off Josh and give them even more reason to beat us."

Mark slowed and glanced back at Josh. "Something about him bugs me. He doesn't talk a lot, but he's probably thinking to himself how he's better than all of us."

"He's not like that. You don't know him—" I cut myself off before I spilled how well-acquainted Josh and I had become. "I mean, I've talked to him here and he's never been snotty like Stephanie."

He peered down at me, and a trace of suspicion crossed his face. "Well, I don't care if he's the nicest guy on Earth. I don't wanna be his friend. Once we make the Olympic team, then I'll be glad to have a beer with him."

*He doesn't drink,* I almost said out loud.

I didn't want to be Josh's friend either. I wanted a helluva lot more. And Mark would kick my ass if he had any idea I felt that way.

# Chapter Nine

"Ladies and gentlemen, we have a full flight today. We ask that you stow your bags and step out of the aisle as quickly as possible so we can get on our way to Denver. Thank you."

I shoved my backpack under the seat in front of me and slipped my laptop into the seat pocket. The four-hour flight would hopefully be enough time for me to complete the essay for my Boston College application. We only had a forty-minute connecting flight from Denver to Colorado Springs for camp at the Olympic Training Center, and that wouldn't be long enough to even power up my computer.

I was buckling my seat belt when Josh stopped at my row of two seats and looked at the empty aisle one. "22B. That's me."

*Say what the what?* The federation's travel coordinator had made our arrangements, and when Mark had sat a few rows behind me, I'd assumed Team Cape Cod would be scattered throughout the plane. Somehow I'd won the seat lottery!

"You don't know how relieved I am that you're not someone holding a screaming baby," I said.

He sat and pressed his palm to his chest. "I'm hurt that's the only reason you're happy to see me."

I laughed, probably too nervously. "I didn't mean for it to sound that way."

"That's a relief because if the president of my fan club isn't excited about sitting next to me, then I'm doing something wrong."

"Don't worry. You're keeping this fan very happy. I'm going to miss my Thursday 'Over the Rainbow' this week."

"Think there's a piano at the Olympic Training Center?"

I pretended to give it some thought. "Probably not."

"Maybe I can just hum it for you tomorrow night."

I broke into a huge smile. "That would be utterly amazing."

Em and Sergei passed us on their way down the aisle, and Em gave us a long and interested look. I gave her a little wave in return. *Nothing to see here... keep moving.*

Josh stored his bag under the seat and tapped my laptop. "Did you bring a movie to watch?"

"No, I need to work on my college essay."

"Wow, you're ahead of the game."

"I'm applying for early acceptance, so applications are due November first. I know it's only the end of July, but I want to get it all done before the season starts."

"What's your essay about?"

"How living with the twins has enhanced my interest in being a child psychologist."

Josh nodded. "That's really cool. It sounds interesting... and very early acceptance-worthy."

I spun my bracelet around my wrist. "I hope so. My grades were good, but my SAT score wasn't fabulous."

"Are you applying to any other schools?"

I shook my head. "BC is the only place I've ever wanted to go. I grew up going to football games and hockey games there with my dad. I know the campus from front to back."

A mom with three kids loaded down with bags squeezed through the aisle, and Josh leaned slightly toward me to avoid being hit.

"I'm keeping my fingers crossed for you." He buckled his seat belt and cleared his throat. "If you um… if you decide you do want to look at other schools, UCLA has a great psych program, and I guarantee the weather would be better. And I could help you learn the campus front to back."

He smiled, and my voice got lost somewhere in my throat. Was he seriously suggesting I move to California? Even if I didn't have my heart set on BC, UCLA's non-resident tuition plus living in California would probably cost a bazillion dollars. But I beamed on the inside that he wanted me there.

"That would be a blast, but I don't think my college fund would agree, unfortunately."

The flight attendant announced the door was closing, so I checked my phone to make sure I'd turned it off. I sat back and put my arm on the seat divider, not realizing Josh had done the same. The soft hair on his forearm tickled my skin, setting off goose bumps from my wrist to my shoulder.

I quickly pulled away. "Sorry."

"You can have it," he offered.

"No, I'm good."

*Liar.* There were way too many intensely incredible things overwhelming my senses right now, and I wasn't sure I'd be able to focus on writing my essay. Josh's sweet cologne lightly teased my nose, and his leg was less than an inch away from touching mine. Even his soft voice was giving me heart palpitations because it was so close to my ear.

I took my iPod from my bag and set it on my lap. I was going to have to immerse myself in music while writing to block out all the distractions.

"Wanna switch?" Josh asked as he pulled his own iPod from the pocket of his cargo shorts. "Could be fun to discover new music."

I hesitated but then handed mine over. "There may be some um… some Disney songs on there."

He grinned. "I won't mock your Disney songs if you don't mock my gangsta rap."

"Dude, I love me some gangsta rap. You'll find a bunch of it on my workout playlist."

The video screens dropped from the ceiling for the safety announcement, and Josh and I stopped talking to listen. As the plane approached the runway, I lifted the window shade and watched the raindrops stream across the glass. It would be nice to have a change of scenery for a few days and to see my skater friends. I wasn't looking forward to seeing Kyle, though. The sting of what he'd done was a dull memory now, but I hoped being around him wouldn't bring up the hurt again. I still couldn't stop kicking myself for almost sleeping with him. Whenever I got into another relationship, I was going to make damn sure the guy was "the one" before I'd take that step.

The plane zoomed up into the air, and as soon as the chime rang, I set up my laptop on the tray table. Josh stretched one long leg into the aisle and plugged his ear buds into my iPod.

"If you want to switch back just poke me," he said.

I bit my lip as my mind went to all the places I'd like to poke him.

*Get to work! This essay needs to rock.*

I took a deep breath and popped in my ear buds. The words started to flow from my fingers as I jammed along to the music. Josh's playlists included a lot of alternative bands I hadn't heard before, and I noted the songs I liked in a separate document so I could download them later.

I felt Josh's shoulders shake, and I looked over to find him laughing to himself. I bumped his arm, and he showed my iPod currently playing The Muppets' "The Rainbow

Connection." He pulled out one ear bud while I did the same.

"Do you have a thing for all rainbow songs?" he asked.

I laughed. "Hey, rainbows are awesome."

"What about puppies and unicorns? How do you feel about them?"

"I'm a big fan of them, too."

"And gangsta rap."

"What can I say… I'm a complex and unpredictable girl."

His smile deepened and shone in his eyes. He opened his mouth, and I thought he was going to say something, but he slipped the bud back into his ear.

Over the next few hours I managed to crank out a strong first draft and even had time left to compare notes with Josh on which songs we enjoyed discovering. When we boarded our connecting flight, I was disappointed he and I weren't seated together, but we were barely in the air before we landed anyway.

Our large group filled the shuttle from the airport to the Olympic Training Center, and after we checked in with the federation staff, we headed to the dorms to find our rooms.

Liza stopped when she saw her name on one of the doors. "I'm rooming with Marley!"

Marley and her ice dance partner Zach had trained on the Cape for years before they'd moved to Seattle, so I was glad Liza had been paired with someone familiar for her first camp. I continued down the hall but came to a halt at the sight of my name.

Next to Stephanie's.

"Oh, fun," she said over my shoulder.

I marched back down the hall to Em and Sergei's room and swept through the open door. "Did you put me and Stephanie together?"

"You might find some common ground if you spend a little time together," Em said.

"There's nothing we could possibly have in common

besides skating. She's evil, and I don't trust her around my stuff. She's liable to tamper with my skates or my costumes…"

"She's not going to do that. Maybe if you reach out to her, she'll surprise you."

I folded my arms. "Yeah, I'm sure she's secretly dying to be my BFF."

I went back to my room, where Stephanie was unpacking her Louis Vuitton luggage. I hauled my rolling bag onto the empty twin bed and hung my garment bag in the closet.

"Don't even think about touching my stuff," I said.

She stepped back from her suitcase and put her hands on her hips. "Why would I touch your stuff? All you have is cheap jewelry and knock-off clothes."

Heat blazed from my face up to my scalp. Stephanie knew my mom had made almost all my jewelry because I'd peddled Mom's creations at the rink. It was one thing for her to insult me, but insulting my mom's hard work went beyond cruel.

"I'm proud to wear this jewelry. My mom puts her heart into every piece." I tried to keep my voice steady. "They mean a lot more than anything you buy with your daddy's credit card."

Her face darkened, and she tossed a pair of sneakers onto the concrete floor. "Like you wouldn't love to have that credit card. If anyone needs to worry about protecting their things, it's me."

"I know this might shock you, but not everyone is obsessed with money and having expensive crap. If you spent less time focusing on material things and more time learning how to treat people decently, you'd have a lot more friends."

"I have plenty of friends at home."

"I can only imagine what that group is like." I shuddered.

Mark pushed our half-open door and stuck his head inside. "We need to go down to the welcome session."

I shut my suitcase, grabbed my purse, and brushed past

Stephanie, not waiting for her to join us.

**\*\*\*\***

A couple of hours later I returned to the dorm, fired up from the keynote speech given by one of the country's most decorated skaters. I was also feeling good because I'd avoided saying more than hello to Kyle, and I'd enjoyed a fun dinner catching up with friends I didn't get to see often.

After my shower, I retreated to my room with the plan to ignore Stephanie. It was the only way to maintain my positive mood. I could only hope she'd deem me unworthy of her attention, and she'd likewise pretend I wasn't in the room.

"Please tell me you don't snore," she said as I picked up my hand lotion and sat cross-legged on the bed.

I sighed. So much for that hope.

"No, but oh how I wish I did," I said.

She flipped off the overhead light, sending us into total darkness, and the lotion I squirted missed my hand and landed who knew where.

"Hey! I was still doing something here."

"We have to get up early, and I don't want to feel jet-lagged while skating tomorrow." Her bed squeaked as she climbed onto it.

"I just needed a few more minutes," I said through gritted teeth.

I patted the blanket and felt the dollop of misfired lotion. My eyes adjusted to the darkness as I slowly massaged the soothing liquid into my hands.

Burying myself under the covers, I took my phone from the nightstand and turned to face the wall. The message light blinked, and when I saw the text was from Josh I smiled against the pillow.

Josh: *Just checking that you and Steph haven't killed each other.*

I pulled the blanket higher over me and the phone. Stephanie would most definitely murder me if she knew I was texting with her brother.

Me: *I'm gonna sleep with one eye open.*

Josh: *She sleeps like the dead so you should be safe for the night.*

Me: *Can I ask you something?*

Josh: *Sure*

Me: *Why is she so mean?*

A long minute passed with no response, and my neck tensed. Perhaps I shouldn't have been so blunt.

Josh: *If you met my mom, you'd have a good idea.*

Me: *They're a lot alike?*

Josh: *Exactly alike*

Yikes. The idea of a Stephanie clone gave me an ice-cold chill. Good thing Josh and I weren't going to date because Mommy Dearest would surely hate me.

Me: *What's your dad like?*

Josh: *He's very smart, very outgoing.*

I could picture that. I vaguely remembered his parents from competitions — they didn't exactly hang with my parents' crowd — but I'd seen photos of them when I'd checked out Stephanie's Facebook since Josh didn't have one. I could totally see his dad as a smooth-talking Beverly Hills attorney. His mom had looked like the stereotypical socialite with too many visits to a plastic surgeon in her past.

Me: *Are your parents going to come for a visit on the Cape anytime?*

Josh: *Probably not. They're always pretty busy.*

What was his mom busy doing? Going to yoga and getting a mani-pedi?

Josh: *I won't keep you up. Big day tomorrow.*

I wasn't ready to say goodnight, but we did have a big day ahead with our short program evaluations and a slew of meetings.

Me: *Yeah, I get to show off my tango moves. Thank you again for helping me. It made a world of difference.*

Josh: *You're welcome. I'm glad you trusted me not to sabotage you ;)*

Me: *Like the time you tried to kill me by inviting me to hot yoga? ;)*

Josh: *LOL well played*

I closed my eyes for a moment and imagined him lying in bed typing on his phone, one arm resting above his head, his wrinkled T-shirt riding up just enough for a glimpse of his tight abs. Knowing he was just down the hall made the vision even more real.

I opened my eyes and saw the red light flashing.

Josh: *See you in the morning*

Another vision flashed through my mind — Josh waking up, his brown hair messy, his long eyelashes fluttering as his blue eyes opened to the world…

I gulped and put my fingers to the keys.

Me: *Goodnight*

****

"What do you think they're going to make us do this year?" Mark asked as we left the dorms and headed for the swimming pool. "Water polo? Synchronized swimming?"

I took a hair band from the pocket of my denim shorts and secured my hair into a ponytail. The federation staff had told us to put on our swimsuits for the evening's team-building activity. Every year they split us into groups and made us do some goofy exercise. I had no idea what we could be doing in the pool. I was just ecstatic Mark and I had gotten through our program evaluations with mostly positive feedback. Now we could relax and enjoy our last night of camp.

"I'm glad I just bought a new suit." Liza looked down at

the purple polka-dotted bikini top she wore with her shorts.

"It's super cute," I said.

I wore the green bikini I'd had for two summers, but I liked the way it fit me. I didn't have much in the chest area to show off, and this suit somehow made it look like I had more going on there.

We arrived at the pool, and I shaded my eyes from the late afternoon sunshine. There was no mistaking this was a gathering of skaters from the number of pasty bodies present. I gave Josh a quick smile as we walked past him, and his eyes swept over me and followed me all the way to my chair. *Green bikini, you done good.*

Two of the federation's team leaders called for everyone's attention and explained we would be split into groups of five to build boats with nothing but cardboard and duct tape. We all snickered and then laughed even louder when we found out we had to float the boat across the pool with all five members of our team in it. Points would be awarded for design and execution, and the winners would get the usual camp prize of bragging rights.

We listened as the teams were read, and my stomach turned when I heard my name after Kyle's. Then it did a happy flip when Josh's name came next. Liza and Zach rounded out our group.

"Your old love and your new love," Liza said quietly. "This could get interesting."

I picked up a roll of duct tape. "This makes a good gag, you know."

"See, that's how I know you do like Josh because you always get so testy when I bring it up."

"I'm testy because this isn't something that should be joked about around certain people—"

"Hey, Court." Kyle walked up behind me. "Guess we're working together."

I slowly turned to face him. "Yahoo."

Zach and Josh joined us, both carrying large flattened boxes. They dropped them next to the pool, and the five of us sat in a circle.

"We need a strategy," Zach said. "I was thinking of something like a canoe."

He started sketching his idea on a scrap of paper, and Josh and Liza huddled beside him. Kyle scooted closer to me, and his spicy cologne reminded me of when we'd been a happy couple at camp the previous summer. I'd thought he was such a good guy. Thinking back to how much I'd stupidly trusted him, I recoiled as he invaded more of my space.

"How have you been?" Kyle asked.

"Wonderful," I said curtly.

"Are you seeing anyone?"

Josh glanced up at us, and I looked directly at Kyle. "Nope."

He swiped his shaggy blond hair out of his eyes. "I know I didn't handle things well with us, but maybe I could call you sometime."

"What? Don't you have a girlfriend?"

"We broke up."

My stomach twisted again. I'd meant so little to him that he'd betrayed me for a quick fling. I'd thought he'd ditched me for the love of his life or at least a long-term relationship.

"Are you serious? So you cheated on me for nothing?"

All three of our teammates were now staring at us. Liza's mouth had taken the shape of a huge O.

Kyle turned his back to them. "Can we talk later?"

I gaped at him. "There's nothing to talk about. I don't want anything to do with you. Ever."

I moved over to Liza's side. "Let's figure out this damn boat."

Josh looked down at Zach's sketch, but one side of his mouth curled up. Liza watched me, still wide-eyed. Meanwhile, Zach resumed drawing.

"Alrighty then," he said. "Why don't we calculate how big we need to cut the cardboard?"

Once we figured out the measurements, the boys did the cutting while Liza and I connected the sides of the boat. Pulling hard on the thick rolls of tape helped me let out my disgust with Kyle. He didn't speak to me again, even when we all had to work together to make sure our vessel was secure.

Josh asked me to help him add another layer of tape to one corner, and he peeked up at me while we bent over the boat.

"You okay?" he asked.

I nodded. "I can't believe he actually thought I'd give him another chance."

"He's an idiot." Josh knelt and pressed hard on the boat. "In more ways than one."

He lifted his head, and our eyes connected for just a moment, but long enough for me to see the intensity behind what he'd said. I fumbled with the roll of tape and winced as I had to unstick a long piece from my fingers.

"I think we're good on this end," Josh told Zach.

Zach came around as he inspected all sides of the boat. "This baby's gonna win. She's a lean, mean floating machine."

I examined our creation skeptically. It looked sturdy, but once the five of us got on board, we might be at the bottom of the pool in a few seconds.

We were informed that our group would be first to sail, and our maiden voyage was only moments away, so we carried the boat to the pool. The guys stripped off their T-shirts while Liza and I shimmied out of our shorts, and then we all gathered around our captain Zach.

"Josh, you take the back and I'll take the front," he said. "Kyle, you'll be in the middle, and then the girls can fill in."

Liza went near the front with Zach, so that meant I'd be sandwiched between Kyle and Josh — the guy I didn't want touching any part of me and the guy I wanted touching *every* part of me. Was I being secretly filmed for some sort of reality show?

Josh and Zach carefully climbed into the boat, anchoring each end, and Josh extended his hand to me. I gave him mine and slowly put one foot on the cardboard. When I set my other foot down, the boat wobbled and I swayed with it, stumbling backward. Josh gripped my hand tighter and grabbed my thigh, and his fingertips brushed the edge of my bikini bottom. The sizzling sensation only made me feel more off-balance.

"You um… you got it?" He took his hand off my thigh.

I eased down into a sitting position, settling between his legs, and I realized just how small the boat was. I had no choice but to back up against Josh's chest.

I rocked the boat even more as I inched backward between his blue board shorts, and he held the sides to steady it.

"Sorry," I said.

"You're perfect," he said softly.

I almost swooned overboard.

The temptation to look at him was so great, but I'd die inside even more if I saw those blue eyes right now. His arms rested on the sides of the boat, and it felt like we were sitting in a bathtub together. Being practically naked further enhanced that feeling. There was so much skin-on-skin contact between us that my body couldn't handle it. Goosebumps were popping up everywhere, and Josh had a close-up view of the ones all down the back of my neck.

I turned my head toward him, and my ponytail swung with me. I heard "Pfft" behind me.

"Did I whack you?" I asked.

He chuckled. "It's okay."

Holy crap, he was close. Closer than the airplane, closer than the tango. I could feel the warmth of his body surrounding me. If I leaned back just a little, I'd be flush against him.

*Yeah, that would go over real well with Stephanie and Mark watching us poolside.*

I'd never experienced anything so torturous yet so achingly wonderful.

Kyle positioned himself in front of me, and I squirmed and moved my legs so they wouldn't touch his. That resulted in my calves bumping Josh's. What was another body part when we were already fused together everywhere else?

He leaned over my shoulder, and his hot breath wisped over my ear. "Can we still win if we push Kyle overboard?"

I grinned. "I'm tempted to find out."

"Time to set sail!" Zach said.

We pushed away from the wall and paddled with our hands to steer the boat. All the other skaters lined the pool, cheering and laughing as we drifted away from the shallow end. When we crossed the center line, I felt water on my butt, and I looked down to find a layer of it seeping into the boat.

"Uh-oh," I said.

"Keep paddling," Josh said. "We can make it."

Our arms flapped faster, but our butts were getting wetter. I could sense the rear of the boat starting to sink.

"We're going down like the Titanic back here!" I yelled.

Zach leaned forward, paddling furiously, and we kept up behind him, even as we dipped further into the water. Soon the entire back of the boat would be flooded.

"Hurry!" Liza screeched.

The cheers grew louder, and I zoned into the finish line, smacking hard at the water. The nose of the boat touched the wall, and Zach threw his arms into the air.

"We did it!"

The water overtook us, and we all tumbled with laughter into the pool. I came up for air, and Josh and Zach were slapping hands and shouting, "Teamwork!"

Josh turned and pulled me into a hug, and I looped my arms around his shoulders. He gave me a gentle squeeze, and

I relaxed into him. He was solid muscle everywhere.

*Damn, this feels so perfect.*

It took everything in me not to wrap my legs around his waist and kiss the hell out of him.

As soon as we split apart, I met Stephanie's lethal gaze from the edge of the pool, and the magic was gone. I boosted myself up and out of the water and went in the opposite direction, wringing out my ponytail as I headed for the stack of towels.

I stayed far away from Stephanie for the rest of the event, but I couldn't evade her at the dorms. Dread filled my gut as I neared our room because I knew she was going to come at me full force with snippy comments about Josh and me.

When I reached the room, the door was cracked and I could see Stephanie talking on her phone. I was about to barge in, but I heard her say, "Mom, I told you they loved our programs. Why do you have to keep harping on the one negative thing?"

There was a pause and she let out a deep sigh. "We have time to get new costumes made. We don't compete until September."

More sighing followed another pause. "I don't know why the judges didn't like the costumes. You know how picky they are."

I peeked inside and saw Stephanie throw her suitcase onto her bed. "I have to pack, Mom. I'll call you when we get home."

I backed away from the door to wait a minute before entering. Mommy Dearest sounded like one of those nitpicking skating moms who made their kids' lives miserable. I could see how that may have helped shape Stephanie into the brat she was, but it didn't excuse her awful behavior. Josh had managed to rise above the negativity surrounding them.

I went inside, and Stephanie gave me a cursory glance before returning to packing. She remained quiet, and I wondered if the conversation with her mother had distracted her from what she'd seen at the pool.

After I shoved all my dirty laundry into my suitcase and carefully packed my costumes in their garment bag, I sat on my bed to return a text from Meredith. Stephanie sat on hers and stared at me, so I stopped typing and braced myself for the end of our peaceful evening.

"I'm going to tell you this because I think it'll save you some heartache," she said.

I rested my head on my hand and glared at her. What kind of angle was she taking this time?

"You might think because Josh is nice to you and shows you affection that he's into you, but he knows what we're all fighting for, and he's a smart guy. He knows if he gets you to fall for him, you're not going to be as focused on skating."

My God, there was no limit to the garbage that came out of her mouth.

I sat up straight. "You must think I'm really stupid if you think I'd believe Josh would be that calculating."

"You don't know him as well as you think you do. He'll do anything to get on the Olympic team. It's all he's wanted for so long."

I didn't doubt Josh's strong desire to fulfill that dream. I had the same goal pushing me every day. But the idea that he would cook up a scheme to hurt me was preposterous.

"I know him well enough to know he could never do something so devious. That's all you."

"You believe what you want. I was just trying to give you a heads-up because I don't agree with what he's doing. I'd rather beat you on the ice without any outside games."

I looked down at the bed. There couldn't possibly be any truth to what she was saying. Josh was one of the most genuine people I'd ever met.

*You thought Kyle was genuine, too.*

I shook my head. No, Josh wasn't Kyle. Stephanie wanted

me away from her brother, and making him seem like a jerk was the only way she knew how to accomplish that. I couldn't wrap my mind around that level of shadiness.

I grabbed my shower kit and stalked to the door. "You're really messed up, you know that? When I come back, don't speak another word to me."

# Chapter Ten

My eyes slowly focused and adjusted to the daylight as I padded down the carpeted stairs. Oh, how I loved Sundays and being able to sleep past dawn. I moseyed into the bright kitchen and set my phone on the counter before pouring a heaping bowl of cereal. The house was so quiet since Sergei was at a competition in Germany with Stephanie and Josh, and the twins were spending the weekend with Em's parents in Boston.

Carrying my phone and the cereal down the hall, I headed for my favorite room in the house, the library. Em sat in one of the big leather chairs with stacks of CDs surrounding her and her laptop resting on her knees.

"Morning," she said.

I flopped down on the leather couch. "What's cookin'?"

"I'm planning the Christmas show."

"Already? Aren't we still in September?"

"I know, but I got a late start last year and everything felt so rushed. The next two months will fly by."

I spooned some oat flakes into my mouth and chewed slowly. The *last* two months had flown by. Mark and I had been working tirelessly on perfecting every detail of our programs for our first competition in a few weeks in Paris. I could tango in my sleep now. My time spent with Josh at the restaurant also seemed to have passed quickly. I felt like the big hourglass from *The Wizard of Oz* was hanging over us, counting down the days until Josh had to move back to L.A. Our friendship had continued to deepen, and I'd continued to sense that *somethin' somethin'* simmering between us. But Josh had never made any kind of move, and as much as I knew that was for the best, I still couldn't get him out of my head.

"What do you and Mark want to skate to this year? This'll be your last Christmas show." Em's mouth turned down.

I curled my legs under me. "Maybe we can skate to 'Blue Christmas.' It's kinda melancholy for the occasion, and my mom loves Elvis, so she'd be thrilled."

"I was thinking we can also have a group number with you, Mark, Stephanie, and Josh like we used to do with you, me, Mark, and Chris. We had a lot fun with those."

Skating with Josh? Best idea ever! Skating with Stephanie? Hell on earth!

"It was fun because we all liked each other," I said. "This is a much different situation."

"The four of you can find a way to work together. You're the only senior teams we have, and I think it would be great to mesh your different styles."

The opportunity to skate with Josh was definitely outweighing the pain of sharing the ice with Stephanie. Mark would hate the idea, but I had the feeling Em wasn't going to make this optional for us anyway.

"Can we skate to 'The Christmas Song' by Nat King Cole?" I asked.

It was my favorite holiday tune, and I'd always had a secret fantasy of dancing to it with a special guy. Skating with Josh to it would be the next best thing.

"Sure." Em typed on her computer. "Josh offered to cut all the music for me, so I'm making a list for him. I'll put that on there."

While she continued typing, I picked up my phone and trolled Stephanie's Facebook to see if she'd posted any new photos from Germany. There was one of Josh and her posing with their bronze medals. They'd skated very well, and I was starting to get nervous about competing against them at Skate America in November.

"Is Josh still playing the piano at the restaurant?" Em asked.

"Yeah, on Thursday nights."

"And Stephanie still doesn't know?"

I shoveled more cereal into my mouth and shook my head.

"What's up with that?" Em asked.

I took my time chewing and swallowing. "He just wants to do his own thing without her coming around."

"I guess I can understand that since so much of their lives has been spent together." Em picked up her mug of coffee from the end table. "You've gotten to know Josh pretty well, haven't you?"

I shrugged. "We talk at the restaurant." *And we text. And share long looks that make me crazy.*

"I'm glad you've become friends. Other than when we're doing choreography, he's so quiet at the rink."

"I think he still sorta feels like an outsider there. Not that you and Sergei haven't made him and Stephanie feel like part of the group. But Mark hasn't exactly been friendly, and his buddies have followed suit."

Em pursed her lips and sipped her coffee. "He's such a sweet guy. Maybe working on this group number will break some of the ice between him and Mark."

*God bless her.* She was never going to give up on making the four of us a happy family.

"The only thing that's going to break the ice between them is all of us making the Olympic team. I might even hug Stephanie if that happens."

Em laughed. "I'm going to hold you to that."

"Just remember I said *might*." I pointed my spoon at her.

If all of us did make the team, I'd be so beside myself I'd probably hug everyone within a mile radius. I'd give Josh an extra-long embrace, and maybe it would lead to a kiss...

I chomped hard on my cereal. The whole thing was a dream with slim odds of happening. Rebekah and Evan were two-time champs who wouldn't be easily dethroned, so there was realistically only one place on the team available. I shouldn't be thinking about a Team Cape Cod trip to the Olympics anyway. I had to concentrate on my own skating and making sure Mark and I earned a spot. Nine years of work were riding on it.

****

"Two glasses of chardonnay coming up," I said to Meredith and turned to the back of the bar.

A mellow and not very demanding Friday night crowd had descended upon the restaurant, so I'd had lots of time to chat with Josh and Mrs. Cassar, who'd parked herself next to him. She'd already patted his cheek once, and I'd barely contained my laughter.

I poured the wine and passed the order to Meredith before grabbing the bottle of merlot to refill Mrs. Cassar's glass.

"Joshua was just telling me about the Christmas show," she said.

I bit my lip but couldn't hide my grin. Josh had told me only his grandma called him by his full name.

"I'm almost finished cutting all the music," he said.

"That was quick." I filled Mrs. Cassar's glass halfway.

"Em just gave you the list on Monday."

"There are only a few programs that have multiple music cuts, so it's been pretty easy."

Mrs. Cassar took a sip of wine. "You'll have to remind me when the show gets closer. I'd love to see it."

"You've never come to any of our shows before," I said.

"Well, Joshua invited me. He said you're going to skate together."

Did the fact he mentioned that to Mrs. Cassar mean he was just as excited about it as I was? I'd started counting the days until our first practice.

"Rehearsals should be fun considering how unenthused Stephanie and Mark are about this group number," I said.

"Why can't just the two of you skate together in your own number? That's what I want to see," Mrs. Cassar said.

Josh and I locked eyes, both seeking a response from the other. No way was I going to divulge how much I'd love to do a program just with him. He stayed quiet, too, and I would've killed to know if he was thinking the same thing.

When the silence became too awkward, I decided to answer the question from a different angle. "I think our partners might throw a collective hissy fit if we did that."

I slid down the bar to tend to another customer, and Mrs. Cassar soon waved me back to her with her diamond-ring-covered fingers.

"Dear, can you get me that appetizer I love? The mini crab cakes?" she asked. "Joshua, you'll share them with me, won't you?"

He wiped his mouth on his linen napkin and glanced at his plate full of pasta. "I'm knee-deep in spaghetti here."

She squeezed his bicep. "You'll work it all off skating and throwing your sister around."

I laughed as Josh's face tinted pink. When I returned to them a bit later with her order, Mrs. Cassar was asking him, "How long have you and your sister skated together?"

"Since I was eleven and she was nine. She was really tiny, so we used to play around and do little lifts on the ice, and one of the pair coaches at our rink saw us and told my parents we should try skating pairs."

"You must get along well to have stuck it out this long. My brother, may he rest in peace, wouldn't have put up with me for five minutes much less years and years."

I pretended to organize bottles on the shelves while I eavesdropped on their conversation. It was a trick I'd perfected working behind the bar.

"Off the ice we don't have a lot in common, and we don't agree on a lot of things, but on the ice we've always worked well together," Josh said. "It's the one place we speak the same language."

*Yeah, because off the ice the only language Stephanie speaks is fluent Bitch.*

"If you skated with Courtney…" Mrs. Cassar said my name loud enough to make me turn my head. "You'd have a partner you got along with on *and* off the ice. Wouldn't that be wonderful?"

My cheeks grew warm, and I wished I could crawl under the bar. It was hard enough hiding my feelings for Josh without Mrs. Pair Matchmaker stirring things up. I peeked at Josh, and he raised his water to his lips, but I thought I saw him smiling behind the glass.

"I need to check on an order," I said and rushed to the kitchen.

More of my barstools began to fill up, so I only caught bits and pieces of Josh and Mrs. Cassar's conversation the rest of the night. Almost every time I passed them, Josh was laughing and shaking his head, undoubtedly at another gem from the old lady's mouth.

She left the restaurant about thirty minutes before closing, but Josh stayed until the last customer departed. He'd been doing that lately even on the nights when he wasn't playing piano and was obligated to be there until ten o'clock.

"Mrs. Cassar said she's going to bring all the ladies from her book club to the Christmas show," Josh said. "And she asked if she can come watch us rehearse."

I laughed and untied my apron. "She is so excited about this."

"I asked Em if I could help choreograph the group number, so I'll see if you and I can skate together for a good part of the program." He shoved his hands in his pockets and shifted from one foot to the other. "If that's okay with you."

"Yeah, I'm..." *Contain your gushing.* "I'm cool with that."

I scooted into the kitchen to get my purse and sweater, and after I said goodnight to Meredith, Ronnie handed me a small takeout container.

"Last piece of chocolate mousse cake. Enjoy it on your night off tomorrow," he said.

"Ooh, thanks. See you Tuesday."

I met Josh in the dining room, and he pointed to my container. "What you got there?"

"Chocolate mousse cake." I pushed open the heavy front door. "I scored the last piece."

Josh fell in step beside me as we walked toward our cars parked in adjacent spots. He was quiet, so when he reached over and grabbed my box, I didn't realize at first what was happening.

"Now I have the last piece." He grinned as he held the box over his head and jogged ahead of me.

"What are you..." I set off after him. "You can't take my cake!"

He darted between our cars and continued to hold the container high in the air. "If you can reach it, you can have it back."

I jumped up but didn't have nearly enough hops to reach the end of his long arm. He took a couple of quick steps to evade me, and I put more spring into my feet to jump higher.

On my second leap, I lost my balance and fell forward, and Josh caught my waist with his free hand, pinning me against him.

Our eyes met, and my heart pounded hard. The intense way he looked at me stole my breath. His lips parted, and his gaze traveled slowly down to my mouth, filling me with anticipation. I couldn't think of anything except how much I wanted to feel his lips on mine. My whole body yearned for it. His arm tightened around my waist, and I leaned into him, aching more every second he waited to kiss me.

He looked into my eyes, and as soon as he did, he backed away. A heavy weight pushed on my chest, and I felt like my thirteen-year-old self, being rejected by Josh all over again.

"If this um… if this drops on the ground, no one will get to eat it," he said with a forced laugh.

He gave the box to me, now avoiding my eyes. I clutched it with both of my shaky hands and looked down at the pavement.

"Have a good weekend," he said.

My throat was so tight I couldn't speak. I just nodded and quickly dug in my purse for my keys. The search seemed to take an agonizing year, and when I finally retrieved the keys I flung myself into the driver's seat and tossed the cake onto the passenger side. Throwing the car in reverse, I turned the wheel hard and sped out of the lot.

The first two blocks I steeled my jaw, willing myself not to cry, but the hurt strangling me was too much to hold inside. My breath came out in gasps as tears streamed down my face. I swiped at my blurry eyes so I could see the road, but they just kept filling with water.

I'd tried to accept that nothing would ever happen between us. I'd told myself that I just had to deal with my feelings while Josh was around, and when he'd leave the Cape I could get over him. But none of that logic had mattered when I was pressed against him and he was looking at me with so much desire. I'd never felt so strongly about anyone. I'd wanted him to kiss me more than I'd ever wanted anything in my life.

# Chapter Eleven

"Coco, what movie we watch?" Quinn asked as she climbed onto the sofa next to Alex.

I crouched in front of the large built-in entertainment center and inserted the DVD into the Blu-ray player. "My favorite movie of all time, *The Wizard of Oz*."

"Do it have a princess?" Quinn asked.

*Hmm… Glinda is a witch, but she looks like a princess…*

"Sorta," I said.

"And animals?" Alex mimicked a tiger's claw and let out a little roar.

I pressed Play and sat on the couch beside Quinn. "It sure does. There's a cute little dog named Toto and a big lovable lion."

"You sit in middle," Quinn said and crawled across my lap.

I put my arms around the twins and snuggled them close to me. I was so happy to be babysitting instead of working at the restaurant. After spending the day thinking about nothing but my near-kiss with Josh the prior night, I needed a movie escape badly. I couldn't stop wondering if Stephanie had been right about Josh playing me. What if it was all a big game to him? What if he and Stephanie were in cahoots to mess with my head?

"Why it have no color?" Quinn said as the opening credits rolled.

"It's very old. Even older than your grandparents."

Alex's mouth opened wide. "Dat's really old."

They had lots more comments as the story began ("Dat man have a big nose!" "Look at da pigs!"). When we reached the part when Dorothy was about to sing "Over the Rainbow," I patted their heads.

"This is a really pretty song, so let's be quiet and listen, okay?"

I tried to see only the black-and-white image of Dorothy singing on the farm, but my mind kept picturing Josh playing the song on the piano. Every time he did, he'd look over at me behind the bar, and his eyes would crinkle with his gleaming smile. Once he'd waited to play it as the last song, and I'd given him a hard time, saying I'd been anxious to hear it all night. He'd leaned toward me, his blue eyes shining, and he'd said, "You know it's true what they say. Good things come to those who wait."

Quinn whimpered and buried her face in my side, and I checked back into reality. The villainous Almira Gulch was riding her bike across the TV screen.

"She scary," Alex said and mimicked Quinn's position.

Quinn peeked at the TV with one eye. "I don't like her."

I caressed their silky hair. "She's only in some parts of the movie. There are a lot more happy, pretty parts."

Their tiny hands clung to my pajama T-shirt, but they faced the TV again. They were silent during the tornado, but the moment Almira and her bike transformed into the Wicked Witch and a broomstick, Quinn screamed and both she and Alex clambered onto my lap, quivering with fear.

*Crap, they're probably going to have nightmares for months.*

My mom had let me watch the movie when I was three years old, so I'd thought the twins could handle it. Em was going to kill me.

"It's okay. I'll turn it off." I reached around them for the remote on the coffee table and shut off the DVD player.

They squeezed their arms around me and each other, and I hugged them and kissed the tops of their heads. "Why don't we watch Winnie the Pooh? I know that's your favorite."

It took some coaxing for them to let go of me, but I eventually extricated myself and switched out the DVDs. We watched Pooh and his pals frolic through the forest until the twins started yawning and rubbing their eyes.

"Time to get ready for bed," I said.

After I made sure they properly brushed their teeth and I tucked them into Alex's twin beds, I went back downstairs and stretched out on the couch. Clicking through the TV channels with the remote, I spotted *Pride and Prejudice* and had to stop even though I'd seen the movie at least fifty times.

My heart began to feel heavy again as I watched Lizzie and Mr. Darcy exchange longing looks. All the smiles Josh had given me, all the times I'd caught him staring at me while I waited on customers at the bar... had they really been just for show? How could I have been so wrong about what I'd felt between us?

I hugged one of the green throw pillows and curled into a ball. I needed something sweet. Chocolate. My piece of cake!

I shuffled in my big furry slippers to the kitchen and took the cake from the refrigerator. As I carried it to the sofa, I tasted a dollop of the icing with my finger. I was ready to dive into the rest of it with my fork when the doorbell rang.

*Who could be visiting this late at night?*

After setting the cake on the coffee table, I went to the big front window to peek through the blinds. I jumped back at the sight of Josh's car parked along the curb.

*What is he doing here????*

I looked down at my T-shirt and fleece Minnie Mouse pants. I wasn't even wearing a bra. My attire wasn't suitable for *any* visitors much less Josh.

Did it matter, though? If he was messing with me, I shouldn't care what I looked like in front of him.

I marched to the door and swung it open. Seeing Josh's handsome face made my stomach do its familiar flip-flop, and I gripped the doorknob tighter.

"What are you doing here?" I asked, not hiding my brusqueness.

His eyes darted over me and settled tentatively on mine. "I um... I wanted to give Em—"

The house phone trilled, and I looked behind me. "I need to get that."

I hurried to the kitchen and picked up the cordless phone. "Hello?"

"Courtney? Hi, is Em around?"

Em's mom didn't identify herself, but I always recognized her loud voice anyway.

"She and Sergei are out on their date night."

"Oh, okay. Do you know if they have any plans tomorrow? Mr. Jim and I might drive down in the afternoon."

Josh had closed the front door and had moved slowly from the foyer into the living room. He stood watching the TV, and I noticed he was holding a CD.

"Um... Liza's coming tomorrow to stay for a few days because she's off from school. I don't know of anything else going on, but you'll have to check with Em."

"I'll call her tomorrow after church. Take care, Sweetie."

I ended the call and put the phone on the granite bar that divided the kitchen and living room. Turning to Josh, I said, "You have something for Em?"

"I just wanted to give her the CD for the Christmas show."

My forehead wrinkled. "It couldn't wait until Monday?"

"Well, I… I was out so I thought I'd stop by since I had it in my car."

He held out the disc, and I took it from him. His explanation sounded flimsy at best. Was this another part of his plan — to continue to be in my face so I wouldn't stop thinking about him?

"I'll give it to Em."

I turned back to the bar and placed the CD on it, and I pretended to examine a piece of mail. It hurt too much to look at Josh, and my chest grew tighter every second he was around. A storm of questions brewed inside me and threatened to rain all over him at any moment.

"Court—"

I spun and faced him. "Do you get some twisted pleasure out of rejecting me?"

He stared at me, his eyes wide. "What?"

"Eight years ago you had the chance to kiss me and you didn't, and last night you had an even better chance and you walked away again. Do you enjoy rejecting me?"

"No," he said firmly. "I've… that's not…"

He took a few steps toward me, his eyes never leaving mine. "The time we first met, I tried all night to get up the nerve to talk to you, but I didn't know what to say. You were… you were so pretty and you didn't try to act older like the other girls. And then you picked my name out of the hat, and… I'd never kissed anyone before, so I was afraid I wasn't going to do it right and you'd think I was a total loser. That's why… that's why I bailed."

A large part of my anger melted as I reflected on the words I'd wanted to hear all those years ago. He *had* liked me, braces and frizzy hair and all. The thirteen-year-old in me squealed. But that didn't explain why he'd backed off in the present day.

"What about last night? I know you've kissed a girl now." I paused as a remote possibility came to me. "You have kissed a girl?"

"Yeah… yes," he quickly stammered. "I have, but…"

He moved closer to me, and my pulse raced at the nearness of him. His clear blue eyes searched deep into mine.

"There's never been anyone I wanted to kiss more than you."

The rest of me melted, and the warmth inside me grew hotter. Josh inched forward so there was no space between us, and he slowly lifted his hand to my cheek. His thumb brushed under my chin and along my jaw so lightly, but I could feel his touch *everywhere*.

"I've dreamt about this for so long," he said, barely above a whisper. "I just wanted it to be perfect."

My mouth had never felt so dry. I swallowed and licked my lips, and Josh's eyes went to them. When they looked up, I saw the same desire I'd seen the past night. But none of the hesitation.

His lips touched mine, gentle yet firm, and I wound my arms around his shoulders so our bodies pressed together. He kissed me soft and slow, and I could feel how much he'd longed for this in the way he savored every stroke of my mouth.

He backed me up against the bar and lifted his head as he set his hands on my hips. With one quick motion he picked me up and sat me on the edge. I clung to him, and he eased between my knees, his eyes not breaking their hold for a second.

One of my slippers fell to the floor, and I curled my legs around Josh's waist, just as I'd fantasized doing in the swimming pool. His body felt so tight. His mouth returned to mine, and his tongue slipped between my lips, setting off a breathless moan in my throat.

*I am making out with Josh.*

The boy I'd wanted to be my first kiss was now giving me the most amazing kiss of my life. And it was *so* worth

waiting eight years for.

I buried my fingers in his hair, while his hands slid under my shirt. The heat from his touch burned through me, and I kissed him harder. His fingertips skimmed over my ribcage, tickling my skin, as they moved closer to—

"Coco?"

I broke away from Josh's lips and saw Quinn and Alex hand-in-hand at the foot of the stairs staring at us. Josh pulled back and rubbed his face as he scooted around the bar. I jumped down and straightened my shirt.

"Hi, Josh," Quinn said.

"Hey, Quinn." Josh sounded strangled as he gave her a feeble wave.

"Are you boyfriend and girlfriend?" she asked.

"Wha… what?" I stammered.

"Only boyfriends and girlfriends s'posed to kiss."

*Oh dear God. They've really seen it all tonight. Witches, tornadoes, Josh's tongue down my throat…*

I figured I could ignore her question as I did with many of her others. "Why aren't you sleeping?"

"We see da witch when we sleep," Alex said.

I put my hand on my forehead. Why had I shown them that damn movie? If I hadn't, they'd still be tucked away in their beds, and I'd be at second base with Josh.

"Why don't you go back upstairs and I'll be up in a few minutes to read to you. That might help you sleep better."

"We wanna stay with you," Quinn said with a little cry in her voice.

I glanced at Josh with a pained look, and he gave me a sympathetic smile. I shoved my foot into my lost slipper and herded the twins toward the couch.

"I'm gonna walk Josh out," I said while bundling them under a fleece blanket. "I'll be right back."

"Hurry," Quinn said.

Josh followed me to the door, and I left it half open as we

stepped out onto the porch. The cool, crisp night made me shiver, and Josh cuddled me against him. I wrapped my arms around his waist and immediately felt warmer from his soft sweater and his body heat. I wanted to pick up where we'd left off so badly...

"Can I see you tomorrow?" he asked quietly.

With his strong hands caressing my back, I couldn't form a coherent thought much less speak. I nodded, and he kissed me. And then again... and again until Quinn shouted my name.

"I'll text you," Josh said as he reluctantly released me.

He walked backward across the lawn, watching me the entire way, and his butt hit the mailbox. He grunted and stumbled, and I covered my mouth as I laughed.

"Are you okay?" I called out.

He smiled and gave me a thumbs-up. As he drove away I went inside and stopped in the foyer to take a deep breath.

*Things just got a lot more complicated.*

"Coco!" Quinn yelled again.

I moved slowly into the living room and sat beside her. "Let's go upstairs, and I'll read to you and lay with you."

"You sleep all night with us?" Alex asked, his big blue eyes full of hope.

"I sure can."

Both he and Quinn squealed with delight. There was no way I could sleep anyway. Having the twins with me would be no different than being alone, wide-awake and reliving every single moment of what had just happened.

"Is Josh your boyfriend?" Quinn asked.

Damn, she was nothing if not persistent. I had no idea what was going to come of tonight, but I couldn't have Quinn and Alex blabbing to Em and Sergei before Josh and I figured things out.

"We like each other very much, but we don't want anyone to know yet, so you can't tell anyone you saw us kissing. It'll be our special secret."

"Mommy say no secrets."

Well, I'd already exposed them to enough questionable things that night. So what if I corrupted them a little more? Of course, I might be sleeping on the street if Em discovered my stellar baby-sitting skills.

"This is different because it's just a temporary secret," I said.

"So we no tell Mommy and Daddy?" Quinn asked.

"No, especially not Mommy and Daddy." I pushed the blanket aside and reached for their hands. "Now let's see if we can get some sleep."

I grabbed my phone from the coffee table and noticed the cake still sitting there. After I returned it to the refrigerator, I picked up a couple of books from the library and led the twins to my room. The kids scrambled to get cozy under the comforter, and I slid in next to them as their giggling subsided.

They fell asleep during the second story I read, and my phone blinked just as I set the book on the nightstand. I smiled and picked it up.

Josh: *Is it tomorrow yet?*

I rested my head against the pillow and reread the short text over and over. Josh had said he'd dreamt of kissing me for a long time. How long? Since we were kids? Had I really been on his mind all those years?

I was all aflutter just thinking about seeing him again, but then a wave of fear washed over me. This was real now. Josh and I were *real*. No more secret feelings, no more safely watching from afar. It was all out in the open.

So what now?

# Chapter Twelve

The midday sunshine spilled through the big bay window and bathed the library with light. With the scent of Em's marinara sauce cooking in the kitchen and Quinn beside me rifling through crayons, it felt like a normal Sunday. Except it wasn't. I'd been an emotional mess all morning, especially after Josh had texted me, asking if I could meet him that evening at the beach.

"I make her dress blue!" Quinn rambled to herself as she pressed the blue crayon to her coloring book.

I looked at my phone and the last message Josh had sent me after we'd finalized our plans.

Josh: *I can't wait to see you.*

I sank further into the leather couch and held the phone to my chest. I couldn't wait to see him too, but I was also terrified. I'd slept only a few restless hours as I'd agonized over all the things standing in the way of Josh and me being together. I'd never realistically thought anything would happen between us, so I hadn't prepared myself for this scenario.

"You wanna be blue?" Quinn swiped the crayon on the

stuffed animal next to her.

"Don't write on Alex's monkey," I said.

She giggled. "Monkey say 'What da heck!'"

I just shook my head. In the hallway, the sound of luggage rolling on the wood floor grew louder, and Liza appeared in the doorway with her bags.

"Sissy!" Quinn clambered down from the couch and ran to her.

Liza dropped her bags and swallowed Quinn in a hug. "You're getting so big! You're going to be as tall as me soon."

"Wouldn't take much, Shorty," I said.

She stuck her tongue out at me. "So, what's been going on around here?"

*Oh, nothing. Just earth-shattering developments I can't discuss.*

"Not much," I said.

"How's Josh?" She grinned.

"Coco kiss Josh," Quinn announced.

I shot up into a sitting position. "Quinn!"

"What!" Liza hopped over the arm of the sofa and sat facing me. "When did this happen?"

"Quinn, remember this was our special secret?" I lowered my voice. "You're not supposed to tell anyone."

"You say no tell Mommy and Daddy. You no say no tell Sissy."

I rubbed my temples. Had I really thought a three-year-old could be trusted to keep quiet?

"I need to hear every single detail," Liza said. "This is so awesome."

I glanced at Quinn, who'd returned to coloring her fairy princess. I'd already done and said enough in front of her.

"Let me help you bring your stuff upstairs." I stood and picked up Liza's flowered duffel.

She quickly followed me with her small rolling bag, and I shut the door to her bedroom behind us.

"This can't leave this room," I said.

"I'm not the one you need to worry about. You have Motor Mouth down there ready to spill to everyone." She laughed. "How did she find out?"

I dropped onto the bed. "She and Alex were supposed to be sleeping, but they snuck up on us."

"Oh no!" She laughed louder. "I'm sorry. I know it probably wasn't funny for you, but it's kinda hilarious."

I felt a smile creep across my lips. "The shock on their faces *was* pretty funny. I don't think they've ever witnessed Em and Sergei kissing like that."

"Oh my God, so you guys were like making out? Tell me everything! Did he kiss you first? Is he a good kisser? Was there tongue?"

"Whoa, simmer down, girlie. He did make the first move. That's all the details you're getting."

"Aww, come on! I'm dying here. You know I've never kissed a boy, so I have to live vicariously through you."

Her big blue eyes pleaded with me, and I knew how she felt because I'd been her once. All my friends had gotten their first kiss before I had.

"I'll just say that Josh might be shy, but he knows how to make a girl melt," I said wistfully.

Liza sighed. "He is so hot. I don't know what I'd do if a boy like him kissed me."

I picked up her stuffed teddy bear and petted its fluffy fur. "If only this boy wasn't all wrong for me."

"Why? You don't think you could handle dating him and competing against him?"

"I don't think Stephanie and Mark could handle it."

"Then don't tell them."

"It's not that simple." I set down the bear and paced across the plush carpet. "What happens when Josh moves back to L.A.? Law school is so time-consuming, and I'll be starting BC hopefully. We'd never see each other. And his family would all hate me anyway. He said his mom is a carbon copy of Stephanie."

Liza grimaced with terror. "Maybe his dad's nice. He has to get his sweetness from somewhere."

"I don't know. His dad sounds tough. He has really high expectations for Josh, and I'm sure they don't include dating a middle-class girl who works as a bartender."

"What does Josh think about you guys dating?"

"We haven't talked yet. I'm meeting him at the beach later."

Liza sighed again. "That sounds so romantic."

I collapsed on the bed and held my head in my hands. "I know, and it's going to be so hard to tell him this can't go anywhere."

"Are you sure it can't? Romeo and Juliet found a way to be together."

"And they both ended up dead."

"Well, just stay away from poison and daggers."

I peeked up at her. "Thanks for the helpful advice."

A knock sounded on the door, and Sergei called out, "Lunch is ready."

I slowly trailed Liza downstairs. I normally flew to the table for Em's delicious Sunday lunches, but my stomach was twisted every which way. I knew what I had to tell Josh when I saw him, but I didn't know if I'd have the willpower once he was physically in front of me.

Especially if he kissed me again.

****

When I pulled into the parking lot at Kalmus Beach, I spotted Josh's car right away since it was one of only two cars there. I listened to the blaring music from my radio and took a couple of deep breaths to psych myself up before I shut off the engine and climbed out. The breeze off the water cooled my bare legs under my denim skirt, and I tightened the belt of my sweater. Slipping off my flip-flops, I moved from the roughness of the pavement to the softness of the sand.

Josh stood in the middle of the empty beach, spreading a blanket over the sand. His back was to me, so I stopped and watched him, my heart aching. The wind ruffled his dark hair, and I remembered my fingers knotted there as he'd pressed his lips to mine. It would be so easy to walk up to him right now and reenact that scene.

I folded my arms and curled my toes into the sand as if to anchor myself. Josh turned and saw me, and he broke into the brightest smile I'd ever seen. Inside I crumbled into a thousand pieces.

I walked toward him, resisting the urge to run, and he came forward tentatively. Before I could say anything, he enveloped me in a hug, one arm around my shoulders, the other snug around my waist. My body defied my mind and sank into him. When his lips brushed against my hair, my breath caught in my throat and I pulled away.

"Hi," I said quietly, looking anywhere but in his eyes.

"Hey," he replied just as low.

I noticed the red takeout bag next to the blanket and recognized it immediately. "You went to the restaurant?"

"Yeah, I hope you haven't eaten yet. I got Chef to make your special veggie sandwich."

I hadn't eaten since lunch when I'd forced down Em's pasta primavera, but my stomach still wasn't feeling receptive to food. Josh had been so thoughtful to get one of my favorite meals, though. Add that to the long list of things making it so difficult to walk away from him.

"You didn't have to go to all that trouble," I said.

"It was no trouble." He took my hand and motioned for me to sit with him.

I tucked my legs under me and stared at Josh's hand around mine. My heart ached deeper. We couldn't be the cute couple holding hands and picnicking on the beach. No matter how good and natural this felt.

"I told everyone at the restaurant we were working on something at the rink so there wouldn't be questions about why I was picking up dinner for us," Josh said. "I wasn't sure where things are going with us from here, but—"

"We can't do this," I blurted out.

The brightness that had filled his eyes dimmed, and he loosened his hold on my hand. "I thought last night you felt the same. Did I misunderstand…"

I slowly shook my head. "You didn't misunderstand."

"Then what's wrong?" he asked softly.

"I just… I just think we have to stop this before it starts because there are too many reasons why it could never work out."

He studied me intently, and my face and neck grew warm. I turned away and watched the gentle waves wash ashore. What a beautiful evening it would be if the circumstances were different.

"So you don't want to give us a chance?" he asked.

"You're leaving in a few months. I've done the long distance thing and learned the hard way how painful it can be."

"I would never hurt you like Kyle did." He squeezed my hand.

I looked into his clear eyes and believed he wouldn't, but I still slipped my hand from his grasp. "There's also the Olympics and keeping our heads straight and our partnerships from imploding…"

"I've thought about all those things, too, and I know we could figure it out."

"I guess… I guess I'm not as sure we could." I paused as a swell of emotion pushed against my chest. "And I can't take that risk."

Josh stayed quiet, and he shifted his gaze from me to the

horizon. I had to know what he was thinking, but I didn't feel like I had the right to ask.

"This isn't how I pictured this night going," he finally said.

"I'm so sorry. I never should've let you think last night that—"

"Don't. Don't apologize. Last night was the best night of my life."

A lump choked my throat, and I sat on my hands so I wouldn't reach out and touch him. He looked at me with such hurt, and there was nothing I could do to make his gorgeous blue eyes shine again.

*There is*, I thought as my gaze dropped to his lips.

No, that would be a huge mistake that would only lead to both of us hurting more in the end.

"Maybe I should go," I said.

I got to my feet and walked quickly to the parking lot. When I reached the pavement I glanced back at Josh, and his head was down. I slipped on my flip-flops, not caring about the sand between my toes, and pulled my car keys from the pocket of my sweater.

"Court, wait," Josh said behind me.

I froze and turned to see him jogging to the lot. He stopped and stared at me for a long moment, and I held my breath, waiting for him to say something.

"I don't want to lose you as a friend," he said.

I exhaled. "I don't want to lose you either. I just wasn't sure you'd still want that."

"If we didn't talk anymore, it would make all of this even harder."

He was so right. I couldn't imagine not laughing with him at Mrs. Cassar's craziness or texting him when I heard a new song I thought he'd like. Our friendship had become such an important part of my life, one that would leave a gaping hole if I lost it.

"I'm so glad you feel that way," I said.

He chewed on his bottom lip. "I can't promise things won't be a little weird."

I nodded and fiddled with my keys. "Yeah... like I probably shouldn't stay for a sunset beach picnic."

"What if I vow to stay on my side of the blanket?"

I smiled a little. "I think it might still be too risky."

He stared at me again with those intense blue eyes, making me fidget even more. Pointing his thumb behind him, he said, "At least take your dinner to go."

I unlocked my car and went to open the door. "Let me give you the money for it."

"No way. Friends can buy friends dinner." He backpedaled toward the sand. "Hang on and I'll go get it."

He returned a few seconds later with the takeout container, and I pulled open my door and stood behind it. Couldn't hurt to have an actual shield between us.

"Are you gonna stay?" I asked.

"Yeah, it's so peaceful." He stuck his hands in his pockets. "I really wish you could stay, too."

It physically pained me to stand my ground and not follow him back to the beach. But I just knew what would happen if we sat on that blanket with the sea breeze tickling our faces and the sky darkening around us. Maybe one day we could do it as friends, but the memory of our kiss was too fresh. The electricity still crackled too strongly.

"I think it's probably best if I go." I paused as I caught the unmistakable disappointment in his eyes. "But I'll talk to you later?"

He nodded. "For sure."

When I started the car, I turned up the volume on the already blasting music. I needed the noise to fill my head and shut out all the conflicting thoughts. But it didn't work. As I watched Josh disappear in the rearview mirror, my eyes brimmed with tears. I wasn't just driving away from the beach. I was driving away from something that could be so wonderful. If only it made sense.

# Chapter Thirteen

"Court, you know how long this stupid group rehearsal's gonna last?" Mark asked.

I tightened my skate laces and looked up at him in the doorway of the locker room. He had one hand on the frame and one on the phone to his ear.

"I think only about an hour. I have to get ready for work after," I said.

"An hour's long enough." He moved the phone to his mouth. "Zoe? Hey, I should be there about four."

I stood and checked my reflection in the long mirror on the wall. I'd worn my favorite hot pink tank and black leggings for the occasion. Josh and I might be just friends, but I was still ridiculously excited about skating with him. It was like I enjoyed torturing myself.

"K, Babe. Love you," Mark said and ended his call. "Why do we have to rehearse so early for the show anyway? It's two months from now."

"I think Em's just stressing about coordinating everyone's schedules. You and I will be in Paris next week, and then all of us will be in Lake Placid for a week next month. She wants to make sure it gets done."

He shoved his phone in his skate bag. "Stephanie better check her attitude at the door 'cause I'm not dealing with her bitching for two months."

"Uhh… I wouldn't hold my breath on that."

We went out to the ice, where Josh and Em were showing each other various steps and arm movements. It amazed me how Josh could make a simple lunge look so sexy. I set off near the boards to do a quick warm-up and also to work off some of my jittery energy.

When Mark and I circled over to Em and Josh, Stephanie finally appeared and glided slowly to our spot at center ice. She crossed her arms, pursed her lips, and audibly sighed. Mark frowned at me and rubbed his forehead.

*Attitude checked at the door? I think not.*

"Okay, the gang's all here." Em slapped her hands together. "Josh and I have put together some ideas, but if anyone wants to contribute during the process, please don't hesitate to speak up."

"Why is he running this with you?" Mark asked.

"Because he asked to help."

"And he's a creative genius," Stephanie added.

Josh's face flamed, and he looked down at the ice.

Mark held up his hands. "Excuse me. I didn't know I was in the presence of greatness."

*Two minutes in, and this is already a disaster.*

Em clapped again, but this time so hard her hands must've stung. "It doesn't matter who comes up with the choreography. All that matters is the four of you bring the choreography to life and make it your own. So let's get to work."

She directed us to form a square with me facing Mark and Stephanie facing Josh. After she explained the opening movements she wanted us to do, Josh chipped in with additional instruction and Em helped him demonstrate the next few steps. When he said, "Then we'll switch partners," every nerve in my body went on alert.

"Why do we have to switch?" Stephanie asked.

"You're questioning the genius's ideas?" Mark said.

Em gave him a warning look I'd seen her give the twins when they misbehaved. "You're switching because it's going to make this number *fabulous*. We'll run through the opening and then Josh, you can show Court your part and I'll show Stephanie and Mark theirs."

"I thought we were all just going to be on the ice at the same time but not skating with each other." Stephanie put her hands on her hips. "Josh is my partner and I should only be skating with him."

"Hey, I'm not throwing a party over skating with you either," Mark said.

"You're all going to do this, and it's going to be the best damn group number in the history of Christmas shows. Understand?" Em said on the verge of shouting.

Mark and I looked at each other, and he lifted his eyebrows. Em rarely raised her voice, so she wasn't messing around. Stephanie didn't say another word. Even she knew she needed to shut it.

We practiced the opening sequence as Em had instructed, and on the last step I ended up face to face with Josh. He gave me a little smile, but he couldn't hide the sadness in his eyes. We'd chatted at the restaurant earlier in the week, even shared a couple of laughs, but that sadness had been a constant. It made me feel like my heart was being stabbed repeatedly by my toe pick.

"Josh, you're good?" Em asked as she skated over to Mark and Stephanie.

"Yeah, I'll... I'll show Court what's next."

After she turned away from us, he raked his hand through his hair. "I should've asked if you were still okay with us skating together."

Okay? I'd looked forward to this so much since the moment Em had mentioned it. There was no way I was giving it up. No matter how much it hurt to touch him and not be able to really *touch* him.

"It's... it's fine. I wouldn't want to make this process more pleasant for Stephanie anyway." I smiled.

"I'm glad I won't be home tonight to hear her complain."

"Do you have any new songs planned for tonight?"

"Maybe." His blank expression didn't give anything away.

"No hints?"

"You'll just have to listen carefully."

What was he going to play? Hopefully not some song about broken hearts or people better off as friends. I might break down in the middle of the restaurant.

Stephanie and Mark skated past us, looking less than thrilled, and Josh said, "We should get started."

I nodded and listened attentively as he described the next series of steps. When he took my hand, he went quiet, and I let him lead me into a dance hold as if we were waltzing. I felt like I was floating in his arms across the ice.

We drifted closer together, and my pulse thumped so hard it reverberated in my ears. Josh twirled me around and pulled me even nearer, his palm pressed to my lower back. I drew in a breath and kept my eyes on his chest as I'd done when he'd taught me the tango.

*Do NOT look at him.*

He slowly released me, and I forgot the next step until he guided me into side-by-side stroking. Our movements were perfectly in unison even though we'd never skated together before. We worked up speed as we turned the corner of the rink, and then we both extended one leg for a dual spiral position. Josh wrapped his arms around me from behind, nestling me to his chest, and we glided on matching smooth edges, flying across the ice. My whole body tingled with a thrilling buzz. This was the moment I'd dreamt of when I first discovered pair skating. This was the feeling.

We glided to a slow stop and were met with long stares from Mark and Stephanie, who were in the middle of their own waltz.

"Having fun?" Mark asked tersely.

I thought it best not to answer with my true sentiment of "YES!" They skated away from us, so I was saved from having to give a reply, but I knew Mark would probably give me an earful later.

"There's a dance lift I want to try next," Josh said, sounding very excited. "Ready to give it a go?"

"Sure."

We went over the logistics of his idea, which required me to hook my arms around his neck and let him hold my legs in a full split position as we rotated. We walked through the steps slowly to begin, and I didn't realize how close our faces would be until I locked my arms around him. I could feel his breath on my lips.

*Dear God...*

In an attempt not to gaze into his eyes, I ended up looking at his mouth, which was no less torturous.

*Maybe I should just close my eyes.*

I did my best to focus on the technique, and when we felt comfortable we had the timing down, we took off across the ice to gather speed. All in a fluid motion, I latched onto Josh and pulled myself up, and he held my thighs as I stretched into a split. We began to rotate, and I couldn't help but giggle as we spun lightning fast. I was like a giddy kid on a merry-go-round. Josh beamed a huge smile at me, and I didn't want this to end. I wanted to keep spinning, keep holding onto him, keep seeing him so happy.

Our momentum slowed, dashing my hopes, and Josh set me down. We were both still smiling, though, and Josh's warm hands lingered on my shoulders.

"Hey," Em said as she skated over to us.

"Hey." I put some distance between Josh and myself.

"Looks like it's going well over here." She gave us each a longer look than necessary.

"Yep," Josh said.

"The lift was fantastic. That was a beautiful position you hit, Court."

"Thanks. It was a lot of fun."

"Your partners aren't smiling nearly as much, or at all for that matter, but they're going to look like they're having the time of their lives come show night if it kills me."

We only had a few minutes left, so Em herded us all together and gave us a few encouraging words before dismissing us. Stephanie and Josh skated ahead, and Mark touched my elbow, halting me beside the boards.

"Hold up a sec," he said. "I wanna talk about what's going on with you and Josh."

Blood rushed to my face. Even though I expected him to question me, it sounded like he knew more than I'd thought.

"What are you talking about?"

"He designed the group number so you could skate together because he has a crush on you. I've seen the way he looks at you."

If he'd noticed it, then Em surely had, too. It hadn't stopped her from letting us skate together, though.

"He and Em designed the number together, and they did it this way because it would be an interesting twist," I said.

"Come on, Court. You can't tell me you don't see that he obviously has a thing for you. You seem to enjoy the attention."

"There's nothing going on between us if that's what you're worried about."

It wasn't a total lie. Josh and I had enjoyed five minutes of bliss together but were now sadly done.

"I'm not worried about that. He'd never have the guts to

do anything," Mark said.

My face grew warmer as I remembered Josh's passionate kiss and his hands hot on my skin. Oh, he had the guts. *I* was the coward.

"Just keep your guard up," Mark said. "I don't trust him. He might've also thought up this whole partner switch thing to try to pit you and me against each other."

*Josh doesn't have any shady intentions!* I wanted to scream. *He just wants to be close to me!*

Instead I took a calming breath. "It's just a simple Christmas show number, not an evil plot. Can you stop with the conspiracy theories?"

I skated to the ice door and snapped on my guards. It was going to be a long two months of rehearsals if I had to pretend I didn't love skating with Josh. I didn't know if I could even pull that off. It wasn't a knock against Mark because I'd always enjoyed having him as my partner. When we skated together, I loved the athletic excitement of it. But when I'd partnered with Josh, I'd felt something new, something I couldn't quite grasp yet. All I knew was I wanted more.

****

"How's your steak?" I asked Josh as I refilled his water, making sure not to come close to overflowing the glass.

"It's awesome." He set his fork down. "Who's going to refill my water just the way I like it when you're not here next week?"

I smiled. "I'll leave a note for whoever's working Thursday night."

"Are you getting excited for Paris?"

"I'm excited to compete. It feels like we've been working on these programs for a year. I don't think we'll do much sight-seeing since we did all that the first two times we competed there."

"Yeah, I mean once you've seen the Eiffel Tower a couple times, it's just like any old monument," he said with a teasing grin.

I laughed. "That's not what I meant. I'm just saying we'll be more focused on the competition this time and less concerned with being tourists."

I set down the water pitcher and wiped my hands on my apron. "The Eiffel Tower probably isn't a big deal for *you*, though. I bet your family did a lot of fancy traveling when you were growing up."

"Actually, we didn't. My dad traveled a lot for business, but we rarely went on those trips. We mostly just went to our beach house in Malibu."

"Beach house in Malibu? Oh, that sounds positively awful." I gave him my own teasing grin.

"You've never sat in L.A. traffic with Steph and my mom arguing."

"Okay, maybe that doesn't sound like the best vacation."

He folded his arms on the ledge of the bar. "The house itself is great, though. The piano faces the glass doors to the deck, so I can see the ocean while I play."

"That must be amazing."

"It is. I'd love to show it—" He stopped himself but then finished quietly, "To you."

His sad eyes held me captive, crushing my soul. He took a long drink of water, and I made up an excuse to go to the kitchen. I had to get out of there before I went back on everything I'd said at the beach. After the rush of skating with Josh that afternoon, I was feeling especially vulnerable, and listening to him express his desire to take me to Malibu wasn't exactly strengthening my resolve.

I dawdled in the kitchen as long as I could and kept myself busy on the opposite end of the bar from Josh until he finished eating. He stood and pushed up the sleeves of his gray striped sweater, and I went to clear his dishes.

"I'll give you a hint about the new song," he said. "It'll be the last one."

Damn, so he was going to make me wait all night. Well, he'd earned the right to toy with me after I'd shot him down so quickly.

"I'll be anxiously listening," I said.

I was curious if he was still going to play "Over the Rainbow" for me. It would be the friendly thing to do, but again I couldn't blame him if he didn't.

I didn't have to think about it long because it was the first song he played. Then I turned to wondering if he was sending me some kind of message by leading off the night with my favorite.

The rest of the night dragged by, not helped by a tipsy couple who spent their entire time at the bar alternating between arguing and showering each other with PDA. When the hands on my watch neared ten o'clock, I drifted toward the end of the bar closest to the piano. Josh took a sip of water and flexed his fingers, and I watched him work his magic over the keys.

I didn't recognize the melody at first, but then it came to me — "La Vie en Rose." For my Paris trip. I smiled, and Josh looked over at me and tipped his head. I did a little tap dance and swayed back and forth to the whimsical song as I cleaned up the bar and got ready for close.

I should've known Josh wouldn't play something angsty about our situation. He wasn't that kind of guy.

He was the perfect guy.

My throat tightened, and I rushed around the bar, trying to focus on work. When Josh finished playing and emptied his tip glass, I escaped to the kitchen again to avoid him. I had to get my purse anyway. My tie felt like it was choking me, so I yanked it off and shoved it in my big sack purse.

"You okay?" Meredith asked.

"Yeah, it's just been a long night."

"I know we haven't been able to hang out much lately, but call me anytime if you need to talk."

I could use a friend to talk to. Liza was the only one who knew what had gone down with Josh and me, and she'd gone back to New York. Plus, she was too young to really understand.

"Thanks. There has been some stuff going on. Maybe we can hang out this weekend and I can tell you about it."

A clap of thunder boomed, and lightning flashed through the open back door. Meredith grabbed her purse and gave me a quick hug.

"It's about to pour," she said. "Let's definitely make a plan tomorrow night."

"Sounds good."

I took another minute to collect myself before I went back to the dining room. Josh and I always walked out the front together, and I needed to thank him, too.

"I loved the song," I said as I met him at the hostess's stand. "It was perfect."

"I thought it would be a good sendoff."

He opened the door, and lightning flashed again. A few heavy drops dotted my white shirt.

"I have something else for you, too... for your trip," he said. "It's in my car."

He had a present for me? Thunder rumbled louder, and I looked up at the dark clouds racing across the moon. "We should probably hurry."

"It'll just take a minute." He unlocked his car. "Come inside so you don't get wet."

I didn't think it would be good for me emotionally to be in a small enclosed space with him for even just a minute, but I was so curious about the gift he had for me.

I slid into the car and set my purse on the floor mat, and Josh came around and shut his door. He reached behind his seat and presented me with a small green gift bag.

"It's just a little something to keep you entertained," he said.

I stuck my hand into the bag and pulled out a CD. Since we were on the dark end of the lot, I had to squint to read the cover. There was a photo of Mickey Mouse wearing sunglasses, and the title read *Mickey Unrapped*. I flipped it over and saw some of the song titles, and I burst into laughter.

"Oh my God, are these Disney rap songs?" I asked.

Josh grinned. "They are indeed."

"'Ice Ice Mickey,' 'Ducks in the 'Hood.'" I held my stomach as I laughed harder. "Where did you find this?"

"It's mind-boggling what you can find on the internet."

"This is the most fabulous thing I've ever seen."

"I figured it was the perfect mix for you since you're a fan of both Disney songs and gangsta rap. You can download it onto your iPod for the long flight."

My laughter faded as a deeper swell of emotion took over me. Josh had remembered what I liked and he'd taken the time to look for the CD for me. He could've said "Screw it" and not given it to me after I'd told him we could only be friends. But he hadn't.

"Thank you so much for this." I slipped the CD and the bag into my purse. "You were so sweet to think of me."

I sat back and waited for him to say something, but he stared quietly at the dashboard. The rain fell harder on the windshield, drowning out the silence.

He slowly turned and looked at me. "I think about you all the time."

Another flood of emotion hit me, this time like a tidal wave. Lightning illuminated the car, showing me the wanting in Josh's eyes, and everything I felt for him rushed to the surface. I couldn't fight the resistance anymore.

I leaned across the console and pressed my mouth to Josh's. He responded immediately and curled his hand behind my neck, pulling me closer. His lips were hot and sweet, and they erased all the ache, all the longing. God, I wanted the kiss to last forever.

His other hand touched my thigh, and my pulse raced even faster. I threaded my fingers through his hair and leaned into him, but he still wasn't close enough. I needed to feel *all* of him.

I climbed over the stick shift and straddled his lap, and he groaned against my lips. Our kisses were deep and hungry, drawing all the breath from my body, but I gladly gave it to him. I would give *everything* to him.

His mouth trailed across my jaw with a feathery touch, and the beads of my earring jangled as he softly kissed my earlobe. I felt goose bumps in places I didn't know possible. He ran his finger along my collar and deftly opened the top button of my shirt, giving his lips access to my neck. I tilted my head back, and he sucked gently on my tender skin, turning me inside out with desire. I pushed up his sweater and slipped my hands underneath, feeling my way over his hard muscles.

Thunder vibrated the car, and wind and rain thrashed against the windows, hiding us from the world. Josh kissed my lips, and I brought my hands up to his face. The faint stubble on his cheeks prickled my palms.

He sank his fingers into my hair, loosening my ponytail, and then he slowly pulled his head back so we were looking into each other's eyes. Even in the darkness his spoke so much to me.

"Please don't walk away from me again," he said.

My heart overflowed from the emotion in his voice. How could I turn away from him? From the obviously strong feelings he had for me?

"I won't." I breathed against his lips. "I can't."

We melted into another kiss and were just heating up again when Josh's phone rang in the console. His mouth reluctantly left mine.

"Damn," he whispered.

He fumbled for the phone and glanced at the screen before answering, "Hey."

"Where are you?" I heard Stephanie's voice. "You're usually home by now."

He took a long swallow. "I was um... I was waiting to see if the rain would let up."

"I don't think it's letting up anytime soon."

He rubbed his forehead. "Yeah, I'll... I'll probably leave in a bit."

When he ended the call, I said, "I might be hearing from Em soon, too. She knows I never go out with Meredith on weeknights."

"We still have a few minutes," he said, cupping my face.

Our lips met, and I curled my arms around him. Not until we were completely out of breath did we stop. I rested my head on Josh's shoulder, and he caressed my back with long, slow strokes.

"How are we going to do this?" I asked quietly.

"What do you mean?"

I lifted my head. "I don't think I can tell Mark. He just... he wouldn't understand."

"I know Steph wouldn't understand either."

"Then I think we have to keep this quiet."

He brushed a loose curl behind my ear. "At least for now."

My phone rang, and I reached for my purse. After I gave Em the same excuse Josh had given Stephanie, I turned back to him. Having to hide our relationship from our partners was one of the reasons I'd run from Josh in the first place. But looking into his eyes, I knew I had to do whatever I could to hold onto this. Because this feeling... this special, wonderful, exhilarating feeling I had when I was with him... it was too good to let go.

# Chapter Fourteen

"Coco, you so pretty!" Quinn gaped at me.

I took the last two steps carefully in my red peep-toe heels and squatted as low as I could in my black leather pants. "And you're the most beautiful princess in all the land."

She giggled and waved her glittery wand. She'd had on her Halloween costume since noon. The sun was just about to set, so she didn't have to wait much longer to go trick-or-treating.

"Oh my gosh, Court, you look amazing," Em said as she came down the stairs. "You're the perfect Sandy."

And I had the perfect Danny waiting for me to complete our *Grease* theme, but I couldn't tell Em that tidbit. Keeping my relationship with Josh quiet had been harder than I'd expected, mostly because I was so deliriously happy to be with him that I wanted to tell everyone I knew. Meredith was the only person with whom I'd shared the news.

Quinn skipped down the hall toward Alex the pirate, and I stood and straightened my sleeves. My black off-the-shoulder shirt was just as tight as my pants. It had taken me fifteen minutes to squeeze myself into the outfit.

"I love having Halloween on a weekend so I can actually go out and enjoy it," I said.

"You deserve a fun night out. You skated well in Paris, and you've been working so hard since you got back." Em picked up one of Alex's trucks from the floor. "You're in for an experience in P-town. Sergei and I still talk about the costumes we saw when we went years ago."

P-town, or Provincetown as it was officially known, had a large gay community and the most elaborate Halloween festivities on the Cape. Meredith and I had decided it would be the most fun place to spend the holiday, and the fact it was located on the far end of the island made it the perfect place for Josh and me to go out.

"Meredith's never been either, so we're both preparing ourselves for the craziness." I opened my small red purse and fished out my keys.

"Is it just you two going?"

"Um… Meredith's new boyfriend is coming." I conveniently left out the part about *my* date.

"You don't mind being a third wheel?"

Em watched me closely, and I felt like she might be suspicious. But how could she know? If Quinn had blabbed, she would've said something. I was a terrible liar, so my face was probably red.

"No, it's cool." I fiddled with my keys. "I'd better get going so I can meet them and we can start the long drive. Have fun trick-or-treating."

"We will. Be careful."

I smiled as I headed to the garage. Em and Sergei always gave me my own space and didn't try to act like my parents, but sometimes Em's motherly instincts couldn't be suppressed.

The closer I got to Meredith's house, the more butterflies gathered in my stomach. It happened every time I knew I was going to see Josh. I was especially anxious because this was going to be our first real date. With skating and work taking almost all our time, our relationship so far had consisted of having dinner at the restaurant before my shift and making out in my car for a few minutes after. I was so excited we could finally hang out together as a couple.

I turned onto Meredith's street, and my heart pitter-pattered at the sight of Josh in her driveway. He'd mussed up his hair with gel, and he wore a tight black T-shirt and dark jeans. His sleeves were rolled up, showing off the bulge in his biceps, and I itched with the anticipation of wrapping my fingers around them. We could be as free and affectionate with each other tonight as we wanted. And seeing him now... oh, how I wanted.

Josh turned away from Meredith and her boyfriend Adam to watch me step out of the car, and I fluffed my long curls over my shoulders. His eyes widened and swept over me from head to toe. He met me halfway down the driveway and put his hands on my hips while mine went straight for his arms.

"Holy smokes," he said quietly. "Court, you look... the word hot just isn't enough."

My butterflies fluttered on overdrive as Josh glanced again at my costume. I leaned into him and squeezed his biceps.

"You look pretty indescribable, too," I said.

"I need to see the outfit," Meredith said and instructed me to turn around. "Whoo! *Sex-ay!*"

I surveyed her *Flintstones* costume, which resembled a mini toga. "You're totally rocking the hot cavewoman look."

"I wanted sexy comfort. Being able to wear sandals sealed the deal."

"And I get to not wear pants." Adam spun around in his Fred Flintstone orange toga. "Just kidding. I have shorts on under here."

Meredith walked around to the passenger side of Adam's

car. "Let's get on the road. It's gonna take us an hour to get there."

Josh and I slid into the backseat, and I cozied against him as he draped his arm around me. With the limited amount of time we'd been able to spend together, an hour car ride sounded heavenly. While we all talked and laughed about our childhood Halloween costumes, Josh caressed my hand, tracing wispy patterns on my palm with his thumb. Every stroke he made melted me more inside. I was going to be a puddle of mush by the time we got to P-town.

"What was your favorite costume?" Josh asked me. "I'm guessing Dorothy."

"I was Dorothy a couple times, but my favorite was when I dressed up like my grandma's cat."

"Your grandma's cat?" Meredith cackled from the front seat.

"He was this huge, fluffy orange and white beast named Arthur, but I used to call him Fluffy McFlufferson."

"Fluffy McFlufferson?" Josh's laughter shook both of us, and I started laughing, too.

"I thought Arthur was too boring. Anyway, I loved that cat and pretended he was mine, so my mom made this big orange and white fur ball of a costume for me. All you could see was my little face because everything else was covered in fluff. I had to waddle down the street to trick-or-treat because I was so stuffed up."

Everyone in the car cracked up, and I added, "I was pretty stinkin' cute, though."

Josh caught his breath and grinned at me. "I bet you were. But I'm glad you've moved on to less furry costumes."

He rubbed my leg, and I angled toward him and brushed my lips to his, hinting at what I wanted. He gave it to me in a soft, slow kiss that sent a long, electric shiver down my spine.

I was still buzzing when we arrived in P-town. We found our way to the hub of activity, and I immediately saw what

Em had meant about the costumes. In a stretch of one block, we encountered more feathers, leather, and skin than I'd ever seen. Lady Gaga seemed to be a popular costume choice for the evening, but I couldn't tell if some of the impersonators were men, women, or a mixture of both.

"Hey, Blue Eyes." A guy in a sparkly jumpsuit looked Josh up and down.

Josh blushed, and I covered my giggle with my hand. He got quite a few more catcalls and waggled eyebrows as we walked down crowded Commercial Street. Adam received his own share of comments, most about his bare legs.

"Lookin' good, Danny Zuko!" someone called out as we entered one of the clubs.

Josh gave his admirer a little wave, and I leaned closer to him. "You're actually more like the lead guy in *Grease 2* than Danny Zuko. Remember the smart, quiet one?"

He moved in front of me and pulled me against him. "You don't think I could be the bad boy?"

The passion in his hooded eyes made my knees weak. I looped my arms around his shoulders and held on tight.

"I don't want you to be." I put my lips to his ear. "Sweet, shy guys are *so* much hotter."

He turned his head so our mouths just about touched. A slow smile spread across his, and one soon followed on mine. He kissed me, and I felt an extra thrill that we were standing in a crowded room, happily acting like a couple should.

"You lovebirds want something to drink?" Meredith asked.

"I'll get it," Josh said, loosening his hold on me.

She waved him off. "I've got the first round."

"I'll take a diet soda," I said.

"Regular for me," Josh said.

"Oh, you crazy kids." Meredith laughed as she and Adam headed to the bar.

Josh laced his fingers through mine. "You can get

something stronger if you want. Just because I don't drink doesn't mean you shouldn't."

"I'm good with soda. But I have been kinda curious... is there a specific reason you don't drink?"

He shrugged. "I've just seen a lot of people get messed up from it. People I went to school with and stuff. I figured I'd just stay clean... and it's probably better for training, too."

"That's a good—"

"Hey, I know you." A guy dressed like a vampire pointed at me and then at Josh. "And you too. You're Courtney Carlton and Josh Tucker."

*Crap, I should've known there would be skating fans in a gay club.*

"Hi," I said tentatively.

"I *love* figure skating." He gushed. "I thought you were both *fantastic* at nationals last year."

"Thank you," Josh and I both said.

The guy's eyes darted back and forth between Josh and me and then down to our clasped hands. "So you two are a couple? I heard you were training together now."

"Um... we are but... we're kinda keeping it quiet, so..." I looked at Josh.

"We'd appreciate you not telling anyone you saw us," he said.

The vampire gave us a knowing smile and a better view of his bloody fangs. "I get it. You're on the down-low. There's a lot of that going on around here."

He dropped his voice. "What happens in P-town stays in P-town."

He whipped his cape dramatically and disappeared into the costumed throng. Josh and I just stared at each other, still processing the conversation.

"He probably won't even remember he saw us," Josh finally said.

"Hopefully he's not one of those fans who posts every

little thing on the message boards. I don't want Mark finding out from the internet that we're dating."

"Steph reads every post on the boards, so she would definitely see it."

"Did she question you at all about tonight?"

"I just told her I was going out with some friends. I'd mentioned before that I'd met some people and that's why I stay out late for dinner, so she didn't seem to think anything of it."

Meredith and Adam reappeared empty-handed, and Meredith clapped and steered us toward the exit. "Change in plans. Someone said there's karaoke next door!"

My feet slowed. "Karaoke?"

"Yep, and everyone must sing or you will suffer the punishment of being called a chicken forever and ever."

Josh and I exchanged terrified glances. I could skate in front of thousands of people — millions if you counted those watching on TV — but the idea of singing in front of any amount of people scared the bejeebers out of me.

"You guys are karaoke virgins, aren't you?" Meredith asked.

"Uhh…" Josh mumbled.

Adam grinned and rubbed his hands together. "This is gonna be fun."

He and Meredith hooked their arms around us and walked us next door so we couldn't escape. The club was even bigger than the previous one and filled with even more people. My stomach flip-flopped as I watched three girls on the stage train wreck their way through a Beyoncé song.

"Let's get drinks and then we'll check out what songs they have," Meredith said. "Sure you don't want a cocktail? A little liquid courage?"

Josh took a long look at the stage and then shook his head. "I'll stick with soda."

Well, if he could get up there stone-cold sober, I could

find the guts to do it, too. Maybe this would be a good lesson in courage I could apply to skating later.

"Keep mine the same, too," I said.

"You know what you guys should sing?" Meredith bounced up and down. "'Summer Nights' from *Grease*! I'm sure they'll have it."

The amount of fear gripping me eased a bit. Having Josh on stage with me would make the experience less scary. Maybe even a little fun if I could block out all the people watching us.

After we got our drinks, Meredith and I went to the DJ booth while Adam and Josh searched for an empty table. We found "Summer Nights" right away on the list. I was helping Meredith decide on her duet with Adam when I saw a song that would be the absolute perfect serenade to Josh if I had the nerve to do it.

I chewed on my thumbnail and peeked at the stage.

*You only live once.*

*Just do it.*

I hurriedly gave the DJ my song selections before I could change my mind. Meredith squealed with approval, and I second-guessed whether I should've added bourbon to my soda.

We were behind a number of other wanna-be singers, so we had some time to hang out before our big performances. Since the search for a table hadn't been successful, we congregated near the bar and watched the parade of costumes going onto the stage. Meredith and Adam got caught up in a discussion about punk music with two guys dressed like aliens, so Josh and I had our own fun of rating the outfits and the singers.

A guy clad in a peach beaded dress strutted to the microphone, and I said, "I'm giving him a nine because that looks like a skating costume I wore once."

"Your Madame Butterfly program," Josh said.

I stared at him with wonder. "You remember that? From six years ago?"

He looked down with a shy smile before meeting my eyes again. "You were so beautiful in it."

I thought back to what he'd said about how he'd dreamt of kissing me. It sounded like it had been longer than I'd realized.

"The night you first kissed me, you said you'd dreamt about doing it for a long time. Was it since before you moved to the Cape?"

He set his drink on the bar next to mine and took my hand. "It was since the night we met... eight years ago."

A deep warmth filled me but also a little sadness. "Why didn't you ever talk to me at competitions?"

"After what happened when we met, I didn't know if you'd want to talk to me. I thought about reaching out to you so many times, but I never knew exactly what to say. I wanted to apologize for being an idiot and not kissing you, but I figured you'd probably moved on and weren't thinking about it anymore."

"I would've loved it if you'd reached out to me."

He smiled. "I guess being the sweet, shy guy doesn't always make things the easiest."

I touched his cheek. "All that matters is we're together now."

He rested his forehead against mine, and we stood motionless, quietly breathing in and out, mindless of the loud party around us. As we just enjoyed the nearness of each other, I remembered something else Josh had said and wondered if there had been more to the story.

I tilted my neck back. "Was it really Stephanie's idea to move here or was it yours?"

"It was hers. When she first brought it up, I had some very strong conflicting feelings about it. I knew our coming here would upset you and hurt you, and I didn't want that. I didn't want to be responsible for that. But then the other part of me was ecstatic that I would be near you."

I slowly shook my head. "I had no idea you thought about me all those years."

"I don't want you to think I had an agenda when I came here. I just wanted to spend time with you and to get to know you. And I found out you were everything I thought you would be. Smart and funny and sweet... and even more beautiful."

Passion blazed in his eyes again, and I tugged on his T-shirt, bringing him closer. I kissed him, and he wrapped his arms around me for a full-body embrace. Peach dress guy wailed an awful high note in the background, but the moment was still perfect. I'd never felt so much—

*Don't say love. It's too soon.*

I'd never felt so... so... completely adored. Not by Kyle and certainly not by my couple of high school boyfriends.

"Courtney C! You're up next!" the DJ boomed.

"That's us?" Josh asked.

"That's me. I have a solo first."

"You're doing a solo?"

I nodded. "This song's for you."

I gave him a quick kiss and hurried to the stage. My nervous energy was more excited energy now. After finding out how long Josh had had feelings for me, I wanted to show him how much he meant to me, too. My singing voice might suck, but I was going to work that microphone like nobody's business.

A chorus of whistles rang out as the spotlight beamed down on me. I peered into the dark mass of faces and found the one who made my heart sing.

"This is for a very special someone," I said into the mic.

The music began, and I rocked back and forth to the beat. Josh didn't take his eyes off me as he moved closer to the stage. I glanced at the video screen with the lyrics, but I knew the song well since Mom had listened to lots of 80's music.

I sang quietly at first, but as I watched Josh's smile widen, I gained more confidence. When the chorus came, I belted out the title of the song.

"He's so shy!"

Josh couldn't smile any bigger. From then on I sang the hell out of the song, even seductively swaying my hips. But when I got to the last line which included the words "I'll love him," I skipped over it. I wasn't ready to go there yet, not even in a song.

Loud applause broke out as I finished with a twirl, and I blew Josh a kiss. He held his hand to his heart and snaked through the crowd to meet me as I came down the stairs. Before I could say anything, he took my face in his hands and kissed me.

"I loved every single second of that," he said.

"Even the horribly pitchy high notes?"

"I was too distracted to notice."

I smiled. "Distracted by what?"

His hands caressed my shoulders then slinked around my waist and traveled lower, eventually settling on my hips. "All this."

He might be quiet, but he wasn't shy about showing me how I made him feel, and that said more than any words ever could.

Meredith and Adam blew past us to get ready for their duet, and Josh and I turned to the stage to cheer for them. They went all out, bumping and grinding on each other as they sang "Love Sex Magic." We yelled as much as we could between laughing.

When they finished, we joined them on the stage and asked them to stay as our Pink Lady and T-Bird backup singers. They were more than happy to stay under the spotlights. Josh nervously eyed the audience, and I grasped his hand.

"Just look at me," I said.

He set his eyes on mine, and I got lost in them as the music started. Josh lifted his mic, and he sang Danny's opening line, speaking it more than singing it. I squeezed his hand and followed with Sandy's line, putting a breathy spin on it. Josh grinned, and when his turn came again, he loosened and sang every word with feeling. I got all tingly over how hot his soft, low voice sounded.

Our voices came together for the chorus, and we smiled at each other and closed the space between us. The audience was doing lots of whistling and cheering, but the noise sounded far away. Only Josh and I existed in our magical little bubble.

The more he sang to me, the more I swooned. Then I started to really listen to the lyrics, and sadness crept in, bringing me down from my high. The song was all about a summer fling at the beach. Sandy and Danny knew they had a limited amount of time together, just as Josh and I did. What if we couldn't last once we were apart? What if things were never as good as they were right now?

My voice shook on the final long note, and when Josh hugged me I buried my face in his neck. I'd been in a euphoric state since the rainy night in his car, but I couldn't ignore the reality of our situation. Every day that passed was one day less we had together, and my heart was starting to break just thinking about it.

# Chapter Fifteen

I rang the doorbell of Josh and Stephanie's house and checked out the front of the cottage. I'd done a drive-by once because I'd been curious to see where Josh lived, but I hadn't gotten a close-up look. The house resembled most of the other Cape Cod-style homes on the street with its gray shingles and steep roof, but it appeared to be the smallest on the block.

Josh opened the door with a huge smile and pulled me into a hug. I circled my arms around his waist and pressed my cheek to his chest. He gave the best hugs. They made me feel like I was cuddled in the softest, warmest blanket imaginable.

"I wish I could thank Stephanie for going away this weekend," I said. "I'm so glad she insisted on flying to New York to shop for costume material."

"And I'm glad you switched shifts so we can spend the whole day together."

I looked up at him. "I would've sold my soul for the time off. Considering Halloween was the only real date we've been able to have, an entire day together is like a dream come true."

He bent his head and kissed me, and I stood on the toes of my sneakers to lean deeper into him. He gave the best kisses, too. The heat from his lips reached every inch of my body, stirring desires that were becoming harder to contain.

"We could always skip going to Martha's Vineyard and stay here instead." Josh softly kissed my neck, and I fought even harder to stay level-headed.

His proposal was *so* tempting, but if we were alone in the house all day, things might get hotter than ever between us. I wasn't ready to take that step, not with so many uncertainties looming over us.

"It's such a beautiful, warm day for November. We need to take advantage of it," I said.

"I heard it might rain," he said with a mischievous glint in his eyes.

I smiled. "Not until late tonight. We should be off the ferry and home by then."

He took both of my hands in his. "I do love going out and acting like a normal couple. Halloween was so much fun."

"It was. And today we get to hang out twice as long so it will be doubly awesome."

"Let's get this awesomeness started then." He moved toward the door.

"Wait, I wanna see the house first. Who knows when I'll get to visit again."

"Sure, I'll be your tour guide. It's not too exciting, though." He turned us so we faced the small living room. "This is where Steph spends most of her time, parked in front of the TV. I try to avoid this room as much as I can."

Stacks of fashion and entertainment magazines covered the glass coffee table, and swatches of brightly-colored silk lay on the ivory sofa. Other than those items, there weren't any other personal touches to the neutral-tone room.

"I guess you guys haven't really done a lot of decorating," I said.

"No, we didn't bring much from home."

Seeing the "rental" feel of the place was yet another

reminder that Josh's stay was temporary. I had begun to hate the words "law school."

Josh led me to the short hallway off the living room and opened the second door on the left. "This is my room."

I walked inside and stopped at the foot of the bed. I could smell a hint of Josh's sweet cologne in the air. That plus the cool framed collage of album covers hanging above the bed made me love this room already.

I turned to scan the high-tech-looking keyboard along the wall. Next to it was a bookshelf with a TV and rows and rows of CDs.

"So this is where you practice all your music." I lightly touched the keyboard.

"It's a little cramped, but it's private."

"Did you clean for me or is it always this neat?"

"Let's just say you won't be getting a tour of the closet."

I laughed and noticed a notebook under a pile of CDs on the nightstand. It looked like a sketch pad.

"I thought you said you couldn't draw? Don't tell me you really are a budding Picasso."

He shoved his hands in the pockets of his jeans. "No, that's um… that's where I sketch choreography ideas. Sometimes when I listen to music I make up programs in my head."

"Can I look at it?"

"Yeah, it's… it's kinda messy." He laughed quietly.

I slid the book out and flipped through the pages. Each one had a song title at the top. Some pages contained curvy lines as patterns on the ice with elements like jumps and spins included, while others had just a numbered list of the elements.

"This is so cool. You should show these to Em."

He shrugged and dropped his eyes to the carpet. "I just do them for fun."

"I bet she'd love to look at them, though. They're so

detailed."

I turned to the next page and saw it was labeled "Exogenesis Symphony Part 3," the Muse song I loved. The pattern and elements he'd drawn appeared to be for a pair.

"I imagined doing a program to this song, too." I showed him the page. "I actually dreamt about you and me skating to it."

He looked over my shoulder and smiled. "So did I."

"I wish there was a private sheet of ice somewhere we could really create this."

He wound his arms around my waist. "One day we will skate to it together. I promise."

It was hard not to believe him when I looked into his clear blue eyes, but I couldn't shake the nagging fear that life would get in the way of promises, no matter how heartfelt.

We skipped Stephanie's room and concluded the tour in the kitchen, where Josh grabbed a couple of Stephanie's vegan brownies for us to take on the road. We took my car since I was familiar with the Vineyard, and after the forty-five-minute drive to Woods Hole, we pulled onto the ferry for the quick trip across the Sound.

When we docked in Vineyard Haven, I drove us down the island to Edgartown, one of my favorite spots. We parked and walked past the shops and restaurants to the residential area along the waterfront. Both sides of the street featured elegant captains' homes, most of them pristine white with an American flag beside the front door. As we strolled past them, I basked in the glow of the sunshine and the warmth of Josh's hand around mine.

"Did your dad find out if he can take off next week for Skate America?" Josh asked.

I nodded. "He and my mom are driving to Lake Placid on Thursday. I'm planning to tell them about us because I want to introduce you to them. I know you've said hello to my mom when she's come to the rink, but she hasn't met you as my…"

Josh lifted an eyebrow as I paused.

"Boyfriend?" he finished.

"Yeah. I guess I hadn't used that word yet, so I didn't want to just throw it out there."

"If I could tell people about us, I'd be calling you my girlfriend every chance I got."

I smiled and swung our hands between us. "Did you have any serious girlfriends back home?"

"Very smooth segue there."

"That was pretty slick, huh?" I laughed. "I was just curious. You learned how to kiss like a boss somewhere."

"Having you tell me I kiss like a boss totally makes up for my epic failure at Seven Minutes in Heaven. In fact, I think it's the greatest compliment I've ever received."

I patted his chest. "I'm glad I could make your day. Now, back to my question…"

"What question was that?" He furrowed his brow with exaggerated confusion. "I'm still thinking about showing you more of my boss moves."

"Nice try but not quite slick enough."

"Ah, now I remember. The answer is no. I dated a couple of girls but nothing serious." He angled down close to my ear. "No one could compare to this one girl I couldn't get out of my head."

I grinned and pressed my shoulder to his. I still couldn't wrap my mind around the fact Josh had crushed on me for eight years. I'd been thinking back to all the times we'd crossed paths at events, trying to remember if he'd given any hint of his feelings. But that would've been hard for him to do in the few words we'd spoken to each other.

Our walk led us in a circle back to the commercial area, and we stopped at a café for a quick lunch before returning to the car. I drove us west to the farthest town on the island and up the hill to the lookout for the Gay Head Cliffs. A few people stood along the wood fence taking photos of the popular tourist attraction.

"Whoa, this is a killer view," Josh said as we walked up to the fence.

The Atlantic Ocean and Vineyard Sound stretched in either direction, and below us the sparkling blue water crashed in waves at the base of the tall clay cliffs. Only a small strip of beach protected the clay from the constant onslaught. In the distance the Gay Head Lighthouse stood watch over the picturesque scene.

"This is one of Em and Sergei's favorite places," I said. "They named Quinn after the town here, Aquinnah."

Josh rested his elbows on the fence and swiveled his head to take in the panoramic landscape. "I can see why they love it."

"When Em was competing they used to come here before events to help calm her nerves. I guess we're continuing that tradition since Skate America is next week."

"Are you feeling really nervous about it?"

I hesitated to answer. Josh was my boyfriend, and I wanted to share my worries with him, but he was also my competition. I didn't think he'd gain confidence from my nervousness as Stephanie probably would, but it still felt weird to discuss it with him.

"We had a great start in Paris, but the field next week will be even tougher," I said.

"Yeah, you have to compete against me," Josh said with a devilish smile.

I looked at him with raised eyebrows, but maybe he had the right idea. Perhaps the best way to play the situation was to not take ourselves too seriously. The competition was going to be tense enough.

"And we're going to kick your ass," I said.

He laughed heartily, crinkling the corners of his eyes. "So we're going full out with the trash talk."

"Hey, you started it."

"You know I was just kidding, right?"

"I know. I really do want you to skate great." I put my arm around him. "But I still wanna beat you."

"You're lucky that's one of the things I like most about you — how competitive you are."

"Can you remind Mark of that next time he says I'm going soft by being nice to you?"

"Soft?" He tucked some wind-blown strands of hair behind my ear. "Soft wouldn't tell me she's going to kick my ass."

I slid my hand down into the back pocket of his jeans and squeezed. "And a very cute one it is."

****

"Cancelled?" I repeated to the Steamship Authority employee. "But this is the last ferry out tonight."

"I'm sorry, but no go with these high winds. This is the third trip tonight we've had to cancel."

My hair whipped around me as Josh and I got back into my car. The storm we'd expected was apparently arriving sooner and had brought with it gale-force winds. We were stuck like chuck on the island with no way to get home.

"We'll have to find a hotel," Josh said.

I combed my fingers through my hair to untangle the knots. Spending money on a hotel room hadn't been in my plans for the trip. And would we get one room or two? That could be an awkward decision. But did we have any other options? I rested my head against the seat and thought about the phone call I had to make to Em.

*That's it!*

"Em's aunt and uncle have a summer house here. I've been there before. I have to let her know I'm not coming home, so I'll ask if we can stay there. Well, 'we' being me and Meredith according to the story I told her this morning."

"How are we going to get in?"

"Hopefully they have a spare key under the rug or something."

As we pulled away from the harbor, I called Em and fumbled my way through the lie that I was with Meredith. She gave me directions to the house and said she'd call the neighbor Mrs. Bloom to let her know we'd be coming for the spare key.

A light drizzle began to fall as we drove back west across the island to Chilmark, which wasn't far from where we'd been earlier at the cliffs. When we arrived at the house, I told Josh to slink low in his seat so Mrs. Bloom couldn't see him. Even though it was almost ten o'clock at night, I didn't want to take any chances. Didn't need any nosy neighbors reporting back to Em.

Once I had the key, Josh and I ran through the then steady rain and entered the dark two-story house. We slipped off our wet shoes in the foyer and got our bearings. Light from the wall of windows in the open kitchen allowed me to see shapes in the living room, so I turned on the floor lamp beside the sofa.

"There's a piano!" Josh headed straight for the upright that sat next to the large entertainment center.

"You can give me a private concert."

He smiled and tinkled a few of the keys. "I was planning to do that at my house when we got back tonight, so this is perfect."

I looked around the cozy living room. Unlike Josh's house, there were personal touches everywhere — photos of Em's family in frames of all shapes and sizes and DVDs, books and games spilling out of the entertainment center.

"We should make a fire," Josh said as he walked toward the stone fireplace in the corner of the room.

I put my hands on my hips. "What do you know about fireplaces, California boy?"

"One of my buddies at our old rink... his parents had a cabin up in Big Bear, and we used to build fires there all the time."

He expertly moved around the hearth, and I sat on the couch. I'd wanted to avoid being alone with Josh all day at his house, and here we were, about to be alone *all night*. I chewed on my thumbnail as I watched him stack logs onto the burning tinder.

I didn't know what he was thinking about tonight. If he was like any other guy, he had to be thinking sex was a definite possibility, especially with the romantic atmosphere. Of course, this was a guy who had taken eight years to kiss me, so maybe he didn't have any expectations. But it might be better if I just put my feelings out there and avoided any awkwardness later.

Or I could end up making *everything* more awkward.

Sweat collected on my palms, and I scrubbed my hands on my jeans. *Should I say it or not?* My knees jiggled in time with the quick beat of my heart. *Tell him, already!*

"We're not having sex tonight," I blurted out as I shot to my feet.

Josh was returning the poker to the set of tools, and he dropped it, loudly clanging the brass.

"Wha... what?" he stammered.

"It's just that we're alone here on this island with the rain and the fireplace, and it's all very romance novel-ish, and you know what happens in the books in those scenes, and I'm not ready to go there, so I thought I'd get that out of the way now in case you were thinking something might happen." I caught my breath after spouting the longest run-on ramble in history.

He stood motionless, his eyes still a tad wide. After a few seconds of tense silence, he came over to me and slid his hands inside my collar, tickling the nape of my neck. The care in his touch slowed my anxiety.

"I'm happy just being here with you," he said. "We don't

have to do anything."

My body relaxed, and I wound my arms around his waist. "Well, we can do *some* things."

A slow smile spread across his face. "Just so you know, I wasn't plotting to seduce you with my piano-playing and fire-building."

I laughed, and he continued, "I'd be lying if I said I wasn't thinking about… possibilities, but I'm no stranger to waiting, so we don't have to rush anything."

I hugged him tight. "Sorry for making all this drama out of it."

"Don't ever be sorry for telling me how you feel. That's another one of my favorite things about you — you're not afraid to speak up."

I bit my lip. Should I give full disclosure? I wanted him to know where I was coming from and why I felt the way I did, and the only way to do that would be through complete honesty.

"While we're laying it all out there, I um…" I loosened my hold around him so I could see his face. "I've never slept with anyone, so that's part of the reason I want to make sure I'm ready before…"

His lips curled upward. "I haven't either."

"Oh." It wasn't a complete shock, but I still needed a moment to process. "I guess we're more than just karaoke virgins together, then."

His smile opened wider. "And we know how that turned out. We rocked that stage hard."

"We did. We were smokin' hot."

He grasped my hips and gazed intently at me. "Proof that the first time can be amazing."

The passionate intensity in his eyes slayed me. I leaned into him, and our lips met halfway. One long breathless kiss led to another and another until I finally broke away.

"You promised me a concert," I said between pants.

Josh squeezed my waist. "I thought we could get started on those 'some things' you said we could do."

"All in good time. Since you're a pro at waiting." I grinned.

"I do have a new song I think you're going to love. If I was plotting to seduce you, this would definitely do the trick."

"Oh really?" I turned him toward the piano. "I'm *so* ready then."

He settled onto the bench, and I took one of the blankets from the couch and spread it over the carpet. As I grabbed a couple of throw pillows to make myself even more comfy, Josh warmed up with a few easy bars.

He looked over at me stretched out on the blanket. "I'll start with one of your classical favorites."

I knew the piece from the first notes — "Clair de Lune." My eyes stayed on Josh's hands as he played. They were a beautiful instrument themselves, gliding so smoothly over the keys, applying both strength and softness when needed. *I would happily be his human piano...*

When the song ended, I applauded and Josh gave me a little bow.

"And now for something new," he said.

He rubbed his hands together and stared long and hard at the keys, studying them for a quiet minute before he set his fingers on them and began to play.

I listened closely and soon recognized the music as part of the score of *Pride and Prejudice*. Josh must've remembered that the movie had been playing in the background when we'd shared our first kiss. The melody was one of the most gorgeous parts of the soundtrack, and I closed my eyes and imagined us skating to it.

After the music stopped, I opened my eyes and found Josh watching me.

"I hope I didn't put you to sleep," he said.

"No, I was just having a little daydream about us on the

ice. I love that piece so much." I got up and sat on the bench with him. "The movie will always be special to me now."

"I recognized the movie when I was at your house because Steph watches it all the time, so I looked up the soundtrack. It has great music for skating."

"It's so amazing how you can just listen to a song and learn how to play it so perfectly. It's like magic."

"Do you wanna learn how to play a few notes?"

I nodded eagerly. "Can we do the beginning of the Muse song?"

He patted his lap. "Sit here and I'll show you."

I scooted onto his legs, and he peeked around my shoulder at the piano. "Your hands will start here."

He delicately placed my fingers on the appropriate keys and then covered my hands with his so he could guide them. I shivered as his forearms rubbed lightly over mine. Slowly he showed me which keys to use, making the music come alive. We repeated the few notes again and again until he let go, and I played them confidently all on my own.

"That was beautiful, Court," he said softly.

I turned to him and nuzzled his cheek. "Would you play the whole song for me?"

We shifted so I sat between his thighs, and with his arms surrounding me, I felt the tension and release in his body as the high and low notes came. My eyes followed every movement of his fingers as they skated across the keys, again imagining them doing the same melodic dance across my skin.

When he hit the final note, he lingered on the keys, and I reached out and touched the back of his hand with my fingertips.

"I love watching your hands when you play." I brushed lightly from his knuckles to his wrist. "They're very sexy."

He buried his face in my hair and then swept the long curls away from my neck, kissing the tender spot below my ear. I let out a soft breath and leaned back against him. He turned me so I was sideways, and our eyes connected, then our lips. As our kisses grew fuller and longer, Josh guided us both from the bench and over to the blanket.

We eased down together on our knees, and my hands slipped under his T-shirt and along his waistband, getting a tantalizing taste of his warm skin. It only made me starve for more.

I nudged up his shirt, and Josh did the rest, tossing it aside. I placed my palm on his smooth chest and felt the rapid thump-thump of his heart. Mine was beating with the same heady rhythm. Leaning forward, I touched my lips to his neck and kissed my way across his tense shoulder. His arms tightened around me, his hands massaging my back more urgently. He laid me onto the blanket, and I opened my mouth to him, drinking in all his hunger and need. His lips felt like fire, and his tongue fanned the flames.

His hand moved down my shirt, opening the line of buttons, and his mouth followed, leaving a trail of kisses from my neck to my stomach. The heat of his breath on my belly made me squirm with desire, and I lifted up, letting Josh slide the shirt from my shoulders. His eyes lowered to my body, and his breaths came harder and quicker. He tangled his fingers in my hair and captured my mouth once more. I fell into him, and we tumbled onto the blanket, Josh pinned beneath me.

I kissed his silky lips again and again and didn't realize he'd unhooked my bra until I felt air on my back. The surprise and a little bit of fear shocked me out of our kiss. I pushed myself up so I was straddling his waist, and I watched a hint of uncertainty skim across his eyes as if he wasn't sure he should've made that move.

I'd never let anyone see this much of me, but I wanted it with Josh. I wanted to press myself to him and feel his heart race even faster. I wanted to see the look in his eyes when he touched me. It scared me how much closer I wanted to be with him, but it was the good kind of fear… the exhilarating kind.

I pulled down the straps and let the material fall away. Josh gazed hotly at me, all uncertainty gone, and he grasped both my hands.

"Come here," he whispered.

I bent over him, and my hair draped around us. His kiss was slow and gentle, as were his hands, thrilling me with every touch. We rolled onto our sides, and I trembled as his fingertips traced the length of my spine.

"Are you cold?" he asked, holding me closer to his chest.

I stared into his beautiful eyes. "I'm perfect."

He smiled and kissed my forehead. The fire crackled quietly behind us but was then overshadowed by the ringing of Josh's phone. He groaned and reached onto the coffee table to take the call. His brow knitted as he looked at the screen.

"Steph?" he answered.

I looked at the clock on the cable box. Why was she calling so late from New York? I curled up and covered myself with the edge of the blanket.

"You're home?" he said.

My eyes grew big, and Josh raked his hand through his hair.

"I um… I'm on Martha's Vineyard. I came for the day with some friends and our ferry was cancelled because of the weather."

A pause followed, and Josh said, "Yeah, we're at a hotel."

I watched as he fidgeted with a book on the coffee table. The number of lies we were telling was multiplying at an astronomical rate.

The conversation continued only another minute. Josh put down the phone and joined me under the blanket, hugging me against him.

"She's home?" I asked.

"She flew back early because of bad weather in New York tomorrow."

"And I guess she saw your car was there but you weren't."

He twisted one of my long curls around his finger. "I don't know how much longer we can keep this a secret."

"I know. I hate lying to Em and Sergei. I'm just dreading Mark's reaction."

"After Skate America we'll have to decide what to do."

I hooked my arm around him and closed my eyes. The truth had to be told, but I wanted to hang on to our peaceful existence as long as possible. As soon as everyone knew, they were going to hate all over our relationship. Josh and I only had a few months left together, and dealing with constant negativity and people who wanted to split us up wasn't how I wanted to spend the time.

# Chapter Sixteen

The hotel lobby at international skating events was always a fascinating scene with conversations in various languages filling the air. Standing among the loud chatter at the High Peaks Resort, I examined the colorful practice and competition schedule on the bulletin board. I was so antsy to get the ball rolling and compete the next night. I was also antsy to get the meeting between my parents and Josh rolling. There was nowhere in the little town of Lake Placid we could meet privately, so Josh was going to "run into" us in the lobby in a few minutes. I'd told my parents we were dating on the down-low, so they were aware this had to appear to be a casual spontaneous conversation.

"Hey, Honey." Mom came up and put her arm around me.

"Hey." I gave her a hug and did the same with Dad behind her. "Did you get settled in?"

"The room is beautiful," she said. "We have a great view of the mountains."

"It's so pretty here. Liza and I walked all around yesterday and took a million pictures."

Dad pushed his glasses higher on his nose and glanced around the lobby. "So, do you have to send The Piano Man the secret code word to come down?"

"Did you just call Josh *The Piano Man?*"

"Well, I thought we should have a code name for him in case anyone's listening when we talk about you, and your mom said he plays the piano."

I laughed and shook my head. Dad's goofy sense of humor had caused me many moments of embarrassment when I was a teenager. He didn't look like a guy who would crack jokes with his thick glasses and always-buttoned-up shirts, but he'd quietly sneak in the funny when least expected.

"He should be here in a few minutes," I said.

"Are The Piano Man's parents here this weekend?" Mom asked.

My laughter resurfaced. "You don't have to call him that. No one's listening to us right now. But yeah, his mom is here."

"I wish we could meet her and spend more time with Josh. He seemed like a sweet boy when I saw him at the rink... and from what you've told me."

"He is. He's—" I spotted him coming out of the elevator, and my heart beat a little faster. "The sweetest guy I've ever known."

Josh's eyes brightened as they connected with mine, and then he quickly looked away. He walked with purpose toward the restaurant off the lobby but slowed when he approached us, giving us a little wave.

"Hey, Court."

I waved back, laughing internally at the ridiculousness of the charade. "Hey, what's going on?"

"I was just going to check out the dinner menu." He extended his hand to Mom. "It's good to see you again, Mrs. Carlton."

"It's wonderful to see you, too." Mom smiled bigger than

a casual meeting would inspire.

"Dad, this is Josh Tucker," I said.

Josh shook his hand. "Nice to meet you, Sir."

"Same here."

"Are you having dinner with your family?" Mom asked.

"Um… yes. My mom and Steph are supposed to meet me later."

"Maybe we'll see you all in there."

"I was thinking we could take a walk down Main Street and find something to eat there," I said.

If we were in the same restaurant as Josh, I wouldn't be able to stop myself from looking at him. We hadn't been able to spend any time alone since we'd been in Lake Placid, and I was having serious withdrawals from his boss kisses.

"Josh, I hear you graduated from UCLA," Dad said. "That's impressive you finished in four years while also skating."

"It was pretty hectic. I wish I'd had more time to enjoy the college experience. I didn't see much outside the classroom."

Dad rubbed my shoulder. "I'm glad Court waited to start so she'll able to get the full experience at BC. Those were some of the best years of my life."

"Don't jinx it, Dad."

"No such thing as jinxes. We make our own luck, and you submitted a great application."

"Her essay was awesome." Josh smiled at me.

I opened my mouth to thank him, and it hung open as Stephanie and Mrs. Tucker entered the lobby from outside. Both of them carried multiple shopping bags. Stephanie came to a halt, her jaw tightening, but then I thought I saw a sinister smile narrow her eyes.

*Oh, crap. Can I please click my heels together and poof myself upstairs to my room?*

She and her mom came directly toward us. Josh saw

what must have been terror on my face and turned to the door. His face took on its own look of alarm.

"Hello," Stephanie said, her eyes critically scanning my parents and myself.

Between her examination and Mrs. Tucker's equally strong stare, my cheeks burned. It was like they were cataloguing everything about us. I could see Mrs. Tucker's disdain as she took in Mom's bright yellow sweater, handmade knit scarf, and "mom jeans."

"I thought you were shopping," Josh said as he stood in front of us like a protective shield.

"There were only a couple of decent stores." Mrs. Tucker removed her leather gloves and tucked them into the pocket of her stylish white coat, which appeared to be cashmere.

She looked even more plastic than I'd remembered. She had the same shade of creamy skin as Stephanie and Josh, but it was too smooth, too perfect, and her lips had apparently received a recent injection of some sort. No one had lips that full.

"Mom, you haven't met Courtney, have you?" Stephanie asked, sounding way too friendly. Warning bells went off in my head.

Josh slid slightly to the left so he was no longer a buffer between us. I stuck out my hand and then quickly realized Mrs. Tucker wasn't going to reciprocate. All I received in return was a cool gaze. I brought my hand up to my hair and nervously combed the flyaway frizzies.

"It's nice to meet you," I said. *And by "nice" I mean terrifying.*

"I think we met at a competition before." She looked me up and down.

I was ninety-nine percent sure we hadn't, but I wasn't going to start a dispute. "Perhaps we did."

Mom leaned around Josh and smiled at his mom. "Hi, I'm Courtney's mom, Karen, and this is my husband Tom."

"Bethany Tucker," she said, still not offering a handshake.

I finally realized who she reminded me of — Meryl Streep in *The Devil Wears Prada*. She had the same frosty, piercing stare that could make grown men cower in fear.

"You must be so proud of Courtney," Stephanie said to my parents. "How she works almost every night to pay for her skating."

So her fake nice behavior was a ploy to make sure her mom knew we weren't wealthy. I shook my head in disgust. *Classic Stephanie.*

"Mom, Courtney works as a bartender," she added.

Mrs. Tucker hummed quietly as she eyed me once again. "You should give the staff here some tips. The martini I had last night tasted like well brand. It was terrible."

"Well, if the service is bad, they make up for it with the beauty of the rooms," Mom said. "I'm not going to want to leave here."

Mrs. Tucker smoothed her shoulder-length brown hair. "My room is ridiculously small. I was expecting a lot more from a resort."

Mom's smile never wavered, and I wondered what she was thinking behind it. She was familiar with Stephanie's attitude from all my years of competing against her, but I hadn't given her a heads-up on what Josh had told me about his mom. And speaking of Josh, one of his eyes was twitching, and his lips were pressed together in a tight line. He looked like he was going to lose it at any second.

"We were headed out for a walk, so… it was nice meeting you." I tipped my head at Mrs. Tucker and urged my parents toward the exit.

"Wait, Hon, we need our coats," Mom said.

"Oh. Yeah. Let's go up and get them."

I turned around toward the elevator and high-tailed it out of there. Behind me I heard Mom and Dad echoing my "nice to meet you" sentiment.

I punched the elevator button, and Mom and Dad caught up to me as the doors opened.

"Good quick thinking, Court," Dad said. "I didn't know how we were going to escape from Cruella de Vil."

"Tom," Mom scolded him.

"What? All she was missing was a pack of Dalmatians."

I rubbed my hands down my face. "She was even scarier than I'd expected. And I had pretty grave expectations."

"I can see where Stephanie gets her... personality. They say the apple doesn't fall far from the tree," Mom said.

"Then what happened to Josh? A tornado must've blown his apple across the orchard," I said.

My phone chimed at the same time the elevator stopped on my floor, and I told my parents I'd meet them at their room in a few minutes. I clicked on my inbox and read the text.

Josh: *I'm so sorry. They weren't supposed to be back so soon.*

Me: *It's okay. Why not knock out all the awkward meetings at once?*

I slid the card key into my door and went to the desk for my coat. Liza's team jacket lay draped over it. I knew Em must've had a hand in making sure the federation assigned Liza and me as roommates.

My phone dinged again, and I read as I slipped my arms inside my pea coat.

Josh: *Your parents are really nice.*

What could I say complimentary about his mom? She hadn't burned the flesh off my face? Maybe I should just keep the conversation away from her.

Me: *They like you a lot.*

Okay, so maybe Mom and Dad hadn't said that (although I knew they would once they got to know Josh), but compared to Cruella and Cruella Jr., he was freaking Prince Charming.

Josh: *My mom is rude to most people, so please don't take her behavior personally.*

That was *so* much easier said than done. I shivered at the memory of Mrs. Tucker's sharp gaze boring an icy hole into me. If she was that repulsed by me as just a random skater, how much was she going to hate me as Josh's girlfriend?

\*\*\*\*

"Show time, go time," Mark said, holding his hands up for a double high five.

I slapped them and exhaled a long breath. We were next to take the ice in the short program event, also known as two-and-a-half minutes of high stress. Missing one or two elements in the short could bury a team in the standings.

Em walked with us through the dim backstage corridor to the entrance to the brightly lit rink. Sergei was already out there with Stephanie and Josh, who'd just finished skating according to the applause. I shed my navy Team USA jacket and handed it to Em, and I rubbed my bare arms to stay warm. My sparkly black dress only had thin straps over my shoulders. Mark matched me color-wise with black pants and a black button-down shirt, sleeves rolled up.

I bounced on the heels of my skate guards as we marched out under the lights. The arena wasn't large, and the seats weren't close to being filled. Pairs hadn't been a marquee event since Em and Chris had retired. The ladies would bring in a much bigger crowd the next day.

Stephanie and Josh exited the ice, and I watched their body language for a hint of how they'd skated, but they both wore poker faces. Mark nudged me from behind, and I hurriedly removed my skate guards and stepped onto the ice, glancing back at the boards. Sergei smiled as he hugged Stephanie, and a twinge of jealousy twisted my stomach. It was still bizarre seeing Em and Sergei with Stephanie and Josh, giving them the same hugs and nods of approval. Mark and I needed to perform better than they had. We had to show

Em and Sergei who the top team in our camp was.

I circled the ice, lightly pumping my legs to warm up, and Mark skated to my side as the announcer read Stephanie and Josh's score. The new judging system had been in place long enough where I knew what the numbers meant, and their score was one of the best they'd ever received for the short. An extra kick of adrenaline made my legs move faster.

Mark took my hand and pressed hard. "Ready to show them who's boss?"

It was uncanny how after nine years of skating together, our thoughts on the ice often echoed one another. His use of the word "boss" brought another thought to mind, though — one of Josh kissing me passionately as we lay beside the fire.

I rattled my head. Now was not the time to think about such things. Now was the time to put all my emotion into skating a fierce tango. Em and Sergei smiled at us from behind the boards, and we took matching deep breaths, preparing for our introduction from the PA announcer.

"They represent the United States. Ladies and gentlemen, Courtney Carlton and Mark Phillips."

We glided to center ice amid warm applause and assumed our starting pose of the traditional tango hold. With Mark's head bent close to mine, I whispered, "Let's do this," more as a reminder to myself than to him.

The sharp beats of Tanghetto's "Enjoy the Silence" began, and we moved across the ice still in dance hold. When we reached the boards we broke apart and switched to side-by-side stroking, building up speed for the triple twist. The cold air blew across my face, but not a hair strayed from my perfectly pinned bun.

We flew backward into the entrance to the twist, and I stabbed my toe pick into the ice. Mark tossed me up into the air, and all my muscles tightened as I spun three times above his head. After the final rotation, I opened up and fell into Mark's waiting hands for a smooth set down. *One element done*

— *check.*

We twirled around and quickly transitioned into our footwork sequence, where we hit all the steps sharply, further deepening the tango mood. The tension of the steps heightened the adrenaline coursing through me, and I felt ready to burst as we approached the side-by-side triple Salchows.

*Calm yourself. Free and easy into the jump.*

We pushed off on identical back inside edges and completed three rotations. Mark was a blur next to me until my right foot hit the ice for the landing, and I saw him do the same at that precise moment. Perfect unison, perfect execution. I internally pumped my fist. The Salchows had been known to abandon us at the most unfortunate moments.

We attacked the second half of the program with the same intensity, and we came out of our death spiral and struck our ending pose right on the final beat of the music. Mark looked for another high-five, and I smacked his hands even harder that time.

As we hugged, I caught sight of Josh and Stephanie sitting in the kiss and cry. They'd stayed there to watch us skate. Josh was clapping, but Stephanie just glared at us. They departed backstage as Mark and I arrived at the boards and exchanged hugs with Em and Sergei.

"That was so strong, guys." Em squeezed my shoulders.

"Everything felt really crisp," I said as we took seats on the bench in the kiss and cry. "We never let the tango feeling drop for a second."

"The timing on the lift was better than Paris, too," Sergei said.

We always sat in the same order to wait for our score — Em, Mark, me, then Sergei. Em reached across Mark to hand me my water bottle, and I took a long swig. How would the judges score us compared to Stephanie and Josh? Our program component scores, similar to the old "artistic" mark, had always been about the same, but we'd usually beaten them on the technical score. Now that their technical ability had improved, how would the numbers shake out?

"The score please for Courtney Carlton and Mark Phillips," the announcer said and paused. "The short program score..."

Another pause ate at my nerves. I clutched Mark's knee, and he put his hand on top of mine.

The announcer read the total, and I nodded with excitement as the details of the technical and program component marks flashed on the video screen. We'd earned our personal best short program score.

The standings appeared on the screen, and our names showed above Stephanie and Josh's. My head bobbed with even more vigor, but then I peered closer at the numbers and did the quick math. Only an eighth of a point separated us. We were virtually tied going into the free skate the next night.

The next group of teams crowded around the ice door for their six-minute warm-up, so we escaped backstage. We turned the corner to meet the media, and I overhead Stephanie speaking to a reporter.

"Our number one goal is to make the Olympic team, and we're in the perfect position to do that. We're skating the best we ever have."

They sure were. It was starting to hit me just how much of a battle nationals was going to be. And it made me feel a little sick to my stomach.

We had to give sound bites next, so we stood behind Stephanie and Josh to wait our turn. When they finished, we came face-to-face, and Stephanie lifted her chin and moved past us, nothing said. She'd apparently decided to drop her friendly act from the previous day.

"Great job," Josh said.

Mark was standing next to me, but Josh looked only at me. His electric blue shirt made his eyes pop even more brilliantly.

*Damn, the competition should not look this good.*

"You, too," I said.

Mark placed his hand on my back and steered me in front of the reporter. We answered question after question from each media outlet, most about how we got along with our new training mates ("Great" was our standard vanilla answer). Our final interview found us next to Stephanie and Josh again, and we both concluded at the same time. We all walked in awkward silence toward the locker rooms, stopping to see the final standings on the monitor. We'd finished in fourth and fifth places, which I'd expected, but happily the two-time national champions were a mere one point ahead of Mark and me in third.

Stephanie pivoted and blocked my path, and when I tried to go around her she stepped in my way.

"It was a great competition, don't you think?" she said.

*What is her angle now?* Josh and Mark both watched us warily, likely wondering the same thing.

"Yes. Yes, it was."

She folded her arms over her jacket. "So, are you and Josh going to have a private celebration later like you did last weekend on Martha's Vineyard?"

My body went numb, while my brain fought to think quickly. It didn't succeed as all I could utter was, "What?"

"I went to the Vineyard with friends," Josh said.

"Oh, cut the crap. The only friend you have is Courtney. Or should I say *girlfriend*?" Stephanie practically spat at me.

"What the hell is she talking about?" Mark asked.

"I don't know what you think you know…" Josh said with less conviction.

"I've seen all the texts and the pictures, including your cute little matching Halloween costumes."

*Oh my God.*

Josh's jaw clenched. "How did you get on my phone? It's

always locked."

"It wasn't hard for me to sneak a peek when you were punching in the password once. Then all I had to do was wait until you were in the shower to grab it."

"You had no right to do that."

"I had every right when you've been lying to my face every day!"

"Court, you'd better start talking right now." Mark fumed.

I was still too overcome to speak. Stephanie had read our texts. Our private, heartfelt words. Since Josh and I hardly saw each other alone, we'd been relying on our phones to stay connected. To share our feelings. My stomach turned at the thought of Stephanie seeing all of it.

"Your partner's waiting for an explanation." Stephanie waved her hand at me. "Go on."

Anger rose in my throat, tightening and burning. She'd calculated this, waited until we were in the middle of the competition to drop this bomb.

"I'm not going to talk about this here or in front of you," I said.

Mark took my elbow. "We're gonna talk about it *somewhere*."

"What's going on?" Em asked as she and Sergei entered our circle of intensity.

"Ask Courtney and Josh," Stephanie said. "They're the ones who've been sneaking around together and lying to all of us."

Em glanced from me to Josh and back again, but she didn't look shocked. With her pursed lips she looked more annoyed.

Sergei stepped forward. "You all need to get changed and get on the bus. We'll deal with this at the hotel."

Other skaters and coaches watched us with curious looks as everyone in our group appeared on the verge of exploding.

We slowly dispersed, and Josh slid next to me. His eyes were still dark with fury.

"I'm so sorry," he said.

"It's not your fault."

"Court, let's go." Em pointed me to the ladies' locker room.

Josh and I parted, and I blew past Stephanie to get to my bags. The night had started off so promising, and now it was all shot to hell. Mark wanted to strangle me, and who knew what Em and Sergei had to say. I'd never been a violent person, but visions of punching Stephanie's snotty face played over and over in my mind.

# Chapter Seventeen

Em and Sergei were waiting for us in the hotel lobby. None of us had spoken a word on the short ride down Main Street.

"Stephanie, Josh, let's get a table in the restaurant." Sergei motioned for them to follow him.

"Our mom is waiting to have dinner with us," Stephanie said.

"You can let her know you're having a meeting," Sergei said tersely.

Stephanie moved a step slower than Josh but dutifully trailed after Sergei. That left Mark and me with Em, and I guessed she and Sergei were tag-teaming us.

"I have to check on the twins," she said as she unbuttoned her coat. "Can you get a table for us? On the opposite side of the restaurant please."

Mark and I followed her orders and slid into a booth near the back of the room. The place had a cozy lodge ambiance with its light-colored wood and burning fireplace, but I wasn't feeling very cozy with Mark glaring at me. I knew my parents would be looking for me, so I texted Mom that I'd see them in the morning. I had no idea how long this was going to take.

"Are you texting *him*?" Mark asked.

"I'm texting my mom," I said and tossed the phone into my purse.

He stared at me for a long minute. "What the hell, Court? We've been partners half our lives, and you betray that for some guy?"

"I'm not betraying our partnership."

"You're dating our biggest competition. You don't think that's a problem?"

The waitress came to the table, and Mark told her we needed a few minutes. She seemed happy to leave after spying the intense looks we were giving each other.

"If my dating Josh was a problem, we wouldn't have gotten our best ever score tonight," I said.

"That was just one short program. What's gonna happen at nationals when the Olympic team is on the line? Will you be okay with beating Josh? Crushing his dream? Because that's what you'll have to do."

"We can both make the team. No one has to have their dream crushed."

I sounded like one of Em's rah-rah Team Cape Cod speeches.

"And that's the problem right there." Mark smacked his hand on the table. "You shouldn't care what happens to anyone else. You should only be concerned with how you and I are going to get on the team."

"I'm not saying I'm concerned with both of us making it. I'm just…" I held my head in my hands. "You're twisting my words."

"I don't think I am."

"What do I have to do to prove I'm still just as focused on our partnership and our goals?" I saw his mouth open for an immediate comeback, and I hastily added, "Besides breaking up with Josh."

"Why do you want to date him anyway? Isn't he moving back to California?"

*Thanks for the reminder.* It wasn't as if that didn't weigh on my mind every day.

"We have some things to figure out, but—"

"Is it really worth getting involved with him when it might be over in a few months?"

The knife twisted deeper into my gut, hitting all my biggest fears about our relationship. I slapped open my menu and pretended to read.

"We don't know what's going to happen," I said quietly.

Em marched up to the booth and made me scoot over so she could slide onto my side. "Have you ordered yet?"

"I'm not really hungry." I shut the menu.

She reopened it. "You have to eat."

"See, now you're not taking care of yourself," Mark said. "And you say this isn't a problem."

"I wouldn't be feeling sick if you weren't ragging all over me," I barked.

He leaned forward. "I'm just trying to tell you—"

"Zip it. Both of you." Em flagged down our waitress. "Can I get a glass of merlot?"

Mark and I both stuck to water, and we all silently examined our menus until the waitress came back to take our orders. After she walked away, Em took a long sip of her wine and slowly set down the glass.

"Court, I wish you would've been honest with us," she said. "I had my suspicions about you and Josh, but I wanted you to come to me."

"How did you know?"

"Have you forgotten that Sergei and I snuck around for a year? I know all the signs."

I avoided her gaze as I folded my straw wrapper into tiny squares. "I'm sorry. We didn't want to keep this from you, but we knew there was going to be backlash from some people."

"You think?" Mark snapped.

I looked up at him. "If I'd known Stephanie was going to turn this into a circus, I would've told you from the beginning."

"Sergei is talking to Stephanie about how she handled things," Em said.

Mark snorted. "Did he draw the short straw?"

Em ignored his comment. "I want to make sure this isn't going to be an issue between you two. Whatever needs to be said should be said now and then we need to move on."

"So you're okay with her dating Josh?" Mark asked.

"I'm going to trust that Court and Josh have entered into this relationship carefully, and they're prepared to handle competing against each other." Her big blue eyes focused steely on mine.

I'd been coached by Em and Sergei for so long that I knew all their strategies, all their ways of getting the responses from us they wanted. The purpose of her statement was to make me think long and hard about whether I'd made the right choice. It was also to show Mark she had confidence in my decision, whatever that might be.

"I think tonight Josh and I proved we can handle it," I said.

"Then as long as you maintain that professionalism, I don't have an issue with this," Em said.

Mark let out an angry laugh. "Of course you don't. You dated Sergei when Chris didn't want you to, when everyone thought it was a bad idea."

My eyebrows shot up, and Em shot Mark a dark glare.

"I don't appreciate the attitude, and that was a very different situation. There were a lot more issues since Sergei was my coach. Those issues don't apply here." She turned to me. "I don't like that you lied to all of us, though. That part I do have a problem with."

"I really am sorry we didn't tell you. I realize now it

would've been better to be up front with everyone."

"We need to have honesty and trust between all of us in order to work as the best possible team," Em said.

I nodded and made eye contact with Mark. "I know, and I promise it won't happen again."

He tapped his thumb on the table as he mulled over my apology. When he didn't say anything, I fidgeted in my seat, anxious he was going to tell me he didn't believe me.

"Mark, do you trust that Court will put your partnership first?" Em prodded him.

He gave me a hard look. "You swear you're not gonna flake on me?"

"I've wanted to be an Olympian since I was ten years old. I'm going to fight for this with everything I have," I said slowly, making sure he heard the resolve in every word.

"But what if Josh breaks up with you right before nationals?" Mark asked. "What if that's part of the plan? Stephanie stirs up the first round of trouble here, and then he goes in for the kill when it's crunch time?"

I groaned and covered my face. "How many times do I have to tell you Josh is nothing like Stephanie? He's not using me. He's had a crush on me for eight years!"

"Really? That's so sweet," Em said.

"What took him so long to make his move? Jeez," Mark said.

I looked down at the table. "It's complicated."

I wasn't going to get into Josh's shyness and our failed first kiss. That wasn't anyone's business but ours.

"And getting involved *now* isn't complicated? He picked the worst time possible," Mark said. "I'm telling you, if he does anything questionable, anything to hurt you—"

"He won't," I said firmly.

"Josh is a good guy." Em backed me up.

The waitress set down our plates, and I took a bite of my sandwich. My stomach felt a little more settled than it had when we'd started this conversation. Now to get through the meal peacefully...

"I'm holding you to your word." Mark picked up a French fry and waved it at me. "And I'm still gonna keep an eye on Josh. And his evil sister."

"You're a great partner to look out for Court," Em said.

*Looking out is one thing. Being insanely paranoid is another.*

Em steered the conversation toward less volatile topics the rest of dinner, so we were all in a calm mood when we left the restaurant. Then we saw Stephanie, Josh, and their mom standing in the lobby.

I could feel Mark tense beside me. Just seeing Stephanie's face again stirred up fury in me, too. But no way in hell was I going to confront her with Mrs. Tucker there.

"If I go upstairs, you're going to play nice, right?" Em said.

Mark crossed his arms and widened his stance. "Of course."

Em passed them on her way to the elevator, and she stopped and spoke to them for a few minutes. Mrs. Tucker actually cracked a smile, though it looked like the phony one Stephanie often wore.

Mark took a call from Zoe on his cell, leaving me standing alone as he wandered over to the empty sitting area. I shuffled my feet and took out my own phone so I wouldn't look like an aimless fool. I wanted to talk to Josh, but the idea of approaching him in front of his mom sounded as appealing as diving into an ocean full of sharks.

I glanced up as Em departed, and Mrs. Tucker's smile had evaporated. She was speaking to Josh while also treating me to more of her icy looks. Every one of them made the hairs on the back of my neck stand up. I tried to figure out a way to get to the elevator without going past them, but I'd have to learn how to walk through walls.

Josh turned away from Stephanie and his mom and came

toward me, and I froze from the iciest of Mrs. Tucker's glares. Josh took my hand and intertwined our fingers, but I pulled away.

"Maybe we shouldn't... here." I looked over at Mark, and he was observing us just as intently as Mrs. Tucker was.

Josh grasped my hand with both of his. "I've waited too long to be with you to watch you from across the room."

His warmth washed over the coldness I felt from the people staring at us. He stepped even closer and bent his head.

"I'm not happy with how this came out, but I'm happy it's out," he said.

"I am, too. I just... I don't want Mark to get riled up again. And your mom... I assume she knows about us?"

"Yeah, Steph took care of that." His voice quickly went from soft to hard.

"Shocking," I said bitterly.

Stephanie and Mrs. Tucker apparently had endured enough of seeing Josh and me together because they disappeared from the lobby. Not before one last haughty glance at me, though.

"What did your mom say?" I asked.

He hesitated and shook his head. "It doesn't matter."

"That bad, huh?" I chewed on my lip.

"I don't care what she thinks."

"You must care a little. I mean, she's your mom."

He looked down at our hands and gently pressed mine between his. "Her way of looking at the world is so narrow and so different from mine that I don't... I don't understand her at all. So whatever opinions she has about my life, they don't hold any weight with me."

My heart hurt for him. He deserved to have a mother who was just as caring and wonderful as he was. I couldn't imagine growing up with a mom as cold and judgmental as his. I wanted to give him a hug but not in the middle of all the lobby action.

"Walk with me to my room?" I said.

We got into the elevator, and I wrapped my arms around Josh. As he held me tight, the craziness of the night slipped from my mind, and all that remained was the perfectness of how our bodies fit together. I'd missed that feeling so much in the few days we'd been in Lake Placid.

The elevator chimed, and we walked hand-in-hand to my door. Liza was probably asleep since she had an early practice, so we stayed in the hallway.

"How did things go with Mark?" Josh asked.

"We came to somewhat of an understanding. Em was awesome. She really supported me."

"Yeah, Sergei was the same. Well, after he lectured me about lying and gave Steph an even longer lecture about manipulating the situation."

"She deserved a lot more than a lecture."

Josh pinched the bridge of his nose. "I still can't believe she looked at my phone."

"I *hate* the idea of her reading our texts. It's like she invaded the most private part of our relationship." My throat ached, and I swallowed hard. "God, the things we wrote about that night on the Vineyard..."

I squeezed my eyes shut. We'd texted how we wished we could lie next to each other again, touch each other...

Josh rested his forehead against mine. "I'm so, so sorry. I should've been more careful."

"You didn't know she'd go to those lengths."

"I told her the only reason I'm still speaking to her is because we skate together."

I hugged him again, even longer and tighter. He was saddled with two cold-hearted people in his life. I didn't know how he put up with Stephanie on a daily basis. Mark might drive me nuts sometimes, but he was a good person. He would never be intentionally hurtful like Stephanie had been.

"Tomorrow is going to be pretty important," Josh said.

I looked up at him. "We have to do well to prove none of this is affecting us on the ice. Em and Sergei are going to be watching us closely."

He nodded. "We just have to do exactly what we did tonight."

*And if we do that, hopefully Mark and I will come out on top again.*

Even though we'd joked around with the trash talk before, I didn't want to say that to him. It didn't feel right after all the drama of the evening. I kept thinking about what Mark had said about crushing Josh's dream. I had to put that out of my mind or switch the focus to crushing Stephanie's dream. That was definitely something I had no problem using as motivation.

****

The moment I saw Josh's face, I knew he hadn't skated well.

His eyes were filled with disappointment as he and Stephanie came to a stop at the boards after their free skate. I raced onto the ice and tried to push aside my sinking feeling by carving deeper edges. *How they skated doesn't matter,* I reminded myself. *This is about you and Mark and what you need to do.*

Unfortunately, I couldn't plug my ears to block out Stephanie and Josh's score, and it confirmed there had been mistakes. Big ones. I shook out my arms to keep the blood flowing and kept my head down as I glided past the kiss and cry.

*Don't look at them. Don't think about them.*

The short filmy skirt of my burgundy dress flapped over my thighs as I picked up the pace. Mark joined me and took my hand, and we made one more lap around the rink before receiving our introduction. We opened our arms to acknowledge the crowd's cheers and settled into our starting pose. I had to face the kiss and cry as Mark and I stood back to back, and I saw Stephanie gesturing animatedly at the ice. Josh totally ignored her as he quietly watched us.

I closed my eyes and took a deep breath, and a few seconds later the music began. Saint-Saëns' Organ Symphony was a beautiful piece that hadn't been used much for skating, but I'd fallen in love with it the first time Sergei had played it for us. The sweeping highs and lows gave me a sense of power and strength in every movement I made.

We knocked out the triple twist in the opening section of the program and set up for our side-by-side triple-toe-double-toe-double-toe combination. Our path took us straight toward the kiss and cry at the end of the rink, and I was looking directly at Josh as we sped toward the jump. Stephanie had left the scene.

*See the jumps! See the jumps!*

I quickly pulled my eyes down to the ice and visualized the perfect combination. In the next instant, I picked into the ice and spun three times, keeping my arms tight to my body. As soon as I landed safely, I jabbed my toe pick into the ice again and whirled into a double, repeating the motion once more for the third jump. Beside me Mark landed a few seconds later, making our combination slightly out of unison, but we'd completed it cleanly from what I could tell. I let out a small breath of relief.

With one of the biggest hurdles out of the way, we relaxed more into the choreography, and I soaked in the power of the soaring music. We nailed the triple Salchows and both throw jumps and flew through our hardest lift. Em and Sergei clapped loudly in support as we skated past them, and I felt as if we were flying even faster than usual.

I moved to Mark's side, and he grabbed both my hands for the lasso lift. He swung me up and around to get me over his head, but his right hand slipped, and my balance was gone. All my muscles seized as I felt myself losing control and heading downward.

Mark held onto my left hand with a fierce grip, and I collapsed onto his shoulders, practically choking him with my right arm. I slid off his back, slowly loosening my hold on him, and we glided in a stunned daze for a few moments before reconnecting our steps with the music.

We managed to get through the remaining lifts without another disaster, but all I could think about was how many points we'd lost on the aborted one. It was the kind of mistake that didn't happen often, but when it did, it was a killer.

As soon as the music ended, Mark dropped his head and muttered to himself. I gave him a hug and patted his shoulders while he continued to quietly curse.

"It was a fluke," I said. "There's nothing we could've done."

Sergei and Em told us the same thing when we reached the boards. We sat in the kiss and cry, and I jiggled my knees as we endured the long wait for the score. I wanted so badly to ask Sergei what kind of mistakes Stephanie and Josh had made, but I thought it best not to bring them up at the moment.

The announcer piped up, and I gritted my teeth, bracing myself for the numbers. We'd done everything besides the lasso lift well, so there was hope we'd still be ahead of Stephanie and Josh in the standings.

The score appeared below our faces on the monitor, and my shoulders relaxed. We'd maintained our position in the standings, though by a small margin. Mark and I hugged again, and Em put her arm around me as we walked backstage.

"You really held it together after the lift," she said. "You guys haven't missed one like that in a long time."

"It shocked me for a second, and then I knew I had to get my butt in gear. I didn't want to give you any reason to doubt my focus."

"I could see your determination from the start. I wasn't worried at all."

I slowed and fiddled with the zipper of my jacket. "What um… what happened with Josh and Stephanie?"

Em's mouth turned down. "Josh fell on both jumps."

"Oh." The sinking feeling I'd had earlier returned.

The federation's media coordinator ushered Mark and me to the waiting journalists, and I caught a glimpse of Josh speaking to a newspaper reporter. His expression was still grim. Had he fallen because his mind was on other things? When we'd talked that afternoon, he'd seemed just as determined as I was to overcome the outside distractions.

I didn't see him again until I got on the bus and noticed he and Stephanie sat ten rows apart. Josh was staring out the window, and I hesitated in the aisle, not sure if I should bother him. When I had a bad skate, I preferred to stew alone.

I started to move past his row, but he turned and said, "Hey."

"Hey." I stopped and pointed to the empty seat. "Can I…"

"Yeah. Sure."

I stowed my bag in the row across from us and held my breath as Mark came down the aisle. He gave us a long look but kept walking.

"Rough night," I said.

"Steph thinks I screwed up on purpose to get back at her."

"She can't be serious."

"Oh, she's serious. You know, because I don't have any pride in my skating, and I would throw both of us under the bus for revenge." His voice was laced with anger.

"That's the most ridiculous thing I've ever heard."

He propped his elbow up on the window and pushed his fingers through his hair. "My timing was just off on both jumps. It's frustrating because I'd been so consistent lately."

"Em and Sergei will help you fix it," I said as I touched his thigh.

He covered my hand with his. "What happened on the lift?"

"Our grip just slipped a little and we lost it."

"You skated great otherwise." He rested his head against the seat and turned so he faced me. "You were so damn beautiful out there."

All the frustration had left his eyes, and he looked at me like I was the most gorgeous thing he'd ever seen. He quickened my pulse faster than any workout could.

"I really wanna kiss you," I whispered.

His lips eased into a smile. "I have no objections."

Even though the bus was dark, we were hidden between the seats, and no one sat around us, I felt a little weird about engaging in PDA there. We were still competitors, both coming off less-than-stellar performances.

"After dinner," I said.

He held his chest as if he'd been shot. "Kicking a guy while he's down."

"What's an hour or two when you waited eight years to kiss me the first time?"

"But now that I know how freaking incredible it feels, I want it all day, every day." He leaned closer to me.

I gave his leg a squeeze. "I promise it'll be worth the wait."

"You won't consider the fact I have to endure dinner with Steph and my mom? Don't I deserve something good before the torture?"

"Why don't you have dinner with me and my parents?"

He sat up straighter. "You're sure that's okay?"

"Of course. They want to get to know you better. The only thing is... will your mom be mad if you ditch her?"

He shrugged. "It's not like we have tons to talk about."

"Then we'd love for you to join us."

He smiled and angled toward me, and I placed my finger on his lips. "Later."

****

I popped the key into my door and found Liza sitting on her bed with a room service tray. I rolled my bag next to the TV armoire and pitched my jacket onto my bed.

"Why aren't you having dinner with your mom?" I asked.

Liza poked at her salad. "She was making me crazy."

"Uh-oh."

"She thinks she knows everything I'm feeling because she used to compete like ten million years ago. She doesn't get that I'm not her."

"I'd stay and eat with you, but I have to meet my parents and Josh."

Her eyes lit up. "Aww, he's having dinner with you?"

"It's nice not having to sneak around anymore."

My phone dinged, and I quickly read the text. "My mom said they got a table already, so I'd better go."

"Tell your boyfriend I said hi," Liza said as I opened the door.

I smiled as I always did whenever I thought of Josh as my boyfriend. I started down the hall, and my smile flew away when I saw Mrs. Tucker exiting her room. Making a speedy pivot, I tried to race back to my room, but she called my name. I slowly turned around and approached her.

"Hi," I said.

She was wearing stiletto boots, so she had a big height advantage over me in my fake UGGs. It gave her the opportunity to look down on me literally and figuratively.

"So, you're dating my son," she said.

She sounded as pleased by that as someone talking about

a natural disaster.

"Yes… I am."

"And what do you hope to gain from this?"

I wrinkled my forehead. "What do I hope to *gain*?"

"This is obviously not going to be a long-term relationship, so I'm concerned you're using Josh for your own competitive advantage."

*Didn't I just have this conversation? Oh, yeah, with Mark, who thought Josh was using ME.* We were being smothered with paranoia from all sides.

"I would never take advantage of Josh's feelings for me," I said. "I care about him a great deal."

She tilted her head slightly to the side as if that helped her get a better angle to scrutinize me. "You can't blame me for worrying. Josh is very sensitive, very thoughtful. He doesn't open up to people easily."

"Maybe he doesn't open up to people because his family never made him comfortable with doing so."

Her eyes narrowed in the same way Stephanie's always did when she was pissed. She took a step forward and towered over me even more. *Why did I have to open my big mouth?*

"Who do you think you are? You don't know a damn thing about my relationship with my son."

*I know he feels like you're from two different planets.*

I moved backward to regain my personal space. *Don't you dare say that out loud. You've already dug your grave deep enough.*

"You're right. I… I don't know you. I just know what Josh has… expressed… to me…" My mouth dried up as Cruella stared me down harder.

"I'm sure you think you're an expert because you've known him what, a few months? Well, I can play that game, too. I can tell you what I've learned about you in the few minutes I've spoken to you. You have no manners and no class, and I'll be glad when Josh comes home and leaves you behind where you belong."

She left me standing in the hallway, my heart pounding. I'd had slim hope before of her accepting me, but that hope was now obliterated. Tears misted my vision, and I shook my head and blotted the corners of my eyes with my fingers. I wasn't going to let that woman make me cry. It was what she wanted — to make me feel like I had no place in Josh's life.

I sniffed back the tears and took a deep breath, but I knew the truth. Her words wouldn't have gotten to me if I wasn't already terrified. Terrified that exactly what she wanted was indeed going to happen.

# Chapter Eighteen

"Only three weeks until show time." Em clapped her hands, ending the giggles of the novice skaters on the ice. "Let's get serious."

Josh joined me on the first row of the bleachers and pulled on his skates. "Em's cracking the whip today?"

"The kids are having a little too much fun with the props," I said.

"It's hard to believe Christmas is in a month. It seemed so far away when we started rehearsals."

I stared at the ice, where Em fumbled with two giant candy canes. Christmas was coming too fast, too soon. Once the holidays passed, we'd be staring down the barrel that was nationals.

"I can't wait to give you your Christmas present," Josh said.

I snapped out of my daze. "You have my present already?"

"I don't have it in my possession, but I have it picked out." He grinned like an excited little boy with a secret.

"Can I get a hint? Let's play twenty questions!"

"Nope. You're not getting any hints."

"Not even a tiny little one?"

"My lips are sealed."

"Hmm..." I leaned close to his ear. "I bet I can make those lips do whatever I want later tonight."

His eyes widened. "I need to hear more about these plans."

"We should do something after my shift. It's the first weekend we don't have to lie about where we are."

"Why don't we go to my house? We can listen to music, I can play for you..." He tapped his fingers along my thigh as if it was a piano.

"Won't Stephanie be there?"

"We'll be in my room." He dropped his voice. "With the door locked."

I smiled and lifted one eyebrow. "Trying to lure me into your bedroom. Maybe there is a little bad boy in you."

He gazed at me with the look he always gave me right before he kissed me — the one where his eyes flashed to my mouth then settled deep into mine. My lips parted on instinct, and I took in a small breath.

"Court!" Em called out.

We both jerked our heads toward the ice and fidgeted as though we'd been caught doing something questionable. Em and Sergei didn't have a problem with us dating, but they probably didn't want us being obvious about it at the rink. We'd done a good job since being back from Skate America, so one momentary slip should be excused.

"Can you put these in the storage room for me?" Em passed the candy canes over the boards.

When I returned from storing the props, Mark and Stephanie had arrived with their standard surly faces for rehearsal. We all got on the ice, and Em clicked on the music. After we went through the motions of the opening, we split into pairs, and Josh and I were all smiles. Even after a month of practicing with him, I still tingled every time he took my hand for our duet.

We swept into the waltz, and I marveled again how natural I felt following Josh's lead. He was so light on his feet, and it carried over to me, making me feel like I was breezing over the ice with no effort. As we soared through the spirals, I closed my eyes, focusing solely on the sensation of flying in Josh's arms. After spending almost my entire life on the ice, I hadn't thought it was possible to discover a new spark, but I was living it every time Josh and I skated together.

We came out of the spirals and stroked hand-in-hand to set up for the rotational lift. Mark and Stephanie were a blur as we sped past them. I curled my arm around Josh's neck, pressing myself up as he lifted my outstretched legs, but something felt off. We were going too fast, and I'd shifted my weight back too far. I couldn't stop my momentum, and I fell backward, taking Josh down with me. He grabbed my waist before we slammed into the ice, shielding me with his body from the hard blow.

"Are you okay?" I asked as I rolled off him.

"Yeah, my butt got most of it." He winced when he stood up with me.

I noticed a few spots of red on the ice and looked at his scraped elbow. "You're bleeding."

"What the hell, man?" Mark shouted as he and Stephanie came to a stop in front of us, kicking up a spray of ice. "You trying to kill my partner?"

"It was my fault," I said.

Mark ignored me and got into Josh's face. "If you wanna show off and do a damn lift, you need to keep her friggin safe!"

Josh gave him a cold stare. "Like you did at Skate America?"

I sucked in a breath as Mark's eyes grew darker. *Oh, Josh…*

"Screw you," Mark growled, taking a threatening step toward him. "I've always protected her."

"Stop!" I moved between them and shoved both their puffed-out chests.

Em skated over and added to my blockade between Mark and Josh. "Alright, boys, settle down."

"Yeah, get over yourself, Mark," Stephanie said. "Like you're the perfect partner. You've almost taken me down a couple times."

"That was your fault. You were too busy bitching to pay attention to where you were going."

"For the love of..." Em threw her head back and closed her eyes.

I waited for her to start audibly praying for us to cooperate. Instead she took two deep breaths and opened her eyes.

"Are you guys okay?" she asked Josh and me.

"He needs a Band-Aid," I said.

"There's some in my jacket on the bleachers," she said.

Josh skated toward the boards, and I followed him. We walked gingerly on our blades across the mat, and I watched Josh wipe his arm with a towel and tear open the bandage.

"You didn't have to egg on Mark like that," I said.

"He shouldn't have been in my face."

"I know. He's just... he's just looking out for me."

Josh pressed the bandage down hard on his elbow. "Does he really think I'd try to hurt you?"

I looked over at Mark, who was drifting solo around the ice. "I don't think so. He's being overprotective because of our situation."

"Well, he needs to chill. I would never let anything happen to you."

I smiled a little. "You shed some blood for me today."

He glanced at his arm and then rested his gaze solidly on me. "I'd do a lot more than that to protect you."

We weren't skating together at the moment, but I got the same tingly feeling I'd had on the ice. And all the responses I wanted to give him would have to wait until later.

When we were happily alone.

****

There wasn't an empty seat at the bar, and I'd been running from end to end all night. It seemed every senior citizen on the Cape had come to hear Barry play the piano. Josh was sandwiched between Mrs. Cassar and grumpy Mr. Mayer, and I'd barely had a chance to talk to him since we'd eaten together before my shift.

"Dear, my dinner should be ready by now," Mrs. Cassar said.

"I just checked with the kitchen and they said a few more minutes. They're slammed, too."

"Give my girlfriend a break." Josh smiled at me. "She's working as hard as she can."

"Girlfriend?" Mrs. Cassar looked from Josh to me and back again. "When did this happen?"

"About a month ago, but no one knew about it until last week," I said as I topped off Mr. Mayer's water.

"Well, it's about time. I was tired of watching you two make googly eyes at each other."

Josh and I both dissolved into laughter. One of my regulars at the opposite end of the bar signaled for my attention, so I composed myself and went to serve the elderly man. I headed to the kitchen next and returned with Mrs. Cassar's grilled salmon.

"Now that you're a couple, I expect this Christmas show number to be dripping with romance," she said.

I started laughing again. "That's our goal."

"What do your costumes look like?" she asked as she cut into her fish. "I need to visualize this."

"I'm in all black with a red tie," Josh said.

"And I'm wearing a red dress I used for one of my programs last year," I said.

Mrs. Cassar set down her utensils. "You can't wear an old dress for this. You need something special for this special number."

"I'd love to have something new, but costumes are really expensive."

"How expensive?"

"Like a couple thousand dollars."

She took her purse from the back of her barstool and pulled out her checkbook. "Would three thousand be enough?"

I gaped at her. "Mrs. Cassar, you can't... I can't take your money."

"I want you to have a beautiful new dress to wear when you skate with Joshua." She clicked her ink pen and held it above the paper. "So three thousand?"

"You're so generous, but I couldn't. It's too much—"

"Dear, I have more money than time left to spend it. I'll write the check for three grand, and if you have money left over, you and Joshua can use it to do something fun."

She gave me the check, and I pressed my hand to my forehead. "I don't know what to say. Thank you so much."

"You're very welcome."

"I hope my seamstress has enough time to make it," I said as I stared at the number of zeroes on the paper. "The show's in three weeks."

She sipped her merlot. "If she needs more money to put a rush on it, just let me know."

Josh wore the same wide-eyed expression I had. "This is really awesome of you, Mrs. Cassar."

"Thank you again," I said. "I'm gonna put this somewhere safe."

I hurried to the kitchen and stored the check in my wallet.

Em was going to be just as shocked as I was when I showed it to her. She was aware I'd wished for a new dress since Stephanie was having one made. Who knew I had a fairy godmother? I couldn't imagine writing a three-thousand-dollar check like it was spare change.

For the rest of the night I made sure I took care of all Mrs. Cassar's needs before she even voiced them. As she readied to leave, I thanked her profusely until she told me to stop.

"I don't want to hear any more about it," she said. "Just get that dress made — something that will make Joshua want to rip it off you."

My cheeks flamed as did Josh's. He dipped his head and chuckled quietly.

"It's going to be a family show," I said between laughs.

"You can be classy and sexy at the same time." She slipped one arm into her fur coat, and Josh helped her with the other one. "Tell that to your seamstress. Classy and sexy."

I nodded obediently. "Got it."

After she left, I looked at Josh and shook my head in disbelief. "That was insane."

"I knew she was excited about us skating together, but that took it to a whole new level," he said.

"If you were my full-time partner, she might've bankrolled *all* my expenses." I laughed.

I went back to work, and Josh watched the Bruins game on the TV behind the bar while I prepared for closing. He also waited for me to change out of my uniform and freshen up so I didn't reek of food.

I drove behind Josh to his house and met him at the front door, hoping Stephanie wouldn't be in the living room to greet us with a scowl. I hadn't spoken to her since she'd outed us in Lake Placid. Knowing she'd seen our texts made me feel like she'd read my diary, and I hated her having any kind of power over me.

I entered the house tentatively at Josh's side, and my

shoulders relaxed when I saw the quiet living room. From the left end of the house I heard a shower running.

"Do you want something to eat? Drink?" Josh asked.

"I'll take some water."

He poured a couple of glasses, and we retreated to his room on the opposite side of the house from Stephanie's. It was just as clean as it had been the last time I'd been there except his overflowing suitcase sat beside the closet.

"I haven't fully unpacked from last week either," I said.

"I was going to shove it in the closet, but it wouldn't fit." He laughed as he shut the door and turned the center of the knob.

"You weren't kidding about locking the door," I said.

"I don't trust Steph not to barge in here."

"I don't trust her regarding *anything*."

I looked around, and besides the rolling chair under the keyboard, there was nowhere to sit except the bed, so I slipped off my ballet flats and sat cross-legged on the gray comforter. Josh stared at me as I took a long drink of water.

"What?" I touched my hair. Had I missed brushing a spot after I'd taken it down at the restaurant?

"Nothing. I just… I like seeing you here." His eyes smiled first, then his mouth.

I returned his smile with an even bigger one. "I like being here."

He watched me a few seconds longer before turning to the keyboard. "Would you rather live entertainment or—" He pointed to the shelves of CDs. "Recorded music?"

"Mm… surprise me with a CD."

While he scanned the cases, I emptied my glass and went to the kitchen for a refill. I was headed back through the living room when Stephanie met me halfway. Her hair was damp, and she had on white silky pajamas.

"When I blew the whistle on you, I didn't think about the fact that you'd be hanging around here now." She gave me the scowl I'd expected.

I contemplated ignoring her as I'd been doing, but I couldn't stop the anger from spilling out. "Did you even apologize to Josh for invading his privacy? I know you could care less about hurting me, but that was an awful thing you did to him."

"He never apologized for lying to me. And I didn't exactly enjoy reading your sickening texts."

I slowly shook my head. "You have no clue what it's like to have strong feelings for someone."

"You're kidding yourself if you think you and Josh are going to last. He's had this fantasy of you for years... I have no idea why..."

*How does she know that? Oh, yeah, our texts. Damn her.*

She folded her arms. "But now that he has you, he's going to realize you don't live up to any fantasy. It's only a matter of time."

The coldness in her eyes mimicked that of her mother's, and I wanted nothing but to escape from her, too. I barged past her and returned to the safe haven of Josh's room, locking the door behind me. The mellow music of Keane came from Josh's laptop — exactly what I needed to calm me after my encounter with Stephanie.

"You okay?" Josh paused as he rearranged CDs on the shelf.

"Yeah, I ran into Stephanie."

His face hardened. "What did she—"

"It's okay. I don't want to taint our evening by talking about her, so I'm pretending it never happened. This is our happy place," I said as I climbed onto the bed.

Josh fought to contain his grin, and I realized where I'd sat as I'd made my declaration.

"I meant... I meant this room is our happy place, not necessarily the..." I stammered and started laughing. "You know what I was trying to say."

Josh was now grinning ear-to-ear. "Totally."

He filed away the CD cases, and I picked up his sketch book from the nightstand and flipped to the last page with markings. I smiled as I saw he'd designed a program to the *Pride and Prejudice* song he'd played for me on the Vineyard. The pattern showed multiple lifts, some with names I didn't recognize.

Josh sat beside me, and I ran my finger over the drawing. "Did you make up some of these lifts?"

"I'm not sure if they'd actually work since I haven't tried them."

"Still, it's pretty cool you created them from scratch." I carefully turned the pages and noted the variety of music he'd used for programs — from classical to alternative rock. "If you could do anything other than be a lawyer, would this be your dream job?"

He rested his elbow on his bent knee and raked his fingers through his hair. "It doesn't really matter…"

"Just humor me and pretend you don't have to go to law school."

He chewed his lip. "Yeah, definitely. I'd love to be a choreographer. Maybe teach dance or piano on the side."

"Have you thought about telling your dad that being a lawyer isn't your dream?"

His eyes took on a faraway look. "My grandfather started the firm, and my dad knew from the time he was born that he'd take over one day. He's had that same expectation for me all my life."

"But it's not what you're passionate about."

"I wish it was that simple," he said, messing his hair again.

I shifted the book on my lap so I could turn toward him. "I know you don't want to disappoint your dad, but maybe if you talked to him, he'd understand your heart isn't in this."

"I don't think he'd understand me wanting to chase a

pipe dream." He stared down at the sketches.

"Why does it have to be a pipe dream?"

"I have no significant experience. It's not something I could jump right into and make a living."

"Everyone has to start somewhere. Em and Sergei have a lot of connections and could help you."

He looked up at me, and I didn't see the hope I longed to find in his eyes. I saw thick clouds of doubt.

"It would still be a long shot, and in my dad's opinion, not an acceptable alternative to carrying on the family business."

He lowered his head, and I could sense the weight he felt. The heavy expectations. I put my glass on the nightstand and paged silently through the book. I'd been entertaining the idea that Josh could ditch law school and stay in the Boston area, but that's all it would ever be — a crazy idea. I totally got that he didn't want to let down his father. I felt the same about getting into Boston College. Even though that *was* my dream, it was also very much my dad's.

I slowly closed the book and set it aside. "I just wish you could have the opportunity to do more with all your talent and creativity."

"Because I'm a 'creative genius?'" he joked.

"You are." I looked firmly into his eyes. "It's the only thing Stephanie's ever said that I agree with."

He turned and braced his arm on the mattress so he faced me. "I owe a lot of that creativity to you."

"Me?"

"You inspire me." He brushed his knuckles down my cheek. "More than anything else in the world."

My pulse quickened and I leaned into him, so close our breath mixed. "How do I inspire you?"

His fingertips trailed lightly along my jaw, and his thumb teased my bottom lip. He was inspiring *me* to do lots of creative things, all involving his beautiful body.

"I think about you… how you would look on the ice." He combed his fingers through my long curls. "Your hair is down just like this. It falls around my face when I hold you close."

His hand ran the silky length of my hair and caressed the sleeve of my sweater. "Your arms are bare… and you shiver when I touch your skin."

I shivered then without him having any contact with my skin.

"And when I hold you and we move across the ice, I feel the curve of your body against mine…"

He cupped my hip, and his long, thick eyelashes hooded his eyes. I pulled his head down to mine, and our lips crashed together. We kissed without taking a breath, like it was the first time and the last time. He angled me back onto the bed, his knee between my legs, and I pressed up against him, igniting the heat between our jeans.

Our kiss slowed and deepened, and my hands roamed across his back, exploring all the hard ridges. When he stroked my bottom lip softly between his teeth, I moaned and clenched his T-shirt in my fists. He slowly lifted his head and held me still with his eyes. They were filled with so much affection and wonder and desire.

"I love the way you look at me," I said.

He swept a strand of hair from my cheek. "Sometimes I can't believe I'm finally with you."

My heart raced as did my mind. What if there was some truth to what Stephanie had said? Were Josh's feelings for me truly real or was he caught up in the fantasy he'd had for so long? What I felt for him was most definitely real. More real than anything I'd ever known.

His mouth covered mine, gently coaxing it open, and I drew him further inside, needing to drown my doubt. I let him kiss me and touch me until all thoughts drifted away, and only the warmth of his lips and his hands remained.

# Chapter Nineteen

Outside my changing stall, the loud chatter of skaters getting ready for the Christmas show echoed off the tile walls of the rink bathroom. I picked up my duffel and pushed aside the curtain, and Liza spun around from primping in the mirror.

"Oh my God. Josh is going to *pass out* when he sees you in that dress," she said.

I smoothed the silky red fabric and stepped up to the long mirror to make sure I was tucked in everywhere. The neckline of the dress dipped lower than that on any of my competition dresses. Skinny straps circled my shoulders and crisscrossed over my back, where the material also plunged deeper than usual. This was the sexiest costume I'd ever worn. And damn if I didn't feel incredible in it.

"Let's hope none of the stones fall off while I'm skating. It was just finished yesterday." I fluffed my hair over my shoulders.

"Maybe Stephanie will trip on one of them and fall flat on her face." Liza snickered.

I laughed as I slipped into my Team USA jacket. "As

much as I would enjoy that, I want this to go well for Em. She's put up with so much crap to get this show done."

We squeezed past the little girls spraying each other's hair and went into the locker room to put on our skates. When we'd laced them up and attached our guards, we click-clacked out to the noisy rink. A large crowd packed the bleachers and filled the "standing room" areas around the boards. After a quick scan, I found my parents and Mrs. Cassar a few rows in front of them.

Josh paced next to the lobby doors, stretching his long limbs, and he stopped and smiled when he saw me. "Are you going to wait until right before we skate to show me your dress?"

"Maybe," I said coyly.

"You'd better not. He's going to need a few minutes to recover." Liza giggled and scurried over to a group of the junior girls.

"How about a little peek?" Josh moved closer and tugged on my zipper.

I laughed and closed my hand around his. "I think Mrs. Cassar should see it first since she paid for it. I was going to go tell her hello."

He grabbed my waist before I could get past him. "I think she'd be fine with letting me have the first look."

"Hi, Honey!" Mom waved as she jogged over.

We split apart, and Mom embraced Josh, who smiled at me over her shoulder.

"He gets a hug first?" I said.

"Well, his parents aren't here to give him one," she said as she put her arms around me.

*Oh, Mom. Do you really think his prissy mother would be showering him with affection if she was here?*

"I want to meet Mrs. Cassar and thank her." Mom looked toward the bleachers.

"Two minutes!" Em shouted as she worked her way

through the crowd of skaters fidgeting and buzzing with energy.

"I'll introduce you after the show," I said.

"Okay." She kissed my cheek. "Skate great. You too, Josh!"

The lights dimmed, and Em welcomed everyone to the show before herding the youngest kids to the ice for the opening number. As we watched them skate in circles to "Rudolph the Red-Nosed Reindeer," Josh played with the collar of my jacket, attempting to peek inside. I laughed and swatted his hand.

"Very soon," I promised and went to stand next to Mark, who didn't look like he was having nearly as much fun.

"Last Christmas show ever," I said.

"You remember our first one?" he asked as he straightened his red tie.

"When we skated into the Christmas tree? Kinda hard to forget."

One corner of his mouth twitched upward. "They never let us use props again."

"Well... Stephanie is kind of a prop. Cold and unfeeling."

He choked on a laugh. "I would've much preferred to skate with a plastic candy cane."

Sergei came over with a clipboard in hand and a pen shoved behind his ear. "You guys ready?"

Mark saluted and inched toward the boards, and I hung back to wait for Josh. Stephanie was saying something to him, but he left her in mid-sentence when he saw me unzip my jacket. He stood in front of me and let out a slow puff of air as I revealed the dress.

"Remind me to thank Mrs. Cassar a million more times," he said.

I grinned and tossed the jacket under the stereo. "Are you feeling inspired?"

His eyes swept over me, lingering on my deep neckline.

"I'm feeling a lot of things."

I slowly turned to face the ice, wishing I could see his appreciation of the back of the dress. I soon felt it as he brushed my hair from my shoulder, his fingertips tickling my skin. I shivered, and he curled his arm around my waist, warming me with his body.

"You're up!" Em beckoned the four of us forward.

Our rink manager introduced us, and we formed our opening square, each one of us under a spotlight. Nat King Cole began to croon "The Christmas Song," and my heart beat faster every second I came closer to holding Josh's hand. When he led me into our waltz, I tried to memorize everything about the moment — the feel of Josh's palm pressed to my lower back, the bright light in his blue eyes, the cool breeze whispering between us.

I continued to soak in all the incredible sensations, especially the exhilaration of spinning in Josh's strong arms as we did our lift perfectly. Our faces were just centimeters apart, our lips so teasingly close to a kiss. The magnetic connection between us hummed stronger than ever.

There was something about skating with Josh that made me feel like anything was possible. He'd opened a bud of freedom in me, and it had blossomed into a new appreciation for the sport I'd loved for so long. The simplest push of our blades across the ice gave me an exciting rush.

The program flew by too quickly, and I reluctantly let go of Josh's hand when the music slowed to its end. This would be the last time we'd skate together until who knew when. We could skate for fun after our training sessions, but Em and Sergei wouldn't want us messing around on the ice with nationals coming up. My heart grew heavy knowing I wouldn't have our practices to look forward to anymore.

I glanced over at Mark and Stephanie, and they wore the smiles Em had forced upon them, threatening extra laps around the rink. The audience applauded loudly, accentuated by the squeals and bouncing of Quinn and Alex in the first row. I waved to them, and their screams rose to an even higher decibel. After we bowed and exited the ice, I hurried to change into an old blue costume for my "Blue Christmas" number with Mark.

He and I took the ice after Liza's solo, and the sadness I'd felt earlier resurfaced as nine years of memories filled my thoughts. I saw all our Christmas show programs in a mental slide show — from our cheesy numbers as gawky teens to our sophisticated ones as adults. I smiled through the program, keeping my emotions in check, but when I hugged Mark at the end, a few tears escaped.

Watching the rest of the show and all the cute kids while singing along to the Christmas tunes with Josh brought me out of my funk. After the finale, we headed straight for Mrs. Cassar, anxious to hear her opinion on our long-awaited performance.

"Dear, that dress was *spectacular*." She clutched my arm with her bony fingers. "And the way Joshua was looking at you, I think he agrees."

"I most certainly do," Josh said.

"You need to wear it again later when you're alone," she whispered but loud enough for Josh to hear. I knew he'd heard it because he pulled at the collar of his dress shirt, where his neck had turned a deep shade of pink.

"What did you think of the skating?" I asked, trying to steer Mrs. Cassar's mind out of the gutter.

"It was marvelous. I could *feel* how much you loved skating together. You were both very good with your other partners, but together you were absolutely glowing."

"Yes, you were." Mom embraced me from behind. "You were beautiful."

I introduced Mrs. Cassar to Mom and Dad, and she talked and talked until she looked at her diamond-studded watch and said it was time for her nightcap. Once she left,

Mom and Dad put on their coats to leave, too, but then they both hesitated and exchanged a nervous look.

Mom opened her purse and pulled out a white envelope. "This came in the mail today."

The maroon and gold lettering immediately caught my eye, and I pressed the envelope tightly between my fingers. Wouldn't a college acceptance letter come in a thick packet?

"It's thin," I said warily.

Josh put his hand on my back. "That doesn't mean it's bad news."

"Open it," Mom prodded.

Dad watched me with a cautious smile, and I thought about all the times we'd walked through Boston College's campus. Dad telling stories while I imagined myself as a popular co-ed, kicking butt on both the academic and social sides. Now it had all come down to a single piece of paper.

My hand shook as I tore open the envelope and removed the letter. I unfolded it and hoped to see the word "Congratulations" jump out on the page. It didn't, so I quickly started reading.

*Blah, blah, blah… I regret to inform you —*

My breath stuck in my throat.

I read each painful word that followed, confirming my fear about the thin envelope.

Boston College had rejected me.

"What does it say?" Mom asked.

I handed her the letter and slowly shook my head.

"Oh." Her face sagged.

Dad leaned forward to read. "Did they defer your decision until the regular period in the spring?"

My head shook faster. I didn't trust my voice to come out without trembling. Josh hugged me against him and touched his lips to my hair.

"Honey, I'm so sorry." Mom rubbed my arm.

Dad continued to stare at the letter as if the decision

would change. When he didn't say anything, Mom started rambling about how there were plenty of other great schools. I zoned out somewhere between UMass and Northeastern. All I knew was THE school I'd dreamt about wasn't on the list.

Dad slid the paper into the envelope. "She's right. You have lots of other options."

He was trying to sound positive, but I could hear the disappointment dragging down his voice. I swallowed hard, worsening the ache in my throat.

"Can we talk about those later?" I asked.

"Of course," Mom said. "I hate to leave you right now, though."

"It's okay. I'm okay."

I wasn't, but seeing their sad, disappointed faces wouldn't make me feel any better.

Mom gave me her I-just-want-to-take-care-of-you smile, and Josh stepped back so she could wrap me in a hug. Dad followed, and I knew what I wanted to say but couldn't because I would completely fall apart.

*I'm sorry, Dad.*

I barely took a breath, afraid if I did a flood of tears would be released. As soon as my parents walked away, I turned to Josh.

"Can we get out of here?"

He wasted no time getting his bag and mine from the locker room, and we made a brisk exit so none of our training mates could stop us to chat. The blast of frigid night air was a relief. I'd felt like I was smothering inside the rink with all the people around us and all my emotions forcibly contained.

"Do you want to go to my house?" Josh asked as we pulled out of the parking lot.

I was most definitely not in the mood for any run-ins with Stephanie.

"I think I'd rather go home."

We rode in silence, but the buzz in my head was more

than loud. There were two things I hadn't allowed myself to imagine — not getting into BC and not making the Olympic team. Now everything in my future felt precariously uncertain.

"I always thought I might get deferred to the regular decision period," I said. "But I never thought I would get outright rejected."

We stopped at a red light, and Josh took his hand off the gear shift and placed it on my leg. Usually his touch made me feel warm and safe, but the amount of frustration bubbling inside me kept all my nerves on edge.

"Why didn't I take the SAT again?" I threw my head back hard against the seat. "I know that must've been what hurt me the most."

The light turned green, but Josh had his attention on me, squeezing my leg. A horn honked behind us, and he finally shifted the car into drive.

"Do you have any thoughts about where you might apply now?" he asked.

"Not really. I've never looked at any other schools."

He glanced at me as he curved past a half-frozen pond. "I know you said it might be too expensive, but I'll put in another plug for UCLA."

I shook my head. "My parents can't swing that. They only have so much in my college fund."

"Maybe we can look at the numbers. It might be possible—"

"I can't afford to go to school and live in California," I said with a hard bite. "If you want me close to you, why don't you stay here?"

"You know I can't. I have to start school in the fall."

"But you don't even wanna go!" I tossed up my hands.

He stared straight ahead, his grip tight around the steering wheel. As if I didn't feel bad enough, I'd made myself feel worse by yelling at him. I knew the tough situation he was in, how pressured he felt to follow in his grandfather's and his father's footsteps.

"I'm sorry," I said in a much calmer tone. "It's just... it doesn't seem fair that you have a spot waiting for you that you don't even want, while I can't get the spot I've wanted my whole life."

He slowed the car to a stop in front of Em and Sergei's house and shut off the engine. "I wish I could reverse it so I was the one with the rejection letter and you'd gotten into BC."

"You probably aced the LSAT to get into UCLA."

He fiddled with the key fob hanging from the ignition. "Before I took it I was actually planning to intentionally bomb it so I wouldn't get accepted."

I unbuckled my seat belt and turned fully toward him. "You were really going to do that?"

"For a long time I seriously thought about it. But I couldn't do it. I couldn't face disappointing my dad that much."

"Like I did mine." I lowered my head.

He tipped up my chin. "He's going to support you wherever you decide to go. He just wants you to be happy."

"I know he'll support me, but he had his heart set on this." My voice wavered, and I strained to speak. "God, I just hate this feeling of letting him down."

Josh drew me into his arms and held me as I quietly wept. With tears trickling down my cheeks, I lifted my head from his shoulder and found his lips. I needed to feel something good, something to make me forget the bad.

We were lost in a long, slow kiss when the headlights of Sergei's SUV flooded the car. He turned into the garage, and I waited until everyone had been inside a few minutes before I followed. I preferred to slip upstairs to the quiet of my room if possible.

By the time I took a long shower and changed, the twins

were tucked away in their beds and Liza's door was closed. I wanted to listen to my iPod to help lull me to sleep, but I'd left it downstairs, so I padded down to the living room. Em was in the kitchen, poking through the box of teas, and she looked up when she heard me.

"Hey," she said with a slight tilt to her head and a concerned look in her eyes. "Are you okay?"

I stopped before I reached the iPod. "How did you…"

"I ran into your mom and dad on their way out." She put down the box and hugged me. "I'm so sorry."

I'd finally gotten rid of the ache in my throat, and I felt it creeping back in again. I forced myself to think of happy things like the pure joy of skating with Josh earlier.

"Do you want some tea?" she asked. "I'm trying to find the chamomile."

"That sounds like exactly what I need."

She shuffled through a few packets in the box and exclaimed, "Aha!" when she landed on the two she needed. While she heated matching mugs of water in the microwave, I sat at the farmhouse-style table in the breakfast nook. She joined me a minute later with the tea bags steeping in the mugs.

"I know you haven't had much time to process everything yet, but if you want to stay here and reapply to BC next year, you're more than welcome," she said.

I hadn't even thought of reapplying. I'd need to bring up my SAT score to have any hope of being accepted, and standardized tests had never been one of my strengths. I could be setting myself up for another round of rejection.

"That's so incredibly nice of you, Em, but I couldn't keep imposing on you. You need to have your privacy with your family back again."

"You *are* family, and I've never thought of you being here as an invasion of our privacy. I'm going to miss you so much when you leave! And the twins don't remember a time when you didn't live here. They're going to have major separation issues."

I smiled a little and tugged on the string of my tea bag. "I'm gonna miss all of you, too."

She reached across the table and patted my hand. "Keep it open as an option. We'd love to have you for as long as you want to stay."

"Thanks. It's good to know I have at least one option."

"Are you going to apply to other schools for next year?"

"I'm not sure." I blew lightly on the steam rising from my mug. "Most of their deadlines are probably January fifteenth, which doesn't give me much time, plus there's something else pretty important I need to focus on next month."

"Maybe it would better to wait and apply for the spring semester next year. I don't want you to have any extra stress now."

I set down the mug and pressed my head between my hands. "I didn't plan this very well, did I? What was I thinking, only applying to one school?"

"You were following your dream. There's nothing wrong with that."

"I could've followed it more sensibly."

She put her mug down on the table, too, and gave me one of her determined coach looks. "It won't do any good to second-guess yourself. All you can do is move forward and put all your energy these next few weeks into skating your best. That's something that's still totally in your control."

I nodded, realizing how right she was. I'd already lost one of my two life-long dreams. I couldn't lose the other one.

# Chapter Twenty

"Last run-through of the decade!" Sergei exclaimed as he queued up our short program music.

Mark and I dodged Stephanie and Josh's star lift and positioned ourselves at center ice. We would celebrate the end of the decade later at Chris and Aubrey's wedding, but first we had to finish off our final practice of 2009.

I closed my eyes to get into tango mode, but they popped open when Stephanie shrieked, "Daddy!"

She raced across the ice and threw her arms around Mr. Tucker from behind the boards. Josh took a much slower route and exchanged a much less enthusiastic hug with his father. I hadn't expected to see either of Josh's parents at the rink even though they were in town for Stephanie's twenty-first birthday. He'd said his dad would probably work all day, and his mom would be prepping for the birthday party that night. A bunch of Stephanie's friends from L.A. had flown in for the event at the swanky Chatham Bars Inn.

Mr. Tucker looked about the same as he did in the photos online except for a touch more gray peppering his dark wavy hair. He stood the same height as Josh, which meant he was taller since Josh was wearing skates. His strong posture gave off an air of confidence.

"Court." Mark pulled on my hand.

"Oh... sorry." I turned away from the boards and got into tango hold with him.

The music kicked on, and we powered through the opening steps like we'd done five thousand times before. When we swept past Mr. Tucker, I felt his eyes following us, studying every move. We conquered the triple twist, but during the straight-line footwork I grew tighter with each step. As we set up for the side-by-side jumps, I peeked sideways and saw Stephanie yammering away to her dad, but all his attention was on me. My muscles tightened even more, and as soon as I went up into the air I knew I wasn't coming down cleanly. I barely completed three rotations, and I hit the ice hard with my hip.

I scrambled to my feet and looked up right at Stephanie smugly smiling. I zoomed away from her and caught up to Mark for the throw triple flip, but everything felt rushed. My legs still hadn't reconnected with my brain. I stumbled on the landing of the throw, pitching so far forward I had to brace my palm on the ice to stay upright.

Mark gripped my hand extra hard as we stroked into our side-by-side spins, and I thought I heard him mutter, "Come on." Not in an encouraging way but in an aggravated way.

I pulled myself together for the rest of the program, but Mark still frowned at me as we set off around the rink to cool down.

"Could you be any more distracted?" he said.

"Sorry. There was a lot of commotion going on."

"You wouldn't have cared less what was going on if it didn't involve Josh."

Drops of sweat snaked down my hairline, and I swiped at my forehead with the back of my hand. I shouldn't have let the presence of Josh's dad throw me off, but both his parents seemed to have some mysterious power over me. One look was all it took to paralyze me.

While Mark and I circled the rink, Stephanie and Josh performed a perfect run-through of their short. I didn't stick around to see Mr. Tucker's reaction, but I heard his applause as I made my way to the locker room. It was packed with skaters discussing their New Year's Eve plans. Once I'd switched my skates to sneakers, I escaped to the rink manager's office to listen to a voicemail from Mom.

"Hey, Honey. We might be out at dinner when you get here. I talked Dad into going to the North End, but of course he wants to go early to beat the crowds. I should still be up when you get back from the wedding, though. Have fun, and try not to miss Josh too much."

I disconnected the call and sat on the edge of the cluttered desk. Josh and I had disagreed on whether he should attend the wedding in Boston or Stephanie's party on the Cape. With the long drive between the two, he couldn't do both. He wanted to be my date at the wedding, but I'd insisted he go to the party. I didn't want him snubbing his family because of me. Why add another reason for them to despise me?

I was about to leave the office when Josh and his dad entered the lobby outside. They didn't see me, and neither of them looked happy, so I crept back inside the doorway. It didn't seem like the best time to introduce myself.

"You're not skipping the party tonight," Mr. Tucker said.

"Steph will have all her friends there. She doesn't need me," Josh said.

*What are you doing? I thought we'd agreed I'd go to the wedding alone.*

"Being with your family is important. Going with this girl to the wedding of people you barely know isn't."

"Courtney." Josh's voice was so soft I had to strain to hear. "Her name is Courtney."

"I'm sure she's a nice girl, but she's not more important than your family."

"She's very important."

I rested my head against the cinder block wall and shut my eyes. I could picture the confrontation between Josh and his dad from the shortness in their tones. I imagined Mr. Tucker's imposing figure in his long black coat and Josh's blue eyes flashing with irritation.

"It'll be good for you to be away from her tonight. You need to start putting some distance between you. This relationship can't continue once you're in school. You won't have time for it."

"I'll make time."

"You need to be focused on school, not worrying about a girl on the other side of the country. The sooner you end this, the better."

"I don't want to end it." Josh's soft voice grew harder every time he spoke.

"Trust me on this. You're going to be apart for *years*. I have a lot more life experience than you, and situations like yours have a slim chance of surviving."

Josh was either quiet or speaking so low I couldn't hear. He might've been thinking about the odds of us surviving. I'd been thinking about it so much lately that I'd even done an internet search for "percentage of long-distance relationships that fail." The surveys hadn't seemed very reliable.

I heard Josh talking, and I angled my ear closer to the doorway.

"...know what we're doing."

The swinging door from the lobby to the rink squeaked, so I guessed Josh had walked out on his dad. I waited in the office and didn't go back into the rink until I was sure Mr. Tucker was no longer in the lobby.

Josh came out of the locker room, shrugging on his jacket, and he marched straight toward me. "What time should we leave for Boston?"

I cocked my head to one side. "We talked about this. You have to stay here."

"I don't want to stay here. I want to be with *you*."

"I want to be with you, too, but you rarely see your parents."

"I can see them when I move home. Tonight should be our night." He took one of my hands between both of his. "I want to dance with you and laugh with you and celebrate what's been the best year of my life. And I want to kiss you like a boss at midnight."

I couldn't help but smile. Arguing with him was nearly impossible with his sparkling eyes promising me so much, but I couldn't forget what Mr. Tucker had said. He'd actually made a valid point. I had to start getting used to Josh not being at my side.

"Please just do this for me," I said. "It's the right thing—"

"Do I get an introduction?" Mr. Tucker asked behind me.

I slowly turned and slipped my hand from Josh's. He hesitated and then said, "Court, this is my dad."

"Hi, Mr. Tucker." I stuck out my hand and he shook it, unlike his wife had done.

"It's nice to meet you, Courtney."

He examined me just as closely as Mrs. Tucker had, but I didn't see the same repulsion in his eyes. Perhaps he didn't hate *me* personally as Mrs. Tucker did. He just hated the idea of Josh dating *anyone*.

"I was um… I was getting ready to tell Josh that I'm going to miss him tonight, but I hope he has a great time at the party," I said.

Josh shot me a look that said, *You're selling me out?*

"The Chatham Bars Inn is beautiful," I rambled. "You picked the perfect place for the occasion."

"I'm sorry you can't join us," Mr. Tucker said.

*Right. Because you weren't just telling Josh to dump me*

*ASAP*. But I didn't expect a Hollywood lawyer to be short on bullshit skills.

"I should get going." I looked up at Josh. "I have to pick up my check at the restaurant."

"I hear you're a bartender there," Mr. Tucker said.

"Yes. Did you know Josh plays the piano there?"

Mr. Tucker angled his chin slightly upward. "No, I didn't. It's good you're staying sharp. You can always entertain clients at parties."

Irritation itched my tongue. Of course Mr. Tucker would bring the focus back to Josh's future as a lawyer. Did he even appreciate how gifted his son was?

"He has enough talent to *be* one of those clients," I said.

Josh fidgeted next to me, and Mr. Tucker treated me to a half-annoyed, half-amused smirk. There I went again — jamming my foot firmly into my mouth.

"I'm sure he could be, but that's never been his path," Mr. Tucker said.

"Because you don't want it to be," I said.

My foot was all the way down my throat now.

"Josh understands the importance of our family business, his legacy. Perhaps he hasn't explained it well enough."

I took a deep inhale before I blurted out anything more inflammatory.

Josh slipped his arm around my waist. "Court needs to go, so I'm going to walk her out."

He nudged me toward the locker room, and I threw a token "Happy New Year" to Mr. Tucker over my shoulder. I quickly grabbed my bag and my jacket, and neither Josh nor I said anything until we reached the snow-covered parking lot.

"You shouldn't have brought all that up," Josh said. "It's between me and my dad."

It was the first time he'd sounded annoyed with me, and it caught me a bit off guard. "I'm sorry. I just... I thought an outside voice might make him think."

Josh leaned against my car and shoved his hands in his jacket pockets. He stayed quiet, toeing the slush on the pavement with his sneaker.

"Have you ever felt like you were at the bottom of a huge hole?" he finally said. "In so deep that there's no way out?"

I touched his face with my gloved hands. "You're not stuck. You can get out."

"What if I'm not sure I want to? I've known all my life what my future is, and in many ways it's frustrating, but it's also... it's also safe. I know exactly what to expect."

"You have to decide if safe will make you happy." My breath puffed in the air as I spoke.

He pulled me closer. "You make me happy."

I locked my gaze on him and held it steady. "Then don't leave me."

We stood in silence, speaking only with our eyes. The conflict in his slowly softened, replaced by brightness.

"Come with me to L.A.," he said "I can help you with the money—"

I broke away from him. "No way. I would never take your money."

"It can be a loan. I have a trust fund and—"

"No. Absolutely not."

"You let Mrs. Cassar pay for your dress."

"Only because she wouldn't give in. That was just a one-time very generous gift. I'm not going to mooch off my rich boyfriend so I can live in California."

How could he even suggest such a thing? I would never want to feel dependent on him in that way. My parents would be appalled, and if his parents found out, they'd have me labeled as a gold digger faster than a jet could take me to L.A.

"It wouldn't be like that." He reached out to me, but I unlocked the car and opened the door.

"Don't leave mad." He boxed me inside the door. "I don't want the last time I see you this year to be a fight."

"You should've thought of that before you offered to play *Pretty Woman* with me."

"That's not what was I doing. You're blowing this out of proportion."

"You're throwing around trust funds. That sounds pretty serious."

I ducked into the driver's seat, and he held onto the door so I couldn't close it. "Come on, Court. Don't go like this."

"Please let go." I jerked the handle.

He watched me with pleading eyes before slowly stepping away from the car. I drove out of the lot and turned up the radio to beyond ear-splitting level.

I was upset he thought I'd even consider taking his money, but it was more than that. It was the realization that he didn't want to give up his safe future even when he had the ability to go anywhere and do anything. Even when it could mean the end of us.

****

All around me there was merriment. People dancing. People drinking. People prematurely blowing on the noisemakers we were supposed to save for midnight. The Wharf Room at the Boston Harbor Hotel had been transformed into party central with Aubrey and Chris at the middle of it, leading the dancing. But nothing was holding my attention as much as my phone. I'd reread the texts a hundred times since I'd received them hours ago, debating how and when I wanted to reply.

Josh: *I'm so sorry. I didn't mean to insult you. That's the last thing I ever wanted.*

Josh: *All I was thinking about was finding a way for you to come home with me.*

I put the phone on the small round table where I sat. I was the only current occupant since Mark and his girlfriend were dancing, and Liza was helping Em chase down the little bride and groom, Quinn and Alex. Seeing them in their miniature wedding dress and tuxedo had been one of the highlights of the evening.

I toyed with the pendant around my neck and thought about when Josh had given me the tiny ruby slippers on Christmas. He'd been so excited watching me open the box, and when he'd put the necklace on me, the tickle of his fingertips had made all the hairs on my body stand up.

My hand closed around the pendant, and I squeezed it in my fist. If only it had magical powers like its larger version in the movie. In my dream world I'd be able to touch the slippers and transport myself across the country. Then Josh and I could see each other any time we wanted.

I missed him so much, and we hadn't even been apart a whole day. I'd become too accustomed to seeing him every night. Was this how I would feel all the time once we were on opposite coasts? Would there be a constant ache in my chest that couldn't be soothed?

"Hey, Mopey Face," Mark said as he approached the table. "Come dance with me."

"Where's Zoe?"

"She ran into a friend from high school." He held out his hand.

I glanced at my phone, lingering on the blank reply space, and then dropped it into my silver clutch. Mark led me onto the crowded dance floor, and we found a spot beside Em's parents who gave us warm smiles. The DJ was playing "The Way You Look Tonight," and all the older guests had flocked to the large dance space in the center of the room.

Mark put his hands on my waist, and I set mine on his shoulders. We swayed back and forth robotically until Mark leaned in to talk over the music.

"I'm guessing you're depressed because Josh isn't here."

"That's part of it."

"What's the other part?"

I brushed a speck of lint from his black jacket. "I just keep thinking that this is how it's going to be all the time once he leaves. He won't always be able to fly in for big events, and he won't be able to do the little stuff either, like going to a movie or dinner or just hanging out. Our relationship is going to be all video chatting and texting. And depending on what I do about grad school, we could be apart a long, long time."

"Do you think you can handle that? Being in a relationship with someone you hardly ever see? It didn't work out so well with Kyle."

"Josh would never cheat on me. That I know. But what I don't know is if we can survive being away from each other for that long."

Mark's forehead wrinkled, and I recognized his deep-in-thought look. "Maybe you can try it the next few weeks and see how it goes."

"Try what?"

"Not seeing each other. You're way too preoccupied with all this, and I need your head in the game, Court. Why don't you take a break from each other? Obviously, you'll see him at the rink, but otherwise give yourself some space."

That sounded like the argument Mr. Tucker had made to Josh. *Put some distance between you.*

"You think not spending time with Josh the next few weeks will help me figure out if I want to do the long-distance thing?" I said.

"Maybe. It'll definitely help you get into competitive mode, which is the number one most important thing right now."

I raised one eyebrow. "I don't know if I can trust your opinion. You're just trying to get me away from Josh before nationals."

"That's true. But I do care about you, and I don't wanna see you hurt by another long-distance relationship that falls apart."

The concern on his face was genuine. My feet stopped swaying, and I hugged him tight. Tighter than I usually hugged him. The idea of taking a break from Josh made my heart hurt. But Mark was right. I had to get my head straight before nationals, and every time I was with Josh I rode a roller coaster of emotions. Blissfully happy to be with him one minute and then deeply sad over his impending departure the next.

I looked over Mark's shoulder, and my emotions shot upward as did my pulse. Josh stood at the entrance of the ballroom. He wore a dark gray suit with a blue tie, and his hands were stuck in his pockets as he nervously scanned the room.

"He's here," I said.

Mark turned, and I wound my way through the dancing couples to reach the door. Josh saw me break through the crowd, and he took a few steps in my direction but waited for me to go to him.

"You left the party?" I shouted over the music.

"I had to see you." He came closer and bent his head so he didn't have to yell. "I should've looked at it from both sides and realized how my suggestion made you feel."

"I may have overreacted a little."

"Can we just forget I mentioned it?"

True remorse colored his eyes, which looked darker paired with his indigo tie. God, he was beautiful. Inside and out.

"I'm really glad you're here," I said.

His face lightened into a smile, and he gently rubbed my shoulders, warming me all over. His gaze dipped to my sleeveless green dress, and he wrapped me in an embrace.

"You look incredible," he said.

I smiled. "The necklace goes great with my dress."

He touched the pendant, and his fingers brushed my

sweetheart neckline. It set off another rush of conflicting emotions — from the thrill of feeling Josh's electric touch to the sadness of knowing I wouldn't be experiencing it much longer.

"Hey, Josh!" Liza waved and then grabbed my elbow. "Court, Aubrey's about to throw the bouquet."

"Oh, uh... I think I'll pass." I was quite content where I was.

"You have to come. ALL single ladies." She pulled on my arm.

"Alright, alright." I gave Josh a soft peck on the lips. "I'll be back."

Liza dragged me onto the dance floor, and Quinn raced to stand between us. I moved behind her to shield her from the tipsy bachelorettes bringing up the rear of the group. I'd seen some scrums break out during the bouquet toss, and I didn't want her getting trampled.

Aubrey stood a few feet away, and I marveled for the tenth time that night how gorgeous she looked in her elegant cream-colored dress. It had a simple halter neckline and hugged her slim body — very chic just like her. I hoped to look just as stylish at my wedding someday.

A picture of Josh and me standing at the altar popped into my head, and I didn't realize the bouquet was flying right at me until Liza's arm shot out in front of me. She caught it before I even had time to react.

"I got it!" She jumped up and down and waved the cluster of red roses.

Sergei came over and patted her head. "You're not getting married for at least twenty years."

"*Daadd.*"

All the single guys replaced us on the polished wood floor, and I looked around for Josh and found him talking to the DJ. A loud "Whoo!" came from the jumble of guys, and Mark proudly held up the garter. Zoe sped across the room and practically tackled him with a hug.

Josh walked toward me with a smile, and I asked, "What were you up to?"

He took my hand. "Dance with me."

"I don't hear any music."

He twirled me around, and my short bubble skirt flared. "Give it a second."

Sure enough, music filled the airy room once again, and I knew the song right away — Eva Cassidy's soulful rendition of "Over the Rainbow."

"It's Thursday night, so I had to find a way for you to hear your song," Josh said.

I touched my cheek to his and breathed in his sweet cologne. How was I going to let him go? He'd stolen such a large part of my heart. I needed to see his crinkly-eyed smile every day, hear his soft, sexy voice saying my name. I cinched my arms around his neck, wishing that was all I had to do keep him from leaving me.

When my song ended a party anthem began, and I reluctantly disentangled myself from our embrace. Chris and Aubrey danced into the space beside us, and Chris slapped Josh's back and shook his hand.

"Glad you could make it," he said.

"Congratulations," Josh said. "Court's told me so many stories about you guys that I feel like I grew up with you, too."

"I don't know what she told you, but I was always perfectly behaved," Aubrey said.

"Did she tell you she had a huge crush on me and wrote me a poem once?" Chris grinned.

I punched his arm. "I thought we were never going to speak of that again."

"I remember that!" Aubrey laughed. "It was such a sweet poem."

"I was twelve," I explained to Josh.

"I was honored to be your crush." Chris slung his arm

around me. "Josh, you better treat her right."

"Don't worry. I know just how special she is." His eyes shone at me.

Josh and I left the growing craziness on the dance floor and drifted over to one of the large windows overlooking the harbor. He returned me to the warmth of his arms, and we watched a few early fireworks glittering in the distance.

"How come you haven't written *me* any poems?" he asked with a grin.

"You aren't missing much. I wasn't exactly a poet laureate."

"Give it your best shot." His hands caressed my back, sliding along the silky material of my dress. "I'll get you started. Roses are red, violets are blue…"

*Do you know how much I love you?*

I bit my lip and lowered my eyes. I couldn't say those words. I couldn't tell him how much of my heart he owned. Not when I had so many doubts about our future.

"Roses are red, violets are blue…" I looked up at him. "Forget the poem. I'm just gonna kiss you."

And kiss him I did. So passionately that he said in my ear, "Why don't we go outside?"

I grabbed my coat, and we went out to the waterfront walkway, picking up where we'd left off. Turned out I didn't need my coat because we generated enough heat with our kisses to keep us more than warm. We paused to count down the final thirty seconds to midnight and then got lost in each other again as an explosion of fireworks rained over us.

Josh was headed back to the Cape, so I decided to go back too instead of spending the night at my parents' apartment. Em, Sergei, and the twins were staying at Em's parents' house, so all was quiet at home when Josh and I arrived in our mini-caravan. We'd talked on the phone almost the entire ninety-minute drive, so I hadn't been alone with my thoughts. That was a welcome relief since my thoughts had been eating me alive all night.

I turned on a lamp in the living room and kicked off my silver strappy heels. Josh followed me to the kitchen, loosening his tie, and I poured us tall glasses of water. He leaned against the granite bar while I boosted myself onto it.

"Seeing you sitting there takes me back to the night of our first kiss," he said with a smile.

"You were the last person I expected at my door that night."

"I drove around the block five times first. I kept telling myself that when you opened the door I should just take you in my arms and kiss you."

"Did my cartoon pajamas throw you off?" I laughed.

Josh set down his glass and stood in front of me. The tip of his tie brushed my knees.

"No, they made you even more irresistible. So did the spot of chocolate on your mouth."

"I had chocolate on my face and you didn't tell me?"

"Well, it wasn't there anymore after I kissed you." He bent toward me, and his eyes flashed to my mouth, jump-starting my heart.

"What do you think would've happened if Quinn and Alex hadn't interrupted us?" I said.

He leaned all the way into me. "There would've been a lot more of this."

His lips took hold of mine, and I tugged on his tie, drawing him nearer.

"And this." He kissed my throbbing pulse.

The heat from his lips shot through my veins, and it intensified as he smoothed his hand along the curve of my calf and over my knee. He placed slow open-mouthed kisses down my neck, making me weaker with each flick of his tongue, and when his mouth reconnected with mine, I clung to his shoulders and knotted my fingers in his hair.

Josh's hand inched under my skirt, and his thumb

skimmed the inside of my thigh, stirring all my strongest desires. There was no one to interrupt us now. We didn't have to stop.

But if I couldn't tell him I loved him, I couldn't do *this*. If I gave all of myself to him, I would feel that much emptier when he left.

"Josh," I gasped as I broke our kiss.

He started to pull his hand back. "Sorry, I—"

I clutched his arm. "No, it's… it's not that. I… I want this. I want *you*. I'm just…"

"What is it?" He cradled my face.

"I'm so scared," I whispered.

He rested his forehead on mine and sank his hands into my hair. His breaths hadn't slowed yet, and I watched his chest rise and fall in quick rhythm.

"Tell me why you're scared," he said.

I tilted my head back to look into his eyes. "I don't know what's going to happen to us once you're gone."

"We're gonna make it. It's going to be hard, but we can get through it."

I looked down and played with his tie. "I feel like we're going to be sad all the time and wishing the days away until we see each other. Is that how we want to live?"

"Knowing we'll be together eventually will make all the tough days worth it."

"But that won't be for such a long time."

His face creased with worry. "Are you… are you not sure you want to do this?"

"I don't know. There's so much happening right now. I don't know what I'm doing about school, and nationals is stressing me out already. I'm just thinking maybe I need some time to figure it all out." My voice hitched. "Time alone."

His hands dropped, and he took a small step backward. "How much time?"

"I think through nationals and whatever happens after

that." *Hopefully the two of us competing at the Olympics.* "And then… then we can talk."

"So you just need space. You're not… you're not saying you want to end this." He sounded as afraid to say it as he looked.

"No. I just need this time for myself."

He let out a brief exhale and clasped my hands. "Can I still call you or text you?"

I squeezed his fingers hard as if someone was sticking me with a needle. It pained me to think of having no contact with him.

"I don't think you should," I said.

"So I'll only see you at the rink," he said, quietly strained.

I nodded slowly. "Ronnie let me add the next two weeks to my time off for nationals, so I won't be at the restaurant."

He stood eerily still, staring down at our hands. When he looked up, I saw how much pain this was causing him, too.

"I'll give you whatever you need," he said. "But I just want you to know that no amount of time or space will change how I feel about you."

His voice was thick with emotion, and his eyes glistened with unshed tears. I couldn't stand to see him hurting, so I shut my eyes and pressed my lips to his cheek.

"Thank you," I managed to whisper.

"I have one request — that we don't start this break until sunrise." He brought our hands up to his chest. "Let me stay with you tonight."

"Josh, I can't…"

"I know. That's not what I meant. I just want to have you next to me, to hold you for a little while longer."

All the flutters returned to my stomach. "I don't know if I can have you in my bed tonight."

"You don't trust me?"

"I don't trust myself."

"I promise I won't tempt you."

I angled my head to the side. "Just looking at you tempts me."

His lips twitched into the slightest of smiles. "Come here."

He grasped my hips and helped me down from the bar. With his arms completely enveloping me, he said quietly, "Please let me stay."

I couldn't tell him no, not after he'd agreed to be so patient with me. And it wasn't that I wanted him to leave. I wanted him to stay more than anything. To stay the night. Stay forever.

"Okay," I said.

He kissed the top of my head, and I rested my cheek on his chest. We stood there for how long I didn't know, just holding onto each other. Eventually, I changed into my pajamas and brought Josh up to my room. He took off his tie but left on his shirt, and once we were under the comforter he spooned me against him.

"Don't give up on us," he murmured into my hair.

I tried to take in a deep breath, but I couldn't. My chest felt so heavy, my throat so tight. My eyes watered, and I pressed my face to the pillow so it would catch my tears.

# Chapter Twenty-One

I loosened my scarf and breathed in the damp night air. One of the official nationals shuttle buses would've taken my parents and me from the Spokane Arena to the Davenport Hotel, but I needed to walk. I had so much adrenaline still humming through me after the perfect short program Mark and I had lain down. We were in second place, less than two points behind Rebekah and Evan and less than one point ahead of Stephanie and Josh. Any one of us could grab the two Olympic spots, and I was trying not to freak out like I'd done four years earlier.

My steps grew even quicker as I thought ahead to the free skate the next afternoon. "I wish we'd drawn last to skate."

"You're in a good spot, being second in the final group," Mom said. "You won't be rushed to get ready after the warm-up."

Second was normally my favorite because of what Mom had said, but not in a high-stakes competition such as this one. Stephanie had practically jumped up and down when she'd picked the last spot from the bag at the draw. Skating last gave the judges the chance to compare the team to all those who came before, and if the performance was great, the scores were usually higher than normal. Even if there had been equally great performances from others. It was all about giving the final impression. And Stephanie and Josh were going to have the chance to do that.

We followed the path through Riverfront Park and crossed the bridge over the Spokane River, where the whooshing rapids flowed underneath us. I'd become a fan of walking through the park to and from practice to enjoy the fresh air but also to avoid possibly running into Josh on the bus. We'd exchanged small talk at the rink back home the past two weeks, but now that the competition was upon us, I felt like I needed to be completely in my bubble. Not that he wasn't still on my mind, but interacting with him ramped up all my emotions. The good and the bad.

My phone buzzed, and I pulled it from my jacket pocket to read the text.

Liza: *You guys were so awesome!!!! Sending you lots of virtual hugs!!!! Kick butt tomorrow, Roomie!!!!*

I smiled and put away the phone. Liza was still home in New York because the senior-level events had been split into two weekends, and the ladies weren't competing until the next week. I was going to stay in Spokane to cheer on Liza and be her roommate so she could get a break from her mom. I'd hopefully also be participating in all the celebratory events for the Olympic team members.

*Olympic team.*

*Four-and-a-half minutes away.*

I kneaded my hands and took another deep breath. I couldn't think about it that way. That was how I'd psyched myself out the last time Mark and I were in position to make the team. I had to do what Em and Sergei had been preaching all year — focus on every moment of the program and block out everything else. *Just attack the program.*

"Court?" Dad said. "Did you want dinner now?"

I'd been so lost in space I hadn't realized Dad had been talking to me. "Oh. Yeah. I'm kinda hungry."

We walked past the mall where the Fan Fest was being held, and dozens of red, white, and blue banners and decorations in the store windows advertised the championships. Spokane had dubbed itself "Skate City USA," and the excitement of everyone we encountered in town made the event seem even more special. As if I needed another reason to be pumped up to skate.

Dad opened the glass door to the newer tower of the hotel, and we went straight to the restaurant off the lobby. Since it was the height of dinner time, almost all the tables were full. The hostess led us to the back of the restaurant, and I froze when I saw the empty table where we were headed. Sitting right beside it were Josh, Stephanie, and their parents.

They all looked up, but my eyes locked only on Josh. His eyes brightened as he couldn't look away from me either. We'd done such a good job of keeping our heads down at the arena and acting like the other one didn't exist that I hadn't made any eye contact with him in days. And with my heart slamming against my chest I remembered why.

I quickly pivoted to Mom and Dad behind me. "Let's eat in the bar."

"We can see if they have another table," Mom said.

"No, let's just go." I blew past the befuddled hostess.

No way was I going to sit through an entire meal of awkwardness. I didn't know what Josh had told his parents about us... if he'd told them anything at all. If he had, they were probably cheerleading for Josh to make our break a permanent one.

I hadn't had time yet to decide if that was what I wanted, too.

I went back into the lobby and made an immediate right into the bar. Mom and Dad caught up to me, and we slid into a leopard-print booth.

Mom gave me a concerned smile. "You okay, Honey?"

"Yeah." I slipped my arms out of my jacket. "I knew I couldn't avoid running into them all weekend."

"Have you talked to Josh since you've been here?" she asked.

"No, we're doing our own thing... staying focused."

Both Mom and Dad were staring at me so much that I was glad when the waitress came to take our drink order. I asked for a glass of water and then excused myself to go to the restroom. I was sure my parents would discuss me while I was gone, but I needed a breather for a few minutes.

I walked through the lobby and turned into the hallway to the restrooms. My shoulder rammed into someone's chest, and hands grabbed my arms, squeezing tight. My head popped up, and I discovered that someone was Josh.

As hard as my heart had been beating earlier, it had nothing on how fast it was racing now. Not only was Josh looking straight into my eyes, but he was also touching me. Everything about him was so familiar yet so new. His intoxicating cologne, the warmth of his body, the soft strength of his hands. It was as if he was holding me for the first time all over again.

"Hey," he said quietly.

"Hey," I said even lower.

Neither of us moved. My brain kept telling me to, but the rest of my body firmly refused. I was two seconds away from throwing myself around him when he took his hands from my arms, shocking sense back into me.

"I'm sorry you had to leave the restaurant," he said.

"Oh, it's... it's okay. I just didn't want to have any awkward confrontations."

"Can you tell your parents I said hello?"

"Sure. I'd ask you to do the same, but it might ruin your parents' appetites," I said with a weak laugh.

Josh shoved his hands in his pockets and didn't echo my

laughter. He looked over my shoulder toward the restaurant, his mouth in a tight line. I had the urge to ask how he was surviving dinner with his family, but I stopped myself. I couldn't get into all that. Skating had to be my only concern right now.

"I should let you get back," I said and started to go around him.

"Court, wait." He reached out, and I thought he was going to take my hand, but then he pulled his back. After a long pause, he said, "Good luck tomorrow. I mean that."

He didn't have to say the last part because I saw the sincerity in his clear blue eyes.

"Thanks. Good luck to you, too."

He turned and walked away, but he glanced back at me before he rounded the corner. That one look was enough to twist me up inside again. I went into the restroom and splashed water on my face, letting the drops drip down my cheeks.

*Get it together. Put him out of your mind.*

I closed my eyes and kept my head bent over the sink. There would be time to think about Josh, about our future... *if* there was a future for us. I had to put all of that into a box and lock it away in the back of my mind. The only thing that mattered now was the four-and-a-half minutes I would spend on the ice the next afternoon.

I slowly lifted my head and stared into the mirror until the final drop trickled off my chin.

*Everything you've worked for is there for the taking. So go out there and take it. Make your dream come true.*

****

I strode up to the boards and positioned myself at the ice door. I wanted to be the first person on the ice for the six-minute warm-up. This was our last chance to practice before show time, and I planned to use every second to the fullest.

The arena couldn't be more packed, and there was a palpable buzz in the air. The familiar "final group" buzz, where the anticipation had built all afternoon for this moment. The moment when the four best teams would take the ice and fight for the coveted top two spots on the podium. The two spots on the Olympic team.

I shook my head. *Don't think about that! Focus only on the ice.*

Mark and Em flanked me, and I knew Sergei was with Stephanie and Josh in the group huddled behind me, but I wasn't going to look. All my attention was on the long sheet of ice. I bobbed up and down lightly on my skate guards, wiggled my arms, and did squats, using the boards as if it was a ballet barre. As I bounced along to the 80's pop music blaring over the sound system, I glanced up at the clock on the scoreboard.

*Let's go already.*

The event organizers must've heard my internal plea because one of the volunteers opened the door. I ripped off my guards and pushed off across the ice. Mark and I always stretched our legs individually first and then came together to warm up our elements. Stephanie and Josh stroked hand-in-hand past me, their light gray costumes a blur, and I pumped my knees harder, making my turns on deep edges.

Between the traffic of the other three teams I found Mark, and I reached for his hand. We worked up a world of speed and blew through our triple twist, garnering applause from the crowd. Em nodded to us behind the boards and said, "Salchows."

We hurried out of Rebekah and Evan's path and got ready to set up for our side-by-side jumps. We flew so fast and so strong into them I felt like I could jump through the roof. I had too much energy, and I over-rotated the triple, stumbling on the landing. Em gave us another nod and made a circle motion with her finger to signal we should do them again.

I took a calming breath as I entered the jump the second time, and I landed cleanly on one foot. But Mark had to put his hand on the ice to steady himself. My nerves became even twitchier, and I blew on my palms to keep them dry. Em didn't ask us to repeat the jumps, so the last memory we'd have of them would be less than perfect.

We warmed up both throws and one of our lifts as the clock wound down to one minute. I was about to release Mark's hand to do my final warm-up when the background music changed, and the opening beat of the new song stopped my heart.

"Oh my God," I said.

"What?" Mark looked at me with alarm.

80's songs had been playing all weekend at the practices and events, but hearing "He's So Shy" still completely threw me. I couldn't stop myself from looking over at Josh, and he'd had the same instinct. As soon as our eyes connected, we both turned away.

"What, Court?" Mark asked more urgently.

I shook my head. "Nothing."

I took off on my own and stared up into the purple seats full of people to distract myself, but I couldn't block the damn song from my ears. Flashes of standing on the stage, singing to Josh's captivated smile kept assaulting me.

I hummed our long program music and did some of the corresponding arm movements. Anything I could think of to get my thoughts back on track. Josh was circling the rink ahead of me, and I slowed so we wouldn't arrive at the boards together once the warm-up ended. When the final seconds ticked off and the announcer told us to leave the ice, I met up with Mark, and we let the other teams go ahead of us. Em handed us our jackets and guards, and we found a quiet spot in the corridor backstage for the torturous wait. Sergei ushered Stephanie and Josh to a small room for their even longer and more excruciating wait.

Mark and I sat in identical folding chairs and sipped water as Em fed us positive reminders about our jumps. I soaked in every word she said, watching the sureness in her big blue eyes. She believed we could do this.

Did I believe we could do this?

I closed my eyes and saw us completing each element perfectly. The jumps tight and crisp. The throws high and explosive. The lifts soaring and majestic. We'd done all those things before in practice. It was all possible.

*Yes.*

*We can do this.*

*We WILL do this.*

And our time had come.

Em led us toward the ice, and as the three of us stood at the edge of the tunnel, Mark pulled me into a hug, and I squeezed him hard.

"Leave it all out there," I said.

I felt him nod against the top of my head. The young fourth-place team exited the ice, so it was our turn to take the stage. We made slow laps around the rink while the scores were read, and we stopped in front of Em for her final words of encouragement.

"You're ready." She patted our hands on the boards. "Take control of every moment, and it will be yours. You've got this."

I smiled and inhaled and exhaled a slow breath. We'd done hundreds of clean run-throughs the past nine months. All we had to do was one more.

*Four-and-a-half minutes.*

Mark clasped my hand, and I took a quick glance at my burgundy dress, making sure not a single thread was out of place. I touched my curly hair bun and finally stopped fidgeting when the announcer began to speak.

"They represent the Lighthouse Figure Skating Club in

Cape Cod, Massachusetts. Please give a warm welcome to Courtney Carlton and Mark Phillips."

The large audience gave us more than a warm welcome, and we skated into position at center ice, facing the judges. They watched us intently, one finger on their tiny computers, ready to punch in our scores. I made eye contact with all of them and waited for our music to begin.

Saint-Saëns' sweeping Organ Symphony carried us through the opening and into the triple twist, and we came out of the move with more speed than we'd had going into it. I had a good feeling already, but I had to keep my energy under control. Our triple toe-double toe-double toe combination was next, and I couldn't fly into it like a wild woman.

I pictured a clean combination and jabbed my toe pick into the ice for the first jump. Three rotations later I made the same motion for the second jump and then again for the third, breathing steadily throughout. When I landed the final piece of the combination on a clean edge, I peeked sideways at Mark and saw him in the same stance, riding the perfect landing. I fist-pumped in my head and then zeroed all my focus on the next element — the critical triple Salchows.

We curved with the corner of the rink, still flying with a rush of speed, and we split apart to set up for the jumps. Once again I envisioned myself landing cleanly, and I felt empowered as I pushed off my back inside edge. My body coiled into three tight revolutions, and I opened up my arms as my right blade made smooth contact with the ice. Next to me Mark mirrored my position.

Waves of excitement coursed through me, and I gave the crowd a big smile. We'd gotten through our two most difficult elements like a breeze. I wanted to do a happy dance in the middle of the ice.

*Calm yourself. There's so much more to go!*

The music slowed for the Poco Adagio movement, and my heart rate came down a bit as we took our time with the choreography, expressing the beautiful melody. We sailed through the star lift and the throw triple flip, and my smile grew bigger with each passing second. The crowd's cheers had grown louder, too. Em clapped her hands as we rounded her corner of the rink, and she called out, "Keep fighting!"

After our spins and another lift, Mark took hold of my hips for the throw triple Salchow, and I went through my visualization routine, seeing myself floating through the air. I swung my leg around as Mark propelled me upward, and I pulled my arms to my chest, spinning three times before gravity took over. When my right blade found the ice and I stood upright on the landing, a soft cry escaped my lips.

*We're so close!*

As Mark held me high over his head for our final lift, I took in the entire arena, and my eyes welled. Everyone in the building was cheering us on, and the applause drowned out the music. This was the best performance of our lives. It was so surreal I felt like I was watching a movie of myself.

Mark set me down, and I choked on giddiness and tears as we completed our death spiral and spun into our ending pose. The audience leapt to its feet, and Mark lifted mine from the ice, twirling me around and around in a bear hug.

When we finally looked at each other, we were both laughing and crying. Mark kissed my forehead, and neither of us could speak. We bowed to all four sides of the arena and skated around the numerous stuffed animals covering the ice. Em met us at the boards, her face a mess of tears, and I lost the little bit of composure I had left.

She hugged me with all her might. "I'm so proud of you."

I cried all over her cashmere sweater and then let Mark have his turn. By the time we made it to the kiss and cry, we didn't have to wait long for our scores. I knew we'd be in first place, and I slapped Mark's thigh as the big numbers popped up on the screen. The marks were the highest we'd ever received.

The three of us hugged again before quickly heading backstage. Rebekah and Evan were about to skate, but Mark and I had to chat with the media. We answered questions while keeping an eye on the video monitors. Things were going very well for the two-time defending champions, and my stomach began to tighten. If they bumped us down to second place, then they'd be assured of one of the Olympic spots. And we'd have to sweat out Stephanie and Josh's performance.

The federation's media coordinator steered us from the reporters to the lounge set up backstage. The lounge title was misleading because even though there were couches, there were also TV cameras watching every move we made, so relaxing was not an option. Not that I could relax at the moment with our dream in the hands of the judges, but I would've preferred to wait for the verdict in private. The TV network had other ideas, though. They wanted maximum drama for the viewers at home, and that meant filming us as we watched our competitors on the monitor.

Mark and I sat on the orange couch, and he put his hand around mine. He leaned in close to me so the camera microphones wouldn't pick up his voice.

"We were awesome," he said. "We have to get this."

I nodded and stared at the screen. Rebekah and Evan were all smiles in the kiss and cry. All the good feelings I'd had on the ice were rapidly evaporating, replaced by gnawing fear and anxiety. I chewed on my thumbnail as the announcer prepared to read the scores.

The marks came first and then the placement, and my stomach flipped over. We'd been knocked down to second place. Now our fate depended solely on how Stephanie and Josh skated.

I couldn't bear to watch.

Mark let go of my hand and leaned forward. I mimicked him, holding my head so I couldn't see the screen. I wanted

Stephanie and Josh to skate well but fall just short of our score. That would be the ideal situation. For Mark and me, at least.

There was no way we could be kept off the team after skating the way we had. Stephanie and Josh couldn't possibly top that, could they?

The frequent cheers let me know how the program was going without seeing it. The level of applause was starting to sound like the kind we'd received, and my hands began to tremble. My whole body soon followed. The roar that signaled the end of the program was so loud it sounded like we were standing out there on the ice and not tucked away backstage.

*Dear God, please don't take this away from us.*

I dared to peek up at the monitor, and Em and Sergei were embracing Stephanie and Josh. All of them wore huge grins. Josh swiped at his eyes, and a piece of my heart crumbled. He'd worked so damn hard with Em and Sergei to fix his jumps, and I knew how proud he must feel to have conquered them. I was happy he'd skated great, but it had to end there. Mark and I had to come out on top. We *had* to.

The TV camera pointed right at us, waiting for our reaction to the scores. I moved my hands from my head to my mouth because I had no idea what might fly out when I saw the marks.

The announcer came over the PA system, and every muscle in my body clenched. The scores flashed on the bottom of the screen, and then I saw it. Just as Stephanie screamed and jumped out of her seat.

Second place.

Everything inside me turned cold, and sour bile rushed into my throat.

My dream was gone.

# Chapter Twenty-Two

I wanted to scream.

I wanted to cry.

I wanted to rip off my skates and hurl them at the monitor.

But I couldn't do any of those things. Not with a TV camera in my face, documenting every second of this horrible nightmare.

My worst fear coming true.

On the TV screen Em and Sergei hugged Stephanie and Josh with smiles, but their eyes showed something else. Sorrow. My hands tightened into fists against my mouth. They *should* feel sad. They'd helped rob Mark and me of our dream.

Mark.

I turned to him, and he was staring at the screen in disbelief, too. He slowly looked at me, his face a fiery shade of red, like he was ready to explode at any moment.

"Four hundredths of a point," he said quietly. "They beat us by *four hundredths of a point.*"

The bile in my throat inched higher, and I couldn't swallow it down. "I think I'm gonna be sick."

I rushed past the cameras and ran into the locker room, searching for the nearest trash can. I bent over the edge, but all that came out were sobs. My chest heaved as tears poured down my face. And they wouldn't stop coming. My eyes burned and ached as the river of tears flowed endlessly.

*This can't be happening. This has to be an awful nightmare, and I'm going to wake up and won't even have skated yet.*

The locker room door squeaked behind me, and a female voice said tentatively, "Courtney, we'll need you for the medals soon."

I had no idea who the person had been. Someone from the federation. Medals? I didn't want the damn bronze medal. They could keep it. How was I going to stand on the podium without falling apart?

But I had to go or they would drag me there. I slowly lifted my head and evened my breaths until I wasn't gasping for air anymore. I knew I probably looked like death, so I went to the mirror and confirmed it. My eyelids were so puffy I could barely see, but they opened enough to show me what a mess I was. The whites of my eyes were blood red, and my face was stained with tears. I plucked a tissue from a nearby box and blotted my cheeks, but I couldn't fix my swollen eyes.

*Screw it. I don't care anymore.*

I balled up the tissue and slammed it into the trash. As I swung open the door, Stephanie bowled into me, and I rebounded backward. She stared at me, seemingly speechless for once, and I steeled my jaw. I was *not* going to break down in front of her.

I stepped around her and was almost through the door when she said, "You know it's your own fault things turned out this way. If you'd skated better at Worlds last year, we would've had three spots."

Boiling anger heated my face and my neck, and it had to be let out or I would implode. I spun around and marched directly to Stephanie, stopping an inch from her face.

"You are a horrible, *horrible* person, and you do *not* deserve this."

She didn't move an eyelash. "What about Josh? Does he not deserve it either? I knew you never really cared about him."

The mention of Josh's name added another stab to my heart, and I backed away from Stephanie before the tears could start again. I hurried out of the locker room and came face to face with Em and Sergei, two more people who had me steaming with fury.

Em reached out to me. "Court, I don't know what—"

I jerked my arm away. "You did this."

Her eyes watered, and I choked on my own tears as I said louder, "You did this. You brought them to our rink, and you let them take this away from us."

"Court…" Em croaked.

"You promised me. Four years ago you promised you would do whatever you could to help us make the team." My voice broke with a sob. "How could you do this?"

Sergei put his hand on my shoulder. "We did all we could—"

I pulled back and shook my head. "I don't wanna hear it."

He tried to get me to stay, but I walked with purpose to the tunnel leading to the ice. Mark was there, staring blankly into space, and thankfully alone. He was the only person I could stand to see. The only person who would understand the anger and sadness I felt.

When he looked at me with his despondent gaze, my face crumpled, and he wrapped me in a hug. I didn't think I had any tears left, but they kept coming. I turned my head to the side, and I sucked in a breath when I saw Josh hesitantly coming toward us.

He didn't look like someone who'd just achieved his dream. His mouth was turned down, and his eyes were filled with anguish. My emotions were so torn up and mixed up. There was no way I could handle talking to him. I put my arm around Mark's waist and pulled him with me to the boards.

We watched in silence as the volunteer crew assembled the podium on the ice. I scanned the small crowd that had remained for the ceremony and spotted my parents in the front row across the way. Em's Aunt Debbie and the twins sat next to them. I felt another round of tears building as I thought about the disappointment Mom and Dad must be experiencing. They'd spent so much of their hard-earned money on my skating, all for me to chase this dream, and I had come up short twice. It had all been for nothing.

The other medalists gathered around us, and finally the presentation began. Rebekah and Evan were introduced first, and they skated over to the podium. I continued to avoid Josh as he and Stephanie waited for their names to be called. After they received their introduction and took their place on the second tier, Mark and I skated out to take our bows. We made our way to the podium and gave Rebekah and Evan congratulatory hugs, and I tensed all over as I approached Stephanie and Josh.

I didn't want to hug Stephanie. I wanted to smack the triumphant smile off her face. But I was going to act like a classy competitor. We both leaned in and touched each other's shoulders, giving one another the most affection we could stomach.

I stepped sideways in front of Josh and kept my tunnel vision on his chest, doing everything I could not to look into his eyes. He put his arms around me and held me warmly to his body, but I remained stiff. If I let myself soften against him, all the feelings I was holding in would flood out.

Mark and I moved to our designated spot on the opposite side of Rebekah and Evan, and we applauded the fourth-place team, winners of the pewter medal. Once we'd all received our medals and bouquets of flowers, we had to pose for the official photographs. I tried to force my mouth into a smile, but for some reason I just succeeded in making my eyes water again. As the flash bulbs fired, I fought to think of something positive about not making the team. At least Mom and Dad would save the money they were going to spend on the trip to Vancouver. Maybe they could use it to go on a trip that wasn't skating-related. They hadn't been able to do that in years.

After the photos we were instructed to take a victory lap, and I cut mine short when I reached the spot where my parents stood. Em's aunt had taken the twins a few seats away, probably to give us a minute alone. Dad took off his glasses and wiped his eyes, and I totally lost it. He *never* cried. I gave Mom my bouquet and blubberingly attempted to speak, and she embraced me and let me quietly cry on her shoulder.

"We couldn't be more proud of you," she said through her sniffles.

"Coco!" Quinn squealed.

She escaped her aunt and squeezed between my parents. I dried my face with the back of my hand and leaned down to give her a hug. Alex soon joined us, not wanting to be left out.

"You hear us cheer for you?" Quinn asked. "We yell loud!"

"I did." I nodded as I continued to dab the corners of my eyes.

"Why you cry? You got a medal." Quinn pointed to the bronze hanging around my neck.

I wouldn't be able to explain the Olympic team situation to her without dissolving into tears again. "I um… I'm just happy we skated so well."

We had to clear the ice, so I gave the twins goodbye hugs and told my parents I'd see them at the hotel. When I got backstage, Em and Sergei were talking to Mark, and I caught the tail end of the conversation with Mark saying, "I don't care. I'm done."

Sergei turned to me and spoke gently, "We were telling

Mark you might be named to the World team or the Four Continents team."

Four Continents? That event was in Korea in ten days. No way would I be in any kind of mental shape to compete there. Worlds wasn't until March, but...

"I'm done," Mark repeated. "That was the best we've ever friggin skated, and it wasn't good enough. I'm not doing this anymore. Consider this my official retirement statement."

He stalked off to the locker room, and I stared down at the concrete floor. So that was the end of our partnership. I'd expected a grand finale on Olympic ice where we'd stand on the painted rings and celebrate a decade of skating together.

"Court, can we talk?" Em asked.

I looked up at the woman who'd been my role model since I was twelve years old. My coach. My mentor. My friend. But all I saw now was the person who had broken her promise and had broken my heart.

"I can't," I said, my voice wavering.

I changed out of my costume as quickly as I could and headed for Riverfront Park. The air smelled of rain, and I trudged through the small puddles and paused on the bridge. Resting my elbows on the railing, I closed my eyes and listened to the rushing water, hoping the peaceful sound would ease the tightness in my chest.

"Court?"

I didn't need to open my eyes to know who'd spoken my name. The tug on my heart said it all.

I felt Josh stand beside me, and his hand touched the small of my back. Tears pricked the backs of my eyelids.

"Court, I'm so—"

"Don't." I moved away from him. "Please don't say you're sorry."

He pushed his hand through his hair. "I... I don't know what else to say..."

"You can't be sad. You have to enjoy this and be happy.

Otherwise, what's the point?"

"I can't be happy when you're in so much pain."

I stared at him, letting what he'd said sink in. If our positions were reversed — if I'd made the team and he hadn't — I knew I would be happy. I would feel awful for him, but I'd be more happy than sad. Was I a terribly selfish person? Maybe I didn't know what it meant to love someone after all.

"Then we should continue to keep our distance," I said.

I didn't think he could possibly look any more distraught, but my words brought a new level of sadness to his eyes.

"Are you using this as an excuse to push me further away?"

I lowered my gaze and hugged my arms to my body. If my feelings for him weren't as real as I'd thought, I needed more time to figure out what I wanted. Nothing made any sense anymore.

"It's just… it's best this way. For both of us."

"I know you're scared about the future, but I want to be here for you now."

"You can't. You can't be the one to comfort me." My voice became higher and shakier. "*You're* the reason I'm in pain."

He took a hard swallow. "Court—"

"I can't be around you, and you're better off not being around me."

I left before he could try to stop me. I hurried through the park, trembling from the cold and from holding back the sob in my throat. If I didn't truly love Josh, then why did walking away from him hurt so much?

****

"I'd rather go jump in the ice-cold river than do this," Mark muttered.

I couldn't say I disagreed. We stood beside the Fan Fest

stage outside the mall with our fellow medalists, waiting for the pairs victory ceremony to begin. The event organizers had thought it would be a treat for the fans to see us on stage and listen to a Q&A session with us. They obviously hadn't considered that the medalists who hadn't made the Olympic team wouldn't exactly be in a celebratory mood.

Only a few hours had passed since the competition had ended, and my eyes still felt swollen. I'd redone my make-up so I wouldn't look completely pitiful, but I couldn't hide the evidence of all the crying I'd done. It would've been a lot more convenient if they'd held the event during daylight when I could wear sunglasses.

Josh and Stephanie stood ahead of us with their parents, and I turned so my back faced them. Josh had respected my request and hadn't spoken to me. From what I'd seen he wasn't doing much speaking to anyone. His parents and Stephanie seemed to be dominating the conversation while he quietly observed the large crowd.

The emcee called the four teams up to the stage, and I bundled my knit scarf tighter around my neck. If at any point I felt like I was going to cry, I could choke myself until the urge subsided. The bright lights on the stage blinded me from seeing faces in the audience, but I could hear the loud cheers. Someone began chanting, "USA! USA!" and it quickly spread through the crowd.

I tugged hard on the fringed ends of my scarf.

Mark stuck his hands in his jacket and clenched his jaw. I seriously feared he might go postal if he was asked about the competition. And if I tried to step in, I'd probably have an emotional meltdown. That would be the perfect ending to this terrible day — Mark spewing curse words and me sobbing uncontrollably in front of hundreds of people.

I zoned out while the emcee talked to Rebekah and Evan but lifted my head when he asked Josh about making the Olympic team. Josh leaned into the microphone and cleared his throat.

"It um… it hasn't really sunk in yet. But we're excited to go to Vancouver and represent U.S. pairs."

Stephanie grabbed the mic. "It's an absolute dream come true. This is the best day of my life."

Tug. Tug. Tug.

The emcee came over to Mark and me, and I held my breath. *Please don't mention the Olympics. Please don't mention the Olympics.*

"Courtney and Mark," the gray-haired man said as he glanced at the card in his hand. "How have you enjoyed these championships here in Spokane?"

*How have I enjoyed the championships? Can't you see I'm in a state of total devastation?!*

Mark looked at me, and I scrambled to think of something to say. It was probably best he not speak, but now I had to pull myself together and address the crowd without cracking.

"Everyone has been so nice and supportive," I said. "They've made us feel very welcome here."

The audience applauded as did the emcee. "I'm so glad to hear that. I'd like to take this opportunity to thank you all for letting us share in your triumphs and your Olympic journey. How about another round of applause for these wonderful athletes?"

The fans erupted with cheers, and I managed a weak smile. I couldn't stand to hear the word *Olympic* any longer. And I was going to hear nothing but that over the next week in Spokane. I couldn't take it. I couldn't stay there. Besides all the Olympic hype, Josh would be there all week because he and Stephanie had to perform in the Exhibition and attend the fancy team dinner. I'd run into him everywhere.

As soon as I got back to the hotel I changed my flight to go home with Mom and Dad the next day. I'd promised Liza I'd be her roommate in Spokane, but she would have to understand. She'd texted me how sorry she was after the competition, one of many sympathy texts I'd received from friends and family, some I hadn't talked to in forever.

I paused in the middle of packing and sat beside the pile of clothes on the bed. As I was about to call Liza, my skate bag in the corner of the room caught my eye. I'd flung it there when I'd come back from the arena.

I was never going to roll that bag to another practice, onto another bus, into another arena. I was never going to have the chance to compete again.

My eyes brimmed with tears, and I brought my knees up to my chest. This wasn't how it was supposed to end. I hadn't prepared myself for my final skate, and now it was already gone. I laid my head on my knees and wept again, not because of the four hundredths of a point, but for the huge part of my life that was over.

When I'd cried myself out and cleared my vision to see the phone, I took a deep breath and dialed Liza. It rang five times before she answered with a sad, "Hey."

"Hey."

"How are you doing?"

"Well, I've gone two minutes without crying, so that's an improvement."

"I'm so, *so* sorry."

I reclined back against the plump pillows and stared at the ceiling. "I have to talk to you about next week. I can't stay here. It would just be too hard."

"You're leaving Spokane?" She grew louder.

"I'm sorry. I know you wanted me to room with you so your mom wouldn't, but I have to go home. This place is all about skating and the Olympics and I can't handle it."

"But you said you'd be there." Disappointment laced every word. "We'll stay in the room when I'm not practicing and competing. We can eat room service and watch DVDs. I just got the second season of *Gossip Girl*."

I rubbed my forehead. I hated bailing on Liza when she needed a friend. She was going to be super nervous competing for the first time as a senior at nationals. But I didn't know if I'd be the best company for her with how upset and bitter I was. She needed positive energy around her, and there was nothing positive about me right now.

"I'm really sorry, but I already changed my flight. I'm going home tomorrow."

She stayed quiet for a minute. "Then I guess I'll have my mom breathing down my neck twenty-four-seven."

"Call me anytime you need to talk."

"I don't wanna bother you."

"It's not a bother."

Liza said she had to get to sleep, but I could tell she was just too disappointed to talk. I let her go, but not before apologizing again. After tossing the phone onto the bed, I covered my face with my hands.

*Can this day just end already?*

# Chapter Twenty-Three

I crammed the last bite of chocolate cannoli into my mouth and closed the empty pastry box. I'd discovered one of the perks of no longer being a competitive skater — I could gorge myself on whatever dessert or junk food I wanted. Dad had gone to Modern Pastry after work three times the past week just to get my favorite cannoli and Italian cookies.

Both Mom and Dad had been so caring and understanding. I'd spent the week at their apartment trying to get a handle on all my overwhelming emotions. I hadn't wanted to be alone at Em and Sergei's house, and I wasn't sure when I could go back there. My anger toward them had subsided, but I still didn't know what to say to them. Em had left me voicemails, all of which I'd left unanswered. A phone conversation didn't seem right after everything we'd been through.

"Is the last group on yet?" Mom asked through the cut-out between the kitchen and living room.

I glanced at the TV where the top six ladies, including Liza, had gathered beside the ice. They all wore the same intense face, one I knew very well as the "Oh my God, I'm about to skate the most important program of my life" look.

"They're getting ready to warm up," I said.

Mom and I had been watching the ladies' free skate all evening while Dad worked in the bedroom. Hearing the announcers talk about the Olympics caused twinges of anger to flare in my gut, but I was feeling more anxious than upset. Liza sat in third place after the short program, and there were three spots on the Olympic team for the ladies.

Mom rejoined me on the sofa after the warm-up, and we watched the first four girls in the group skate well, putting the pressure on Liza. She had the most technically difficult free skate planned, so all she had to do was survive her nerves. It sounded so easy, but I knew how hard it was. I still didn't know how I'd skated the best program of my life with so much on the line.

And it hadn't mattered.

My chest tightened, and I picked up one of the blue throw pillows and wrapped it in my arms. How long would it be until I stopped having these emotional episodes? One minute I was fine and then the next I was on the verge of tears.

I let out a slow breath and focused on the TV. Liza smiled as she got a final pep talk from Sergei and her New York coach Sandra.

"She looks confident," Mom said.

"She should be. I swear, she hardly ever misses a jump at practice. She just has to trust her technique and not think too much."

Liza skated to her starting spot on the ice and smoothed the long sleeves of her purple dress. Once she struck her opening pose, the music of Sibelius began, and she gracefully pushed across the ice toward her first jump combination.

Mom and I both leaned forward, and I squeezed the pillow harder as Liza went up into the air. She rotated each triple in the combination so quickly they looked like doubles, and when she landed on one foot, I pumped my fist. Every time she completed another jump in the program cleanly I slapped the pillow and edged further forward. My heart was beating at a nerve-wracking pace.

As Liza set up for her seventh and final triple, I clutched Mom's arm, holding my breath during the jump. Upon the perfect landing I shrieked, "She did it!"

Liza became a purple blur in her ending scratch spin, and the crowd flew to its feet. Mom and I jumped up from the couch and gave her a standing ovation of our own. The camera flashed to the coaches at the boards, and Sergei had both arms thrust into the air. Then it panned to the stands and showed Liza's mom, Em, and the twins. Em was bawling.

I swallowed hard. I wished I was there to hug her and celebrate with her and Sergei and Liza. I was supposed to be there.

My eyes stayed peeled to the TV as I sank onto the couch. Liza skated to the boards with her hands over her mouth, and she dove into Sergei's arms once she reached him. I felt like I was watching the exact scene I'd lived one week ago. The perfect skate at the perfect moment. I pushed aside my sadness and crossed all my fingers and toes that Liza would have better luck with the judges than I'd had.

I gnawed on my thumbnail as the wait for the scores dragged on. Liza would be the youngest person by far on the Olympic team, but she was a junior world champion and one of the biggest future stars for American figure skating. They wouldn't be stupid enough to hold her back because of her senior level inexperience, would they?

The marks came up, and I scanned the numbers for the placement.

Second!

Liza broke down and was smothered with hugs from Sergei and Sandra. I couldn't stop my tears either, and Mom scooted over and put her arm around me.

"I'm so proud of her," I said.

Mom rubbed my shoulder. "I know it has to be a little tough for you to watch, though."

I sniffed and looked down at my lap. I couldn't deny the small pangs of envy that pricked just below the surface of my happiness.

"I wish we could've been on the team together. We would've been roommates in the Village." I wiped my eyes and smiled a little. "But I really am so excited and happy for her."

The final skater took the ice, but I didn't pay much attention to her performance. All I thought about was Liza and Josh and how my feelings toward their accomplishments had differed.

"Why couldn't I have been this happy for Josh?" I said quietly.

"Honey, that was a different situation. You and Josh were competing against each other. It's natural that his success was difficult to swallow."

I was still trying to swallow it. It was like a permanent lump in my throat. But there was another reason for the pain I felt. I missed Josh more than I thought possible. I missed everything about him but especially his friendship.

I had to stay away from him once he returned from Spokane, though. Being around him could bring up all the bad feelings from nationals that I was trying to move past. Plus, I didn't want to drag him down with my issues when he should be enjoying every moment of preparing for the Olympics.

If the two of us were to see each other, there was entirely too much potential for emotional disaster.

**** 

The coffee shop hummed with activity on the cold afternoon, and it took me a minute to spot Mark in the back of the room. I gave him a little wave before going to the counter.

When I had my hot chocolate in hand, I met him at the small table he'd secured.

He stood and gave me a tentative hug. "Thanks for driving down."

We hadn't spoken since we'd left Spokane over a week ago, and I was happy when he'd called and asked to meet on the Cape. We'd both needed time to decompress after nationals, but I was ready to talk. Our relationship was one of a few in my life currently in disarray, and I wanted to fix that.

I sat across from Mark and took a tiny sip of my steaming-hot drink. "How have you been?"

He played with the lid on his coffee. "It's been weird not going to the rink. I still wake up early every morning and feel like I need to be somewhere."

"I have the same feeling."

"It's kind of a relief, though. Not having that stress or that pressure anymore."

"Yeah..." I went to take another sip but stopped before I burned my tongue again. "I miss it a lot, though. Being on the ice, in particular."

We sat in silence, both fiddling with our cups. Mark finally set his down and folded his arms on the table.

"I'm really sorry about the way I quit and walked out on you," he said. "You deserved better than that."

"You were upset. Neither of us was thinking clearly at that moment."

"Still. It was a crappy thing to do. I should've apologized when I saw you at the victory ceremony, but I was too mad at the world to think about anything else."

I winced just thinking about that awful day. "It hurt that you didn't talk to me before you said, 'I'm done,' but I didn't blame you for not wanting to skate again after what happened."

"Do you?" He tilted his head slightly. "Wanna skate again?"

I paused and thought about the thrill of competition, the rush of nervous energy that was so scary yet so exciting. It had been such a big part of my life for so long. Saying goodbye to it was harder than I'd expected. But I had to move on. I had to start looking forward to whatever came next.

"It would've been nice to have some closure, but it's probably best that nationals was our final competition. I don't think we could skate any better than we did."

Mark sat back and breathed deeply through his nose. "I still can't believe we lost to them by four hundredths of a point."

"I'm trying not to dwell on that so much," I said, staring down at the table.

"Have you talked to Josh at all?"

I shook my head. "Not since right after the event."

"Are you guys finished?" he asked gently.

"I… I don't know. I've been having a lot of doubts about whether we're supposed to be together. But when I think about not having him in my life…"

Mark took a long draw on his coffee. "Take your time figuring it out. Let yourself get past all this mess from nationals first."

I nodded slowly. "I will."

We talked a while longer and discussed our immediate plans for the future. Mark's were a lot more definite than mine. He was applying to Cape Cod Community College for the fall semester and starting a job at his dad's auto shop the next week. I still had to research which schools I might apply to and decide if I wanted to take a second shot at Boston College.

When I left the coffee shop, I did have one definite plan. There was another relationship I had to repair. I drove across the island with the sun setting in my rearview mirror, and I arrived at Em and Sergei's house with anxiety clawing at my stomach.

I climbed onto the porch and pressed the doorbell, and Sergei looked at me with surprise when he opened the door.

"You rang the bell," he said.

"It didn't feel right… just letting myself in."

He gave me an understanding smile and stepped aside. "Come in."

I took a few steps into the living room, and Em lifted her head from where she was working in the kitchen. The twins also stopped playing with their building blocks.

"Coco, you home!" Quinn ran toward me.

I knelt on the carpet, and both Quinn and Alex threw their arms around my neck. I held them close and kissed the tops of their soft little heads. I'd missed my snuggle buddies and their sweet hugs.

Em wiped her hands on a dishtowel and came around the bar into the living room. Her eyes were so much brighter than they'd been the last time I'd seen her in person.

"I'm so happy you're here," she said. "When you didn't answer my messages, I didn't know if…"

"I didn't wanna talk over the phone," I said as I rose to my feet.

Alex tugged on my jacket. "We made you a present."

"Let's get it!" Quinn grabbed his hand, and they clambered up the stairs.

Em motioned to the sofa. "Come sit."

I took off my jacket, and Em and I sat on the couch while Sergei took the oversized chair. I was contemplating how to begin when the twins came bounding down the stairs with a piece of paper. They held it behind their backs as they stood in front of me.

"Mommy tolded us you sad about the Olympic," Quinn said.

"So we made you dis." Alex handed me the paper.

On it was a crayon drawing of a bright blue ribbon with a gold medal hanging from it. Written on the medal in crooked letters was *Coco #1 Skater*. My eyes pooled with tears, and I put my hand to my heart.

"It say Coco number one skater," Alex said.

Quinn poked the paper. "Mommy help us write it."

I smiled and swiped at the moisture trickling onto my cheeks. "I love it so much. This is the best present ever."

I brought them in for more hugs, and then Sergei took their hands. "Let's let Mommy and Court talk, and you can help me make the salad."

Em went over to her purse on the bar and pulled out a packet of tissues. She took one for herself before offering the rest to me. I hadn't noticed she'd started crying, too.

We both began to speak at the same time and then insisted the other one go first. Em had the final word and gave me the floor. I finished blotting my eyes before I began.

"I said some really harsh things to you, and I shouldn't have taken my anger out on you. That wasn't fair. You and Sergei have done so much for me. You brought me into your home and you've treated me like family…" I took a breath to settle my shakiness. "I know how much you wanted this for me, how hard you worked to make it happen. I couldn't have gotten anywhere close to making the team without you."

Em's chin trembled. "I should've done more, though. I feel so awful that I let you down."

I shook my head vigorously. "You didn't. You did everything you could to make sure we skated the best program of our lives. I couldn't have asked for better coaches—"

I choked on a sob, and Em pulled me in for a long hug. Neither of us could speak as we sniffled quietly. After we finally let go, we both reached for more tissues.

"When we brought Stephanie and Josh here, we truly believed we were doing what was best for you and Mark," Em said.

"I know. I'm glad you brought them here. If you hadn't, I

never would've gotten to know Josh." I mopped up more tears. "I don't know what's going to happen with us, but I wouldn't give up the past six months for anything."

Em's forehead creased with concern. "He's been asking about you. If I'd talked to you."

My heart swelled. "Has he said anything else?"

"I asked him why he hadn't talked to you himself. He said he needs to let you heal because right now when you look at him all you see is what you lost."

I lowered my eyes. "When he looks at me, I think he feels guilty about making the team. That's why it's best we do our own thing for now."

"Are you staying in Boston a while longer?"

"I think so. I don't really have a reason to be here. Ronnie had already let me take off the whole month of February in case—" I cleared the pain in my throat. "I can spend the time off doing my college applications."

Em chewed on her lip as she stared at me. "I have an idea for another way you can spend the time. I've been thinking about it the past few days. You're probably going to think I'm crazy for suggesting it, but I want you to hear me out."

I lifted both eyebrows. "I'm a little scared."

She hesitated, making me even more curious. "I think you should come to Vancouver with me."

"What?" My mouth hung open.

"Let me explain." She touched my arm. "Stephanie and Josh can only have one coach in the Village, so Sergei is staying with them. I'm renting a condo downtown, and I have an extra bedroom since Liza was going to go with me and the kids if she didn't make the team. I also have her ticket to the Opening and Closing Ceremonies, all the skating events, and more. And Aunt Deb is going too, so I'm not just asking you to go so I'll have a babysitter."

She smiled, and I slowly closed my jaw. She was asking me to go to the place where I'd expected to have the best time of my life. But I'd be there as an outsider, not the honored guest I'd hoped to be.

"Em, I've just gotten to the point where I can say the word Olympics without breaking down."

"I know. You're thinking, 'Why would I want to do this?' But even though you can't compete there, I want you to experience the rest of it. I think you'd have an amazing time. My family says the best trips of their lives were the ones they took to the Olympics and not just because they watched me compete. They loved the magic of everything about it."

A trip to the Olympics? Could I really handle that? What if I got there and all the reminders of my failure sent me spiraling into depression?

On the other hand, how many opportunities would I get like this in my lifetime? The Olympics were something I'd always wanted to experience. This would just be a little different from how I'd dreamt it. I'd also be able to support Liza and make up for bailing on her at nationals.

"And don't worry about the plane ticket," Em said. "I'll take care of it."

"I couldn't let you—"

"You're not fighting me on this. I'm inviting you as my guest, so I'm taking care of it."

I let out a long puff of air. "This is such a generous invitation."

"You can think about it. Just not too long because we leave in two weeks." She smiled bigger.

An alarming thought occurred to me. "Would we be traveling with Sergei and…"

"No, they're leaving a few days earlier."

I breathed easier. "If I go, I don't want Josh to know I'm there. He doesn't need me messing with his head before he competes."

"Of course. Whatever you want." Em's big blue eyes widened with hope. "So you're leaning towards going?"

I folded my tissue into a square and then opened it and refolded it. How could I say no to this incredible opportunity Em was offering me? This might be the closure I needed.

"I really want to be there for Liza since I wasn't in Spokane," I said. "And I feel like I'll have a lot of regret later if I pass this up."

"Yes!" Em swallowed me in a hug.

"I can't believe after everything that happened I'm still going to Vancouver."

"I know it won't be the same as being an athlete there, but I promise just being there will be so much fun. We're going to have such an awesome time."

She squeezed me tighter, and I rested my chin on her shoulder. Mark and I were good again, and all was right between Em and me. That left only one relationship to fix. It just happened to be the most complicated one of all.

# Chapter Twenty-Four

I hadn't broken down yet.

We'd been in Vancouver two days, and I couldn't take two steps without seeing the Olympic rings, but I'd been okay. I'd actually been really excited. The whole city teemed with an energy of celebration. There were so many people from all over the world on the streets, wearing their country's colors and proudly waving flags. It was impossible not to be happy in the party atmosphere.

But I was about to face my biggest emotional test so far.

Em and I sat in BC Place with over sixty thousand other people, watching the Opening Ceremony. The twins were back at the condo since Em didn't think they could sit through the four-hour event. We'd enjoyed thirty minutes of opening fanfare, and now the moment had arrived.

The Parade of Nations.

This was the moment I'd dreamt of so many times. Marching into the packed stadium with my fellow athletes, decked out in red, white, and blue. Representing the U.S. on the biggest stage of the sports world. It was the experience every Olympian remembered and talked about years later.

The first country, Greece, entered the building to raucous cheers, and I felt the familiar tightening in my chest. I breathed deeply and blinked back tears. I was *not* going to let this get to me anymore.

Em rubbed my shoulder. "You okay?"

I smiled and nodded wordlessly. As each nation's delegates paraded around the floor of the stadium, Em got me to critique the uniforms with her, and I found myself relaxing and enjoying the pageantry of it all. The obvious excitement of the athletes was contagious.

With the end of the alphabet nearing, my relaxation ended and my pulse quickened. The U.S. delegation would be coming through the large tunnel soon, and with the aid of my binoculars, I was going to see Josh for the first time in four weeks. It felt like it had been four years.

The blue-and-yellow-clad contingent from Ukraine marched in, and I inched closer to the edge of my seat. My eyes were glued to the tunnel opening, waiting for the first glimpse of the American flag.

"Sergei texted me that they're in the middle of the group on the right side," Em said as she adjusted her pair of binoculars.

We were sitting at the top of the first level of seats, so we had a good view of the floor. Out of the darkness of the tunnel the stars and stripes appeared, and a huge roar went up from the crowd. Behind the flag bearer a throng of athletes dressed in navy jackets, white pants, and patriotic knit hats entered the arena.

I wasn't thinking anymore about how I wanted to be out there with all the other athletes. My heart was racing too much from the anticipation of seeing Josh. I peered through my binoculars, trying to find him among the hundreds of uniformed bodies.

"I see Liza!" Em cried.

"Where?"

"There's Sergei! And Josh next to him!"

"Where?" I sounded panicky. "I don't see them."

"Liza's in front of Sergei, holding up her phone. Look for the purple case."

My eyes darted over the sea of navy jackets until a spot of purple jumped out at me. I swung the binoculars behind Liza and found the face I'd longed to see. To touch. To kiss. When I looked at Josh, I didn't see what I had lost. I saw everything I'd won from knowing him. The tears welling in my throat weren't from pain this time. They were from happiness.

Josh's smile beamed so bright I could see the sparkle in his eyes from a football field away. He had his camera in one hand taking video and his phone in the other taking photos. He looked completely awestruck. I felt myself grinning along with him and becoming antsier that I couldn't run down and be with him.

"Did you find him?" Em asked.

"Uh-huh," I said, never taking my eyes off his gorgeous face.

Em's phone buzzed in her lap, and she laughed while reading the text. As Sergei walked beside Josh, he blew a kiss in our direction.

"I told him where we were sitting," Em said.

Both Sergei and Josh looked up at our section, and I slunk down behind the man in front of me. I didn't think Josh would be able to see me crammed between so many people, but just in case...

Sergei said something to Josh, and Josh stared down at his phone, his smile fading. What was he thinking about? Was he thinking about me?

Stephanie grabbed his arm and held her camera up to take a photo of the two of them. Josh's smile reappeared and stayed on his lips for the remainder of the team's march. I followed him with my binoculars into the seats, and he sat between Stephanie and Sergei, still looking all around with wonder.

I finally tore my eyes away from him when the parade ended and a couple of Canadian pop singers took the stage. A host of musical acts, dancers, and acrobats followed, each one outdoing the other in the spectacular production. One of the acrobats was a young boy who performed to the song "Both Sides Now," and I immediately got lost in the lyrics. Listening to them made me realize I'd been looking at everything from only one side. I'd been so focused on what I would be missing when Josh moved away that I hadn't thought about what I would still have.

I couldn't give up our incredible connection because I was scared of the future. Even if Josh was thousands of miles away and I couldn't reach out and touch him, I would still be able to feel him in my heart. And that was enough. Because unlike the lyrics of the song, I *did* know what love was all about. For a while I hadn't been so sure, but being apart from Josh had helped me understand. My love for him was greater than any physical distance between us.

Now I just had to tell him.

****

"I see Josh!" Quinn pointed to the ice.

I saw him, too. There were seven other skaters on the ice, but they could've been aliens for all I knew. Josh was the only person who mattered. He looked amazing in his fitted gray shirt and pants, and I had to check my chin for drool.

Josh and Stephanie glided away from Sergei at the boards and wove between the three other pairs in their warm-up group. They'd skated a clean short program the previous night and were in seventh place. With the number of great teams competing, that was an awesome accomplishment. Em had been all smiles when they'd received their scores.

"Daddy!" Alex yelled toward the boards and tried to

stand on Em's lap.

The ladies in front of us gave us annoyed looks, and Em held Alex down. "Daddy's working, Sweetie. We'll see him in a little while."

I leaned forward and observed closely as Stephanie and Josh warmed up their jumps. Each one was clean and crisp. Josh held all the landings with beautiful strength before moving on to the next element.

I hadn't realized how much I'd missed seeing him on skates. I could watch him do simple crossovers all day long. He appeared focused and confident, and I turned all gooey inside when he gave Sergei a smile. It wouldn't be much longer before I could get close to that smile. I knew Josh would have a bunch of press obligations that night, so my plan was to call him the next day and ask to meet. I grinned to myself as I thought of the text he'd sent me after our first kiss — *Is it tomorrow yet?*

Stephanie and Josh were first in the group to skate, and I kept my eyes on them throughout the entire program, unlike when they'd skated at nationals. They interpreted the ballet music with wonderful grace and fluidity, and they mixed in strong technical elements. I understood how the judges had given them high scores in Spokane.

They deserved to be on the Olympic team. But I hadn't told Josh that or even congratulated him. I had to do that as soon as I saw him. I had to tell him how proud I was of him.

After Stephanie and Josh received their scores, Em left with the kids to see Sergei, and I stayed to watch the rest of the event. When I got back to the condo later, they hadn't returned, so I went out on the balcony. The weather in the city had been almost spring-like during the day, and the night air was chilly but pleasant. I loved sitting on the balcony because I could hear the sounds of the people partying on the streets below, even twenty-two floors up. I could also see the Olympic Village lit up right across False Creek. Every day I looked over there and wondered what Josh was doing. I hoped he was having the time of his life.

The front door opened, and Em and Sergei came in carrying the sleeping twins. I went inside and shut the sliding glass door.

"Are you staying here tonight?" I asked Sergei.

"Yeah, I miss tucking in these two." He patted Quinn's back.

Em shifted Alex in her arms and walked toward the master bedroom. "Court, can you set the DVR for the TODAY Show? Stephanie and Josh are skating on it tomorrow."

"Oh really?"

"I would've loved to take the kids to the show taping, but it's at four in the morning."

I picked up the TV remote. "Yeah, there's no way those sleepy heads will be awake."

"Have a good night," Em said as she disappeared into the bedroom.

Sergei echoed her and closed the door behind them. I turned on the TV and scrolled through the guide to set the recording, and the wheels in my brain started to spin.

After I finished with the TV, I grabbed my laptop and pulled up the TODAY Show website. The show taped on Grouse Mountain, not far from the city, and free tickets were given to the first one hundred people who showed up.

*I can be one of those people.*

My fingers flew over the keyboard as I searched for a local taxi company. I couldn't wait any longer to see Josh. What better way to do it than to surprise him?

I copied the number for the cab and looked at the time. I had a few hours before I needed to leave, so I decided I should take a nap. If Josh was going to see me for the first time in a month, I didn't want bags under my eyes.

I set the alarm clock and stretched out over the comforter, but I felt too jumpy to sleep. What if Josh wasn't excited to see me? What if his feelings for me had changed during our time apart?

My thoughts kept me restless until I finally succumbed to exhaustion. When I opened my eyes, I peered at the clock, and a jolt of panic shot through me. I'd either slept through the alarm or it hadn't sounded. I was thirty minutes late!

I jumped off the bed and hurried to the bathroom to get ready. While I brushed my teeth I wrote a note to Em and Sergei, letting them know where I was headed. Then I called the taxi while I put on my make-up.

The lobby of the building was deserted as I paced in front of the glass doors, waiting for the cab. When the car arrived and we started toward North Vancouver, the dark streets were just as quiet. All the partyers had called it a night.

The cab pulled into the parking lot at the base of Grouse Mountain, and I groaned at the long line of people already there. I needed to be on the first gondola up the mountain so I wouldn't miss the start of the show. As I took my place at the back of the line, I tried to count the number of people ahead of me, but it curved past the ticket office.

When the group began to move forward, I craned my neck to see if the gondola still had space. I reached the front of the line, and my heart sank at the sight of the tram packed with people. The guy in charge held up his hand as a stop sign and said something to his co-worker. She responded, and he called out, "Two more!"

I hopped up and down and raced onto the tram, squeezing between bodies and the doors. All personal space considerations went out the window. We lifted into the air moments later, and I gazed out at the lights of Vancouver drifting farther away. I thanked God I was neither claustrophobic nor afraid of heights.

We became shrouded in darkness as I assumed we were passing through the trees, and then everything suddenly became bright and white. Unlike the city below, the mountain was covered with snow, and the huge TV lights illuminated the entire area.

The doors opened, and the frigid air shocked my face. Half of the crowd swarmed the chalet while the other half went over to the fire pit. I followed the group to the pit because the small ice rink was just beyond it.

And so was Josh.

My stomach danced with both nervous and excited flutters. I hid behind a few people and peeked at Josh putting on his skates. I couldn't go up to him now when he was about to be on TV. We needed more time to talk. I would wait until after he finished with his appearance, and then I would surprise him.

Josh's parents came out of the chalet, talking to two of the show's hosts, and I ducked deeper into the crowd. I definitely did *not* want them to see me first. After schmoozing for a few minutes they went back inside, probably to stay warm. I was starting to lose feeling in my own face.

Josh and Stephanie warmed up on the rink while the hosts joined us at the fire pit and the cameras began rolling. My legs were freezing through my jeans, and I bounced lightly, both to keep warm and to let out some of my edginess. I couldn't wait for everyone to stop yapping so Josh could skate.

Finally, the cameras shifted to the rink, and Stephanie and Josh did a short routine. They also led a couple of the hosts around the ice. When the segment ended, everyone cleared the area except Josh and Stephanie, who sat to change out of their skates. Stephanie finished first and headed for the chalet, and a minute later Josh zipped his bag and stood. My pulse pounded hard.

*This is it. Time to put your heart out there.*

I broke away from the crowd and walked through the snow straight toward Josh. He looked up and gaped at me with wide eyes.

"Court... what..."

Being face to face with him stole my breath and my voice. As I struggled to speak, he rushed forward and took me into his arms. I gasped with a cry and locked him in my embrace. Tears trickled down my cheeks, and I buried my face against his scarf.

He kissed the top of my knit hat, and I sighed at how perfect I felt being in his arms again. I could stay in that spot forever and be completely content. But I had to share all the things I'd longed to say to him.

I lifted my head and held his gaze. "I watched you skate last night, and you were so amazing. I was so happy for you. You deserve to be here. I should've told you that weeks ago."

He slid his gloved hands between my scarf and my chin, his fingers tickling the nape of my neck. With his head bent toward mine, his mouth so close, I lost my train of thought.

"There's something I should've told you weeks ago, too. Something I've known for so long." His thumb caressed my cheek, and his eyes looked deep into mine. "I love you, Court. God, I am so in love with you."

My breath caught in my throat, and I thought my heart might burst from fullness. I pressed my mouth to Josh's, and the warmth of his kiss heated my entire body. He brought all the feeling back to my frozen lips and then some.

We slowly came out of the kiss, our lips still touching, and I said, "I love you, too."

He smiled and kissed me again before wrapping me in the longest, warmest hug I'd ever received. When he pulled back to look at me, I kept my arms tight around his waist, not wanting to ever let him go.

"There's something else I need to tell you," he said. "I wasted so many years being afraid to take a chance and tell you how I felt about you. I don't want to waste more years being apart from you and living a life I don't really want. All because I was afraid to take another chance."

I felt my eyes grow big. "Are you saying..."

"I'm not going back to L.A., and I'm not going to law school."

I stared at him, wondering if I was dreaming all of this. I'd hoped for so many months Josh would stay with me, but I'd accepted that wasn't going to happen. And now he was saying the words I'd wanted to hear so badly.

"Are you really not leaving? What are you going to do?"

"I'm working on something, but I don't want to say anything yet. You'll be the first to know, though. I promise."

I laughed and put my hand to my forehead. "I can't... I can't believe this. I came here to tell you I was happy to do the long-distance relationship because I just wanted to be with you, no matter how far apart we were."

"So, should I move back to California then?" he asked with a crooked grin.

"No!" I hugged him closer. "I'm fully on board with this life decision you've made."

"Good. Because I can't imagine my life without you."

He brushed his lips over mine, and I drew him in for a long, sweet kiss. When we broke apart, I noticed some of the people by the fire pit watching us instead of the show. That reminded me of a couple of people who wouldn't be so entertained by us.

"Have you told your parents you're not going to school?" I asked.

"Not yet. They're going directly to the airport from here, so I'll talk to them when I go home after the Closing Ceremony." He took my hands and laced our fingers together. "Are you in Vancouver for just a few days?"

"No, I'm here the full two weeks. Em gave me tickets and invited me to stay with her."

"That's awesome. Then you should come to L.A. with me when we leave. I'm just going for a couple days." He squeezed my hands and smiled. "I can show you all my favorite places."

"Ooh, can I see the beach house?"

"That's number one on my list."

I grinned and rested my forehead to his. The morning couldn't possibly get any better.

"I can't wait."

"Speaking of the beach, let's get out of here and go someplace warm," Josh said.

"That sounds fantastic."

We walked around the TV cameras, and as we passed the chalet I asked, "Should you tell Stephanie and your parents you're leaving?"

"I'll text Steph. I don't want to see anyone but you right now." He curled his arm around my waist.

We only had to wait a few minutes for the tram to arrive, and since everyone else was still watching the show, we had the entire car to ourselves on the return trip. There was plenty of space for us both to sit, but Josh pulled me onto his lap. Away from all the people and the lights, he gave me a deeper, hotter kiss, making me feel like I could float down the mountain.

I'd been wrong. The morning had gotten even better.

# Chapter Twenty-Five

I held up my phone and snapped my fiftieth photo through the windshield. "This is the most beautiful highway I've ever seen."

Josh smiled and turned up the radio, just the way we both liked it. To the left of the winding highway, the Pacific Ocean glimmered under the midday sun, and its white-capped waves splashed over the rocky shore. I put away the phone and rolled down my window halfway to catch some of the fresh sea breeze.

Every moment since the morning on Grouse Mountain had been pure bliss. Josh and I had traveled all around Vancouver, watching events and cheering on Team USA. We'd gotten the biggest thrill at the ladies' free skate, where Liza finished in fifth place, cementing herself as one of the early favorites for gold in four years. When the Olympic flame had been extinguished at the Closing Ceremony, I'd shed quite a few tears from the overwhelming gratitude I felt. I couldn't have had a more incredible Olympic experience even if I'd been a participating athlete.

Josh curved the rental car onto a side road that also ran

along the ocean, and I gawked at the steep incline as we drove up the hill. A large house came into view, and my jaw dropped even further.

"I thought it would be like one of those little cottages down by the water," I said.

"I guess I didn't mention how big it is. It's not technically on the beach, but it has the best ocean views."

We parked behind the house, and Josh helped me with my huge suitcase. When he unlocked the door, he let me step inside ahead of him, and my mouth fell open once again.

"Whoa," was all I could manage.

The foyer opened to a large living room, which looked especially massive because of the wood-beamed vaulted ceilings. Straight ahead was a wall of glass windows and doors, and there was nothing but crystal blue water in the distance. In the corner of the room next to the patio doors sat a black upright piano. Josh's piano.

"This is… ridiculous," I said as I did a full three-sixty.

"Do you like it?" Josh grinned.

"Do I like it? If anyone would answer no to that question, they should have their sanity checked." I walked over to the glass wall. "How can this just be a *vacation* house? If I came here for vacation, I'd never want to leave."

Josh slid open the doors, and the sounds of waves lapping onto the beach and seagulls squawking floated into the living room. We went out onto the patio, and Josh stood behind me and hugged my waist.

"Now that you're here with me, I could definitely stay here forever," he said.

I leaned my head back against his chest and closed my eyes. The soft breeze caressed my face while Josh's lips caressed my hair. *This must be heaven.*

We stood quietly in our embrace, soaking up the warm sunshine and the peaceful comfort of each other. After the busy morning at the airport and the cramped flight, I couldn't think of a better way to unwind.

"Have I told you today how much I love you?" I said.

He turned me to face him, and he placed a gentle kiss on my mouth. As he gazed into my eyes, I saw how much *he* loved *me*. No words necessary.

"There's something I need to ask you," he said, taking my hands. "Something very important."

I tilted my head to the side, curious over his serious tone. He watched me another minute and then began to lower to one knee. My pulse went into a full sprint.

*Oh my God.*

"Josh…" I whispered.

He stopped before his knee reached the deck floor, and he stood tall again with a smile. "That's not it."

I exhaled and swatted his arm. "You almost gave me a heart attack!"

"I'm sorry, I couldn't resist." He laughed and pulled me close, turning serious once more. "Not now, but one day…"

A long shiver ran down my spine, and I smiled. "One day."

"I do have something to ask you. And it is important." He paused and wet his lips. "Will you skate with me?"

"Of course. Anytime, anywhere you want. You know I've been dying to skate with you again since the Christmas show."

"That's not exactly what I meant. I meant will you be my partner and compete with me."

My eyes widened. "What?"

"I know you wanted to start school, but I think we could be amazing together. When we skated together for the show, we only uncovered just a little bit of what we could do."

He was serious. He wanted to team up and compete. I'd just started to come to terms with saying goodbye to my competitive career.

"I… I don't know what to say. I always planned on retiring now. I don't think I can ask my parents to put any more money into skating."

"They won't have to."

"Josh, I'm not letting you pay—"

"I'm not. We have a sponsor." He smiled. "Mrs. Cassar wants to fund both of us, all our expenses. She said her accountant told her she needs more charitable write-offs."

I gaped at him. "Does she know how much money that is?"

"I laid it all out for her, and she didn't bat an eye. She was too enamored with the prospect of us skating together all the time."

My mind raced with the possibilities. Being able to skate without worrying about the cost. That was a very appealing thought. As was skating with Josh every day. I'd still have to work to pay for living expenses, but I could cut back my schedule. Thinking about Mark, he was clearly done with the sport, so the door was open for me to skate with a new partner. The big question was — could I put myself back in that crazy competitive world after so many disappointments?

"I know you're probably trying to wrap your head around this, and it's a lot to think about," Josh said. "But we don't have to commit to four more years. We can take it one year at a time."

I continued to silently process everything he was proposing, and he rambled on, "Mrs. Cassar even said I can live in her guest house rent-free, which I'll definitely need since I'll be supporting myself. I was thinking I could start giving piano lessons and maybe do choreography for some of the kids at the rink. Em said she'd help connect me with some students. Oh, and she's very excited about the idea of coaching us. Thrilled is more like it."

He grinned and held my hands. "Have I sold you on it yet?"

"You're doing a pretty good job."

"Well, if you need even more convincing, just think about

us on the ice together every day." His voice lowered. "Feeling that connection, creating beautiful movement together."

He angled his head closer, and I bit my lip. "It's all incredibly tempting."

"I would be so honored to be your partner," he said.

He looked at me with so much love and respect that my eyes welled with tears. I thought back to all our rehearsals and when we'd skated in the show. I'd felt so free and so inspired. I couldn't turn down the chance to explore that further. I believed we could do amazing things together, too.

"My answer is…"

His eyebrows rose high with anticipation.

"Yes!"

He broke into a huge smile and enveloped me in his arms, lifting me off the ground. I laughed as he whirled me around and around.

"She said yes!" he shouted to the sky.

His phone rang in his pocket, and I slowly slipped out of his embrace so he could answer it. "Who dare interrupt our celebration?"

He glanced at the screen. "It's my dad."

I gave him a few feet of space and wrung my hands as he took the call. He was meeting his parents in a little while to tell them he wasn't going to school, and I could only imagine their reaction to that plus the news of our partnership. He shouldn't have to deal with it all on his own.

Josh ended the call after only a minute. "He needs to meet sooner because he has to see some client."

"I really think I should go with you. Especially since you'll be telling them about us skating together."

He closed the space between us. "I love you for wanting to come, but it's better if I do it alone. It's not going to be a pleasant conversation."

"Which is why I should be there to support you." I touched his cheek.

He covered my hand with his and kissed my palm. "I don't want you to get caught in the crossfire. Just knowing you'll be here when I get back is the best support I can ask for."

"So I guess I'm not changing your mind."

"I won't be long." He hugged me tight. "Let me show you around the house so you'll know where everything is."

He took me through the living room to the expansive kitchen featuring top-of-the-line everything, and then we headed upstairs. On the top floor of the three-story house was the guest bedroom and bathroom along with a balcony and more spectacular views.

"Make yourself at home," he said. "Call me if you need anything."

I stood on the tips of my toes and kissed him softly. "Good luck."

After he left, I took a long shower and wandered around the empty house, wondering how I could pass the time to make it go faster. My stomach knotted just thinking about the things Josh's parents were probably saying about me. I picked up a framed family portrait from a table in the living room and looked at Mr. and Mrs. Tucker's practiced smiles. Would they ever accept me as part of Josh's life?

Stephanie's face stared back at me from the picture, and I could already hear her disgust over Josh and me skating together. She was starting fashion design school soon, so it wasn't like she was planning to continue skating, but I was sure she'd be annoyed about Josh having a new partner. Especially when that partner was me.

I set down the photo and nervously fiddled with my phone. When I'd browsed every social media website and flipped through all four hundred of Liza's Olympic photos on Facebook, I pulled up the dial pad and called Em.

"Hey," she answered. "Quinn, can you hand me that pink sweater?"

"Are you busy?" I asked.

"I'm just packing. Quinn's being a great helper." I heard her squeaky reply in the background. "What's up?"

I took a calming breath and tucked my legs under me. Hearing Em's voice always helped settle me.

"You're excellent at keeping a secret," I said.

She paused. "Josh talked to you?"

"You think you can handle coaching the awesomeness of Carlton and Tucker?" I smiled.

"You agreed to skate with him!"

"We're going to try it for a year and see how it goes."

"It's going to go wonderfully. I have the best feeling about this."

I pushed my slightly damp hair over one shoulder. "Now that it's sinking in, I have a really great feeling about it, too."

"When you guys skated together for the show, I couldn't get over how easily you fit as partners from day one. I loved watching you learn from each other. He brings out the softer side of your skating, and you bring out more power in him. I can't tell you how excited I am to work with you as a team."

The door opened and Josh gave me a little smile as he came inside, but he had a faraway look in his eyes like he was still reliving the conversation with his parents. I stood and walked toward him.

"Josh just got back, so I'll talk to you later?" I said to Em.

"Yeah, definitely. We have lots to plan!"

"Have a good flight."

I put the phone aside and gave Josh an immediate hug. "How did it go?"

He breathed deeply. "Not good."

He held onto me as if he didn't want to let go, so I rubbed his back and let him take all the comfort from me he needed. When he finally released me, I clasped his hand and led him to the long window seat next to the piano.

"Do you wanna talk about it?" I asked.

He raked his hand through his hair. "I knew they were going to be upset, but it was just… I realized they really have no faith that I can make it on my own."

"I don't think that's true. I think they're just disappointed you're not doing what they want you to do."

"My dad said, 'You're throwing away everything for what? You've already been to the Olympics. It's time to start your life.'"

I winced as I pictured Mr. Tucker saying those harsh words. There were probably even harsher ones about our relationship that Josh would keep to himself.

"I told him it's not about the Olympics. It's about going after the things that are important to me, the things that make me happy." He brushed my hair from my face and gazed intensely into my eyes. "This is the life I want."

His lips met mine, and I felt his sureness in his kiss. I kissed him back with the same passion, giving him all the love I had for him.

"I have total faith in you," I said. "You're going to be amazing at everything you do."

He kissed my forehead then the tip of my nose and then my mouth. "I'm so lucky to have the best partner on and off the ice."

He reclined against the end of the seat, and I snuggled into his arms, my back to his chest. We were facing the ocean and the piano, and I remembered the fantasy I'd had many times the past few months.

"You know, ever since you told me about this place, I've been picturing you here playing the piano… for me." I looked up at him with a smile.

"Are you asking me to play for you?"

"Yes, please."

He nuzzled my neck. "I would love to do that."

We slowly untangled ourselves, and when Josh took his place on the piano bench, I sat beside him.

"Part of my fantasy was sitting next to you so I can have a front-row seat," I said.

"This fantasy sounds very detailed." He grinned and squeezed my knee. "What else does it include?"

My eyes flickered to his mouth. "We can talk about that later."

He tugged on his collar and couldn't stop smiling. As he set his fingers on the keys, I put my arm around him and touched my fingertips lightly to the back of his neck. He closed his eyes and took a noticeable swallow.

"Am I distracting you too much?" I asked.

His eyes opened, and he turned to me. "You're not going anywhere."

He eventually put his attention back on the piano and began to play the piece that had become one of my favorites — "Your Hands Are Cold" from *Pride and Prejudice*. He leaned slightly forward, and his fingers flexed over the keys, so soft but so in control. I sat mesmerized by the ease with which he created something so gorgeous.

When he hit the final note, I said. "We should skate to that for our first program together."

He gazed at me for a long moment. "I can't wait. I've dreamt of skating with you since the first time I saw you on the ice. The girl in the pink dress with the golden hair and the sparkling green eyes. The prettiest girl I'd ever seen."

I smiled and rested my head on his shoulder.

He lifted my chin, and his eyes roamed across my face. "Now the most beautiful woman."

My lips parted, and he took the invitation, sending shivers down to my soul. His mouth lingered on mine then swept along my jaw to my ear.

"I love you," he said.

I melted into his arms, and I sang inside with my absolute favorite melody, the most gorgeous one of all. The one Josh played on my heart.

# About the Author

Jennifer Comeaux is a tax accountant by day, writer by night. There aren't any ice rinks near her home in south Louisiana, but she's a diehard figure skating fan and loves to write stories of romance set in the world of competitive skating. One of her favorite pastimes is travelling to competitions, where she can experience all the glitz and drama that inspire her writing.

To stay up to date on Jennifer's new releases, join her mailing list: http://eepurl.com/UZjMP

Jennifer loves to hear from readers! Visit her online at:
jennifercomeaux.blogspot.com
www.facebook.com/jennifercomeauxauthor
www.twitter.com/LadyWave4
jcomeaux4@gmail.com

Discover other titles by Jennifer Comeaux:
Life on the Edge (Edge Series #1)
Edge of the Past (Edge Series #2)
Reaching the Edge (Edge Series #2.5)
Fighting for the Edge (Edge Series #3)

Please consider taking a moment to leave a review at the applicable retailer. It is much appreciated!

# Acknowledgements

So many people helped me along my journey to publishing this book. First, I'd like to thank my family and friends for their constant support. You've been my readers and my champions since day one! Sylvianne, thank you for insisting I attend the 2010 Olympics. I knew when we were in Vancouver I'd have to write about it one day. Our adventure on Grouse Mountain was too epic!

I can't thank all my beta readers enough — Teresa, Rebekah, Sarah, Sylvianne, Debbie, Melissa, Heather, Elizabeth, Angie, Jessica, Melisa, Michelle, and Tia. I also have to give a big shout-out to my awesome proofreaders Marni and Christy. Special thanks to Rebekah and my friends Tiffany, Denise, and Kristin for helping me with toddler speak (and three-year-old Claire for giving me a line of dialogue for Quinn)! And Teresa, thank you for always listening to my rambling ideas and for helping me work through all my character and plot concerns.

I owe a huge thank you to my cover artist Sarah Schneider for stepping in when I was panicking over my cover situation. It was so great having someone who'd read the story design the cover! Thank you for all your patience and your hard work!

I also need to give a huge thank you to Alex Shaughnessy and Jimmy Morgan for posing for the cover and Ann Bowes-Shaughnessy for taking the photos. I can't express how thrilled I am to have such a talented pair team on my book! You were all so incredibly generous to volunteer to help!

My final thank you goes to all the readers. When *Life on the Edge* was released I had no plans to do a series or write any more books. I just wanted to fulfill my dream of having a book published. But you asked for more and you inspired me to keep writing! Thank you for being so excited about my characters and for all the kind words you've shared with me. You all rock!

CPSIA information can be obtained at www.ICGtesting.com
Printed in the USA
LVOW10s1343090415

433921LV00004B/123/P